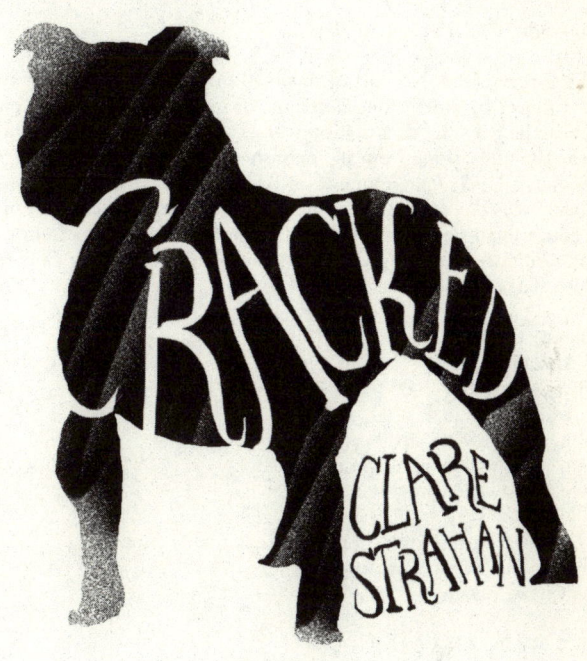

CRACKED

CLARE STRAHAN

ALLEN&UNWIN
SYDNEY · MELBOURNE · AUCKLAND · LONDON

Australian Government

Australia Council
for the Arts

This project has been assisted by the Australian Government through the
Australia Council, its arts funding and advisory body.

First published in 2014

Allen & Unwin
83 Alexander Street
Crows Nest NSW 2065
Australia
Phone: (61 2) 8425 0100
Email: info@allenandunwin.com
Web: www.allenandunwin.com

A Cataloguing-in-Publication entry is available from
the National Library of Australia
www.trove.nla.gov.au

ISBN 978 1 74331 603 0

Cover & text design by Astred Hicks, Design Cherry
Typeset by Midland Typesetters, Australia
Printed in Australia by McPherson's Printing Group

10 9 8 7 6 5 4 3 2 1

MIX
Paper from
responsible sources
FSC® C001695

The paper in this book is FSC® certified.
FSC® promotes environmentally responsible,
socially beneficial and economically viable
management of the world's forests.

Anthe, remember how you spoke the chorus of Leonard
Cohen's *Anthem* to me and inspired the first line of a novel?
Well – here it is.

I'll ring the bells,
my darling friend.

Anthea Joy Simpson
1972–2013

I cracked when I was eleven, but it didn't show. People are so naturally strange, it's hard to tell if they're broken or not, but I'm pretty sure that by the time I finish high school, I'll be a pile of shards, beyond repair.

Over the crest, there it is, Fernwood Secondary College and the continuing joys of Year Ten. Every day is like being submerged in its semolina sand.

Imagine just rocking up, full of gossip, not caring about anything but the latest YouTube. Saying 'Hi' and sitting at my desk exactly as if I belonged. Yeah, that's what I'll do.

No I won't.

For one, my mother hates Facebook (where all good gossip breeds) and refuses to let me on it. And for two, life turns darker and bleaker the closer to school I get.

I don't know why. Maybe it's a pathological condition I've inherited from my father – along with the weird mole on my left shoulder blade?

I have no way of telling.

⁓

By the time I've been to the office for my late pass and am shuffling down the nearly empty corridors to Mrs Sutcliff's Australian History class, I won't look anyone in the eye. Mrs Sutcliff is setting up the TV trolley when I arrive; which doesn't work because someone who 'didn't know what they were doing' – aka Sutcliff – has pressed the wrong buttons or plugged in the wrong cable.

I'm hungry. I haven't had breakfast. I blame Shakespeare.

⁓

Every year my mother directs an amateur Shakespeare production, usually *A Midsummer Night's Dream*. I used to love it and the oldies have fun, but now it's annoying: after being on organisational overload for everyone else, racing around like a maniac doing a million weird theatrey things and the high of the closing night, at home Mum's a zombie, a deflated balloon; empty: like our fridge. And chaotic, like the rest of the place: jumbled with bits of set and great disorganised bags of costumes, and 'cloths' … loads of cloths. But no bananas. No bread. No milk.

'Gods, it's Monday,' Mum said when she shook me awake this morning. 'And you're late.'

When she rushed me out the door she stuffed a few Greek shortbreads – a gift from our neighbour – in my lunch box and scrabbled in her wallet for gold coins. 'I hate to surrender to the culture of pre-packaged dispose-a-food,' she said. 'But you'll have to buy lunch.'

<hr>

Sutcliff abandons the DVD and drones on instead about the riveting details of the Australian parliamentary system. All I can think about is Greek shortbreads. Sutcliff's voice sharpens up to say, 'Clover Jones, put that lunch box away.'

<hr>

Sutcliff has never liked me. She's always ringing my mother to tell her I'm disobedient and insulting.

My mother, the walking dictionary, with her 1930s fashion and pearls. Until I left primary school, I hadn't realised what little clue Mum had about real life. She'd wanted to send me to the Steiner school where I went for kindergarten, but we couldn't afford it and she never got over the disappointment, crying into her pillow at night. At least, I thought that's what she cried about.

She made up for it with her photograph album of my 'stages of development thus far', shared so teachers can get a picture of me as 'a whole person', 'an evolving spiritual being incarnated into a physical body who needs nurture and compassion'; her long letters urging change and the virtues of establishing a 'Steiner-stream' in the state school system; her offers of candles and storytelling. Once, she wrote to the school complaining that Sutcliff had 'undermined my self-esteem and displayed a concerning lack of judgement'.

'Mum, you didn't?'

'Clover, I did.'

'Now she'll really hate me.'

'No she won't.'

But she does. If she could burn a hole in me right now with the glint from her glasses, she would.

'Well, Clover?'

People stare. My stomach grumbles, loudly, like an alien percussion instrument played underwater. Sparks of amusement flicker around the room and the flames creep up my neck.

Rob Marcello cracks his knuckles and says, 'Gross.'

Everyone laughs, even Alison Larder, my red-faced and strange ex-best friend.

Thuggish Pete Tsaparis reaches over to slap Rob on the back. 'Gross, all right, Robbo.'

Rosemary Daniels and her friends smirk behind their make-up.

Sutcliff half-quells them with her hand. 'Clover, is there something you'd like to say to me about this disruption?'

'Fuck off.' That's what I'd like to say.

What I've said.

Silence strikes like lightning. Trung Nguyên drops his pencil case and someone makes the snorting sound of suppressed hysteria. Sutcliff thunders towards me so fast I nearly fall off my tilted chair.

'Up,' she hisses and marches me to the hard vinyl bench outside the principal's office, disappearing briefly inside and then striding off without a backward glance.

Sitting next to me, watching with some interest, is Philip McKenzie.

⸰‿⸰

I haven't been this close to Philip since we had to sit next to each other once for punishment at primary school, and we've hardly spoken since the first day of high school. Mum had insisted on seeing me off at the school gate that first day and she'd cried so hard it was impossible to understand her, but it had sounded like 'I'm sorry.'

'Go home, Mum. I'll be fine.'

She'd straightened her back, blown her nose and walked off, looking brave, our black staffy, Lucille, trotting unconcerned beside her.

Philip had smirked at me and said, 'Your mother's a freak.'

'Yeah?'

But really, I had nothing to say to that.

———⟡———

He looks different. Sort of. He's tall and skinny now and has a few pimples on his neck. He must be fifteen, too. But his face is as smooth-skinned as ever, with its sprinkling of freckles. His rust-coloured eyelashes. His blue eyes, mocking.

———⟡———

Grade Six looms in my mind's eye. Our teacher, Mr Henderson, telling us about his 'maths heroes' and passing around a photo of Albert Einstein. Alison thought Einstein was famous for creating the ultimate wacky-professor hairdo, but apparently he'd worked out some theory as well, the significance of which Mr Henderson was trying to impress upon us at the same moment that a mighty spit-ball hit Philip McKenzie in the head. Mr Henderson glared. 'It's no laughing matter,' he said. 'The Americans took Einstein's theory and turned it into the atomic bomb. A nuclear weapon that even today can destroy the world. Boom! Just like that.'

His eyes swept out the window – Mr Henderson liked to look out the window when he talked;

the distraction of our actual class sitting in the actual room seemed to disturb him – and told us all about it. The A-bomb, tick-ticking away out there, waiting for the right crazy general to press the button and set off a chain reaction that could blow everything to smithereens and leave whatever was left so poisonous it would kill for thousands of years. 'The upside is that these days nuclear power plants are in operation all over the world, making electricity using uranium, and uranium is one of Australia's natural resources.'

'But isn't nuclear electricity radioactive?' I blurted.

Half the class sniggered, and Philip McKenzie flicked a rubber band at me.

'Stupid,' he said.

Mr Henderson jerked around irritably. 'Phil, we do not throw things at each other in class. Apologise to Clover.'

'Sorry, Clover-bomb.'

I managed to score a direct hit with Philip's rubber band on the side of his curly red head. Mr Henderson spun around again, but Alison Larder saved me with her urgency.

'How do we get rid of it?' she said.

'We can't. Nuclear weapons, once they're made, can't be ... unmade.' Mr Henderson blushed. His words had left a silence.

Alison broke it. 'Is it just one bomb? Couldn't we get it? Couldn't we hide it, I mean? I mean, my dad's got a huge garage. How big can it be, one bomb?'

'Oh, no.' Mr Henderson shook his head as though he pitied us immensely and wiped his glasses. 'They called the first nuclear bomb "the A-bomb", Alison, but there are hundreds of nuclear weapons nowadays. Thousands. Bombs and missiles and torpedoes. Enough to destroy the planet many times over.' He rubbed the kidney bean shaped marks on either side of his nose and put his glasses back on. 'What with climate change and whatnot, reducing nuclear arms is not considered the most pressing issue these days.'

And that's when it happened. The crack. I felt it, deeper than my bones. They'd made a bomb that could destroy the world. Okay, I could handle a mistake. But then they made thousands of them? And now it wasn't even *the most pressing issue*. Did that mean everything else was so bad that the world might not survive long enough *to* blow up? We stared at Mr Henderson like desperate rabbits. Well, that was how I'd felt; trapped in the headlights of imminent destruction, small and twitchy with front teeth a little large for my head.

Mr Henderson looked sweaty, I remember. Maybe he'd just noticed our pale faces and feared he'd gone too far, worried what our parents might say. Mine, for one, was likely to complain. Lucky for him, the bell rang.

Philip shoved past me, hissing in my ear. 'That's not really the bell, it's an alarm. They've launched a Clover-bomb at Fernwood Primary School.'

I laughed in a jeery way and it felt better than crying, but aftershocks were pounding me on the insides and Philip McKenzie was right: I thought I might explode.

———

After school that day, Philip stopped opposite me, sitting on his stupid bike in the schoolyard making a fake siren sound.

'Ranga,' I said. Pretty weak, but Alison Larder backed me up, smirking.

Philip was immune. Growing up with clown hair had made him impervious to the insults of amateurs. He just rode one-handed, twirling his finger as if to say 'big deal'.

'Is my hair red?' Philip rode his bike so close, he practically ran over my toes. He was great on that bike and I couldn't ride at all. I shuffled back and stood on Alison, who said, 'Ow.'

Turning impossibly, Philip rode back the other way, circling us. 'Gee – a ranga. I hadn't noticed that, Clover-bomb. You're so clever to point that out. Thank you. You're so kind.'

Like a ginger cat snaking off, he'd gone, leaving a little puff of disdain.

In true me style, I'd run home.

———

Mum was gardening. She seemed small and alone and frail, holding up a lopsided dirt-covered onion. Did she even know we were all going to die?

'Well,' she said. 'What do you think of my onion?'

'I hate your stupid onion!' And I dashed inside. Lucille ran in with me, barking.

Mum gathered us up – Lucille, onion and me – to sit on the couch. She brushed the dirt off and laid her treasure, papery and golden, in my palm. 'What's up?'

I remember my hand curling around the onion. It was a good one, fat, still smelling of earth. Earth. How could the whole earth be destroyed? Were we going to boil to death? Would the seas rise up and sink us? I couldn't find the words to ask, and was afraid of the answers. But Mum wasn't one for letting tears go by without explanation.

In the end, because I didn't know how to explain everything Mr Henderson had said, I blurted, 'Philip McKenzie reckons I'm stupid.'

———

And sitting here now outside the principal's office, I guess he probably still does. He jiggles his leg and I can feel the vibration through the bench.

The leg stops and he says, 'What d'ya do?'

'Swore at Sutcliff.'

'Yeah? Didn't think you had it in you ... Clover-bomb.'

The old name buzzes through me, but his low-key approval flicks a switch and I breathe out; maybe it isn't a nuclear disaster after all.

The clock on the wall opposite us ticks. Loudly. Philip cracks his knuckles. 'So,' he says. 'What happened to you and Alison Larder?'

Why do I feel like crying? I've barely had anything to do with Alison since we started high school and feel embarrassed about half the things we did when we were little.

All through primary school, Alison Larder practically lived at my house. Our favourite thing was laughing. We had this theory that laughter shook the black stuff off your soul. All it took was a certain look from Al and I was hopeless, helpless. We literally fell about: nothing could stop us but exhaustion. And we were always making cubbies, in the lounge under Mum's theatre cloths pegged on string, or in the garden, or up the Golden Ash. And everywhere we went, Lucille came too. Wherever we played, we drew. Especially me. I loved drawing. Sometimes when Alison got sick of it, she'd make up stories (they usually had Jesus in them, but I didn't mind) and I'd draw the pictures and we'd make little books for my mum.

'Well, well,' she'd say. *'Jesus and the Snails*, how lovely.' Or whatever crazy tale it was.

Sometimes we went to Al's, but not often.

The first time I went she whispered, 'You can't put your feet on the seat.'

'But I'm only wearing socks?'

She nodded seriously. 'Even socks can make a mess.'

I reckon Alison's mum would rather have died than let Al climb a tree or have a dog sleep in her bed under the covers. Especially one as smelly as Lucille.

Everything we did at my house made a mess: wet-on-wet watercolour painting; clay modelling; and, when we were very little, 'soapy cooking' with tiny kitchen utensils and grated yellow soap mixed with mud. Al was always wearing my clothes and getting them filthy. Before we went to bed, Mum ran bubble baths that smelled like lavender.

I think Alison loved my mum more than I did.

At the end of Grade Six, just before the school holidays, the longest school holidays that ever were, Alison's dad got some special position in a church in Canberra and her whole family moved away.

'Mum wants to be there for Christmas. Settled in by Christmas,' Al told me, sobbing with the horror of it.

'You could live with us. My mum'll adopt you,' I said.

Alison looked hopeful. 'Maybe my mum will let me bring one of our TVs?'

'And if Mum doesn't like it, we can live in the tree.'

'What about electricity?' Al gazed knowingly at the house. 'I guess we could use an extension cord. Dad's got a really long orange one that's allowed to go outside.'

What would I do without her? I couldn't even climb the tree on my own – one of us had to give the other a bump-up and then the person up the tree had to hook her legs over one branch and feet under another branch and hang half-upside-down to help the other one get up.

I reached down and hoicked her up. 'I'll never have another friend as smart as you, Alison.'

She scrambled for a foothold and then practically ran up the trunk, like a monkey. 'I'll never have another friend with hair as long as you, Clover.'

'You have to stay here. My mum won't mind.'

'We'll be like sisters,' she said.

I felt a stab of jealousy in case Mum loved her more than me, but said, 'We'll be like real sisters.'

'Sisters forever.'

'Sisters until we die.'

Alison said wickedly, 'Sisters until Philip McKenzie dies.' And we laughed until we had to hold on to the tree to stop ourselves from falling out. Then sat in the broad branches and didn't say much until Mum called us in to wash our hands for dinner.

It didn't matter how we cried and hated our parents; they wouldn't agree to our plan. Alison moved away and I headed to high school.

⁓

Fernwood Secondary College drew kids from a few surrounding primary schools and lots of them had been at my school, but I felt like I hardly knew anyone. I blamed Al for my complete lack of ability to make new friends.

On that first day Mum said, 'Just be yourself, love. You'll be fine. You're wonderful.'

Be myself? My wonderful self?

Without Alison, who was that?

Eating lunch the first week at Fernwood Secondary, I discovered my wonderful self – I was a freak.

A pretty blonde girl looked in my lunch box and said, 'Oh.' Then she smiled at me and said, 'Oh well. I'm Katie. Katie Marshall. What's your name?'

'Clover,' I said. 'Jones.'

Katie's face gently wrinkled with confusion. 'Clover? Is that a name?'

Then beautiful, beautiful Rob Marcello with his perfect swept-over hair and deep, chocolaty eyes, sat next to me and said, 'Right. So, Jones, did you watch the footy or what?'

With all the force of my wishes (that I *had* watched the footy; that Rob and I barracked for the same team; that Rob Marcello would sit next to me at lunch for ever and ever and ever) my voice tumbled out in a gush. 'No – but I love footy and would've watched it, but I couldn't because we don't have a television. Mum reckons it rots your brain.'

'You don't have a TV?' Rob said it so loudly, other kids came over to check me out.

One of them was the scariest girl in Year Seven. Her name was Rosemary Daniels, her big brother was a star footy player for Fernwood and she had every SingStar DVD there was and always won because she was 'amazing'.

'What kind of weirdo doesn't have a television?' she said, looking me up and down as if I were a slug, and the other kids laughed.

'She has green turds in her lunch box,' said Katie, and the laughing got louder.

'They're dolmades,' I said, and ran to the toilets, and stayed there until the PE teacher found me and made me go to class.

I was a Steiner-freak who ate home-baked bread and brown rice and didn't have a television.

For the first seven long weeks of high school, I tried to convince Mum that TV was essential to my development as a socially functioning adolescent, but she didn't give in until I said, 'I have no friends,' and cried.

It remains the most disappointing, embarrassing TV ever – not even as big as her stupid dictionary – and is treated like something dangerous, addictive; kept in a cupboard with her favourite anti-TV book, *Four Arguments for the Elimination of Television*. Mum still acts like having it in the house is some great sacrifice.

'Light a candle. Keep this crystal beside it,' she said when we plugged it in. 'It'll help with the radiation.'

I wouldn't have thought anything about the home-baked bread, dolmades and protection from radiation, but at high school I realised that what you ate, what brand you wore and what you watched means everything – 'beeswax candles' and 'biodynamics' signified only one thing at Fernwood Secondary College: weirdo.

But Al and I hadn't known. We'd thought I was normal.

―――

Mum had to get the internet for work when I was in Year Nine, but she refused to let me have Facebook. Halfway through the same year, Alison Larder came back from Canberra, but by then we weren't little kids anymore. Everything had changed. Well, I'd changed. Alison looked almost the same, flat-chested and short, as if puberty had somehow passed her by.

'Say hello to your mum for me,' she said on her first day, after our awkward hello in the milling, noisy school corridor.

I restrained myself from saying, 'Sure, and you say hi to Jesus for me,' and mumbled 'Yeah,' instead.

We haven't really said much to each other, since.

———

But I don't want to say any of this to Philip McKenzie. I change the subject. 'What did *you* do?'

He shakes back his curls, longer now. 'Rode my bike in the hallway.'

'Jeez, Philip, is that all?'

He stretches his legs and crosses them at the ankle. 'No one calls me Philip, except teachers and my mum and dad.'

'What do people call you then?'

'Keek. Keeksie. Kenzo. Any of them names will do.'

'Those.'

'What?'

I shake my head at myself. 'Sorry. My mum always does that.'

'Does what?'

'Corrects my grammar.'

'Oh, right.'

There is a weird little silence. 'You said *them* names instead of *those* names,' I explain.

'Oh.' He shrugs off my grammar correction. 'Well, your mother is definitely weird.'

'It's true.'

'I know. I've seen her.'

'You should try living with her.'

'You should try living with my parents.'

'What's wrong with them?'

'They hate each other.'

The door opens and the principal beckons Philip inside. Keek. I can probably get used to that.

It's not long before the door shoots open and he's ushered out again with a terse, 'Wait there.'

Philip – Keeksie – slumps on the bench with an audible sigh. 'Have fun, CB,' he says as I follow the principal into his office.

CB. Do I actually *like* this acronym of Cloverbomb?

Mr Alberto launches in. 'No mother wants to hear that her daughter is guilty of such foul language and disrespectful attitude. What have you got to say for yourself?'

Mum reckons Berty 'isn't a bad-looking man', but I can't see the attraction. And I'm quite sure he doesn't like the looks of me.

'Sorry.'

Berty looks unimpressed. 'You'll write an apology to Mrs Sutcliff, of course. And ...' he emphasises the 'and' as if I were resisting '... you're suspended for three days. I know Clover Jones fancies herself as "above the law" but this kind of behaviour is not tolerated at Fernwood Secondary College.' He shows me to the door.

What is it with him referring to me as if I'm some other person, some third-party Clover Jones? I should confront him about that, but the thought of more trouble makes me nauseous. Three days of legitimate freedom is excellent, but he's right about Mum; she will not be pleased.

'Wait here. Mrs Fitzpatrick will take you two to the locker bay. It's your lucky day, Phil. Clover is going to help you scrub the floor.'

'What the hell? You can't make us scrub the floor.'

'Unless you want a Saturday morning detention as well, Philip, I suggest you watch your attitude. And yes, I can.'

And he does.

Keek hasn't only ridden in the halls, he's left a massive skid-mark letter K on the locker-bay lino. It's a mighty achievement and tragic that no one is going to see it.

Mrs Fitzpatrick supervises so we can't even slack off. She's the art teacher for the lower school and always seems frazzled. I like her, but she used to be Miss Bell and back then we did charcoal drawing, and perspective and vanishing point and how to create shadows with shading, but since she married Mr Fitz the upper-school drama teacher all we ever do in art is paint sets for his productions. Sometimes I think I'm cursed by amateur theatre.

Using steel wool without rubber gloves is disgusting, but there's an upside because eventually it becomes clear that we have scratched a giant letter K into the lino. Keek and I crack up. After a moment of trying to look serious, Fitzy laughs too. I laugh so hard I swear I can feel the black stuff coming off my soul.

I walk home after school and Keek rides his bike painfully slowly so I can keep up with him.

'Mrs Fitzpatrick is cool,' I say.

'Yeah, Fitzy's all right.'

'Wish she was my Home Group teacher.'

'Yeah, she's all right.'

He lifts up the front wheel with a little hop. 'Maybe you could get transferred or something? Sutcliff'd probably be glad to get rid of you.'

'Whose Home Group are you in?'

'Fitzy's.'

I can't breathe. Keek rides forward at speed, then slides to a halt. If Keek thinks I should be in his Home Group, does that mean …? He rides back to circle around me slowly. 'I can't believe she married Mr Fitz,' I say, my voice still starved of oxygen.

'Mr Fitz's pretty funny – d'ya remember when

he wore a skirt?' He turns and rides in a circle the other way.

'It was a kilt, not a skirt.'

'It looked like a skirt to me.'

'Ranga bastard!' A rock tied up in a grotty head-band hits Keek in the back, making his bike wobble. Across the street, footy boys jog by in a sweaty clump. Pete Tsaparis gives us the finger.

Robbo yells out, 'You were kickin' goals today, Jones – thought Sutcliff was gonna pop a blood vessel. What happened?'

'Suspended,' I call back.

'Good one.'

And they're gone, jogging off round a corner.

My Robbo-burning-cheeks must be practically glowing, but when the wave of elation of being in Rob's line of vision – of having him talk directly to me – ebbs off, they turn another kind of red. 'Pete's an idiot,' I say. 'Are you all right?'

Keek kicks the headband into the gutter. 'They all are.' The rock pings loose and clatters down the drain.

I suppress the blurt of 'Rob's not' and there's an awkward pause.

'I turn off here.' I point. 'I live down there.'

He points. 'I live up there.'

We don't live that far apart. I've seen Keek race away from school on his pushbike, but I've never spoken to him on the way home before.

He sits on his bike, one foot on the nature strip. 'Do you smoke?' he says.

I rearrange my electric-shock eyebrows and have to clear my throat before the word comes out properly. 'No.' A strange thrill stirs inside me and I think of Marilyn Lepace, suspended three times for smoking before she went so magnificently too far and they expelled her. 'Do you?'

'I've been thinking about it.'

'Where would we get them?'

'Easy. My mum smokes. It's one of the things my dad hates about her.'

'So?'

'So...I could steal some from her, dopey.'

We look each other in the eye.

'When?' I ask.

'I'll meet you here. Tomorrow.'

'Where will we go?'

'I dunno. The park?'

'What time do you want to meet?'

'Half-past ten.'

'What if my mum won't let me?'

He gets out his phone. 'Give me your number.'

'My mother doesn't believe in mobile phones. She thinks they give you cancer. We have a landline.'

Keek gives me a look, no doubt recalculating how strange I actually am. 'Nah. We can do it old-school: if you're not here, I'll know your mum didn't let you.'

'What if your mum won't let you?'

He pushes off on his bike. 'My mum won't know.'

'Yes she will.'

A little shake of his curls. 'No, she won't.'

'Yes she will.'

'I'll see ya tomorrow, CB.' He and his bike dwindle as he rides up the hill.

'Okay. See ya, Keek.'

There, I've said it out loud. Maybe now it will stick.

———

Mum paces in the kitchen, banging things. 'I've been on the phone with Mr Alberto.' She throws a spoon into the sink. Something breaks – sounds like glass. She rounds on me. 'How dare you speak to people that way? Every person deserves to be treated with respect.'

Oh yeah, the world's full to the brim with people respecting each other. 'What about me then?' I drop my bag and take off my school shoes. 'What about Mrs Sutcliff respecting me?'

'I think I've heard enough about you, Clover.'

'But—'

'I'm serious. I've been pushing your side of the story for years. I've heard enough. Get to your room and have a good long think about whether it's honouring the best self you can be to treat people with the lack of respect you exhibited today.'

'Yeah? Well what the hell do you think *you're* exhibiting?' I throw my shoe. The moment it leaves my hand, I wish I could snatch it back. It glances off her chest on its way to taking out an indoor plant.

She says, 'Ow,' and stares at me with eyes of thunder.

'Mum—'

'Go to your room.'

My mum doesn't yell often but when she does, it's scary. I go to my room.

———

Later, she comes in with a cup of hot milk and honey. 'Thought you might need something warm and sweet.' She shifts the angle of the page to see what I'm drawing; radiated skeletons crawl from the fractured earth and an onion-angel escapes through a crack in the sky.

I sit up and reach for the milk. 'I didn't mean to throw that shoe.'

'Yes, you did. And I've left the worst of the mess for you to clean up.'

'Sorry.'

'It hurt, you know.'

'I am sorry, Mum. But it doesn't matter what I do, they hate me. Alberto and Sutcliff. It's not fair.'

'I know.' She sighs, deeply. 'Life is rarely fair, but swearing at Mrs Sutcliff isn't the answer.'

Lucille climbs up and settles herself with three turns and a sigh. Mum puts her arms around me and my hot milk.

'Well, what's done can't be undone,' she says. 'What are we going to do with you for three school days? I'm running that creative writing course for new mums at the Community House this week. I guess you'll have to hang out with us. Or shall I see what Mrs T is doing?'

Our family is Mrs Theopopolous's pet project; technically, she's our neighbour, but in reality, she's Yiayia, which means grandmother. She keeps us stocked with jams and preserved fruits and dolmades, homemade from the leaves of her grapevine. She used to try to set my mother up with her married children's unmarried cousins, until (to Mum's great relief) they ran out. All Yiayia's children have moved into their own houses and she complains about how lonely it is since Mr Theopopolous died, but he's been dead for as long as I can remember and her five grown-up children and their spouses always seem to be at her house with their thousand children.

'Yiayia is next door. I'll be fine.'

'I won't be home until about three-thirty. What will you do with yourself?' Mum sounds dubious.

'I dunno. Draw.'

'Are you sure?'

'Mum, do you remember Philip McKenzie?'

'Yes, of course I do. His dad and I went to school together. His mum too, for that matter. They've been going out since, gee—'

'What?'

'God, younger than you. Year Nine.'

'Philip reckons they hate each other's guts.'

'Don't tell me that, Clover.'

I crane my neck to see my mother's face, but it's awkward with the milk and she turns away, which doesn't help. 'Why not?'

'It's none of my business.'

There's something weird about that, but I'm not in a position to push it and the thought of anybody's parents being at high school, especially my own, is vaguely vomit-making, so I press on. 'Anyway, we hung out together at school today.' I'm glad she can't see my face.

'I thought you didn't like each other? But it's good you're finally making friends. I've always thought it was a pity you fell out with Alison, the two of you were such fun when you were little; oh love ...' And she hugs me tighter because I'm crying again, which makes me feel better but guiltier about the smoking. She lets go when Lucille slurps from my half-empty cup.

Keek looks weird out of school uniform. We are dressed strangely alike, in hoodies and black jeans.

His connies are black and mine are orange – a present from Aunty Jean.

'Did you bring them?'

'Yep.'

And there they are, up his sleeve: half a packet of smokes.

'Won't your mum know?'

A visible ache floats over Keek's face. 'She doesn't remember stuff. She won't know if she smoked them or not.'

'My mother remembers everything – she remembers what I ate at my seventh birthday party because it was the first time I had potato chips.'

Keek gives me a look.

Why is my mother such a freak? Has she passed her freakish genes on to me?

'Where *is* your mother?' he asks.

'Working till three.'

'Then we could go to your house.'

The thought of going to my house with Philip McKenzie and smoking cigarettes stolen from his mother sends shudders up my spine. Mrs T looms. 'It's too risky,' I say, and try to explain, but Keek shrugs me off.

'Yeah, yeah, it's cool, whatever. Let's go to the skate park. Get your bike.'

'I don't have a bike.'

Keek looks at me as if I'm from outer space. 'I've got a mountain bike. You could ride that.'

I don't know what to say. It's like confessing that you can't read, or swim. The words come out slowly, like I'm speaking underwater. 'I can't ride a bike.'

Keek says, 'God, you *are* a freak.'

God. It's true.

I nearly run home, but Keek pats the handlebars and says, 'Oh well, who cares. I'll dink you.'

'Dink me?'

'Don't look like that, CB. It'll be fine.'

'No way.'

'It's about six k's from here to the bowl. Do you want to walk?'

I don't want to walk.

'Right, hop up, then.'

The bike isn't high off the ground, but it's as if I've tripled my gravity – I'm as heavy as lead and can't even jump, let alone hop up backwards. I use a retaining wall to get up on the handlebars. Once I'm there, I feel Keek's breath on my neck. I wobble, and jump off.

He shakes his head. 'You've got to trust me.'

It isn't comfortable, being dinked on Keek's bike. Apart from being scared to death, my legs ache. Grey fur streaks in front of us and I panic. Keek nearly runs us into a tree.

'That cat was freakin' miles away!'

'Forget it, I'll walk.'

'Come on Clover, relax and it'll be fine.' He pats the handlebars again. 'Use that brick letterbox. And this time, lean back further and stick your legs out. But not out, out – down out.'

<hr />

Keek tells me that the paved area outside our municipal library is perfect for skateboarding. It has several sections and the right amount of steps and rails; even a huge curved sculpture that looks like it's been made for the job. So Fernwood council built the skate park to keep the skaters away from the library. They must have wanted to keep them away not only from the library but from respectable people in general because they built it out in the boondocks of the local reserve, miles from anything.

The path leading through the reserve to the bowl is gravel – a terrible surface for skateboards. 'It's so far from the shops, half the time there's nobody here,' Keek tells me as we rattle along.

'Where do they go?'

'There are other bowls, if you catch the train. And they still use the library. Only now you can get fined.'

The bowl is bleak. I like it immediately. It's so completely somewhere no adult would want to be. It's a huge concrete plate with two interlinking bowls sunk into it, adorned with a few crappy tags. Fernwood Reserve spreads around us, green grass and grey gum trees – a strip of ferny bush along the creek is all that's left of Fernwood forest. It's peaceful. The bowl is so remote we can't even see the footy oval.

'But you can hear them on the weekends,' Keek says. 'And they shout when they're training, too. Freaks.'

'Who do you barrack for?' I ask. 'In the real footy, I mean.'

'Don't tell me you like football?'

'Go Bombers!'

Keek groans.

'Well, what do you like?' I climb off the bike and stretch. 'Besides bikes, obviously.'

He scrutinises me, like I'm a bug. 'Do you read?'

Then I know what the look is for. Unless there's a craze – in which case it's essential – reading is definitely not cool. Not getting-around-with-your-face-in-a-classic-paperback type reading. Another happy fact I'd learned from experience. 'Yeah, sometimes,' I say cautiously, hedging my bets.

'I ride and I read. That's about it.'

'What are you reading now?'

'*A Wizard of Earthsea*. Have you heard of it? It's pretty old.'

'Mum's got it. On the "books I loved when I was a kid and think you should love too" shelf of our bookshelves.'

'Have you read it?'

'No.'

'It's good.' Keek leans forward on his bike so the back wheel lifts. It bounces when he drops it back to the concrete. 'What are you reading?'

'My Aunty Jean's given me a pile of John Wyndham. Ever heard of him? He's old too. I'm reading *Day of the Triffids*.'

'Can I borrow it when you're done?'

It's hard to imagine Keek reading a book. I want to see him do it. 'Sure,' I say. 'But I'm warning you – it makes going down the creek give you the creeps.'

There's a covered seat, a bus shelter where no bus will ever arrive. Someone has done a decent job of the bus-stop graffiti and I trace a giant eye with my finger.

Keek pulls out the cigarettes. 'What are you doing?'

'I like how they've done this.' I point to the curving line of the eye. 'See how it's so clean, and it's definitely a spray line and not drawn. That must be hard. And they're good colours, not muddy. I'd be very happy if I could control a big piece of art like that.'

Keek is sceptical. 'Art?'

'Of course it's art.'

Keek waves at the tags. 'I suppose you think they're art, too.'

These particular tags don't seem like art, it's true. 'In principle,' I say.

Keek snorts, mocking me. 'In principle.'

'It's an artistic statement, at least.' Keek hasn't changed after all – he always was annoying.

'What's it saying? "I have a marker".'

'It's saying, "I exist".'

But Keek isn't convinced. 'It's about as artistic as a dog peeing on everything it sees,' he says.

I stare at the bowl. 'That looks scary.'

'Nah.' Keek leaves the cigarettes and lighter on the bench and zooms off on his bike. My stomach lurches to see him zip up and down the curve of concrete, seeming to stop still, suspended in air as he reaches the lip. He jumps out and rides back to me. 'Can't do much. Didn't bring my helmet.'

'Helmet?'

'Shit yeah. Dean Barry cracked his head here about eight months ago and now he's like, brain damaged.'

'I heard that.'

'Yeah. I saw him take the tumble. We laughed. At first.'

It's quiet in the middle of the morning with no one around. I can almost see Dean, airborne, then hear the sickening crunch. 'It's weird, everyone being at school,' I say.

'Why do they have to make it so boring?' Keek bunny hops his bike then gets off and leans it against the bus shelter. 'I wouldn't mind going if it wasn't so fucking boring.'

'Fucking,' I say. It sounds stupid, saying it like

that, but I've never said it as freely as Keek just did. First Mrs Sutcliff, now this. No wonder my mother is worried. I say it again, more loudly. Then shout it at the top of my lungs. I pull a cigarette from the packet and light it.

'Yuck,' I say, and cough.

Mum's taken pity on me and arranged for me to be transferred to Mrs Fitzpatrick's Home Group. Fitzy actually smiles at me and says, 'Welcome to the class.'

Sutcliff still gets to torture me in history, which is only bearable because it's one of my few classes with Robbo. I mean, Keek's cute in his own way, I guess, but Rob? Rob is *hot*. And you can tell he's nice, too. Underneath.

Being in the same Home Group helps me and Keek make the transition from suspension-buddies to school-buddies without excessive weirdness, despite his rider-friend Cho paying out on him for 'being a complete idiot' for starting to smoke. She unfavourably dissects me and puts out a delicate hand. 'Hi,' she says. 'Do you ride?'

When Keek scoffs loudly and I say, 'No,' she drops my lumpish hand and turns away. Every nerve in my body suddenly strains to justify my existence. 'I'm artistic,' I blurt.

'Congratulations.' Cho shows me her even teeth. 'I'm Burmese.'

'I'm Catholic,' says Keek, and they laugh. I smile, weakly, and retreat into the safety of my notebook to zone them out. I'm still obsessed with drawing onions. This one's words and image, an onion in cross-section with a different sentence in every layer. An onion poem to my father.

***

'Don't shave your thighs, Clover,' says Mum, poking her head into the bathroom at exactly the wrong moment. 'Shins if you must, but you can hardly see that fluff you're calling hair. You'll regret it. Don't do it, I beseech you.'

I beseech you. The lingering effects of Shakespeare. 'What do you want?' I say, irritated.

'There's a boy on the phone.'

There's a boy on the phone?

Because of our stupid landline, I have to trail my soapy legs out to the lounge in a towel. I take the receiver as if it might be toxic. Or Rob Marcello.

It's Keek.

'What are you doing?' he asks me.

'Nothing.' I can't believe I'm blushing over the phone. 'Why?'

'Tell him he can come for pancakes if he wants,' Mum calls from the kitchen.

'Mum says you can come for pancakes if you want.'

'Okay.'

I can't believe it. I'd been completely sure he would refuse my mother's kind invitation. 'They're made with biodynamic whole-wheat flour and we only have raw sugar.'

'Don't you want me to come?'

'Yeah, but – yeah, of course.' How could I explain? 'My house is …' I look around at art and wood and books and strange Steiner-inspired clay sculptures and watercolour paintings Mum's made with her friends, or at her many 'courses', not to mention my own creations from over the years, and sigh. It isn't like anybody else's house that I've ever been to. Nobody else keeps their miniature television in a cupboard. We have a phone with a rotary dial. A typewriter. We still use my dead grandparents' record-player and Mum listens to their vinyl records. I live in a museum and my mother is the chief dinosaur.

'What number is it?' he says.

⸻

My mother and Philip McKenzie chat over pancakes. In true mother-fashion, there's a spray of ivy circling a hand-rolled beeswax candle. Inspired by having a guest,

I suppose, she lights it and trots out an old Steinery grace we used to say at every meal.

> 'We thank the water, earth and air,
> and all the helping powers they bear,
> we thank the people, loving good
> who grow and cook our daily food.
> And at last we thank the sun,
> the light and life for everyone.'

I think I'm going to die, but Keek doesn't seem fazed by pre-pancake poetry, our lack of technology or the overabundance of Lucille, who sits watching his every mouthful with eyes of longing. Mum asks him about his dad and Keek tells her that he works as a solicitor and is addicted to indoor rock-climbing.

My mother clicks her tongue and says, 'The poor man.'

'Let's go to the park,' I say, desperate to get out of our house.

'Yeah, okay. But can I finish my pancake first?' Keek and my mum smile at each other like old friends. Like allies.

We lie in the bowl, looking up at the sky and smoking.

'Your mum's okay, Clover.'

'I thought you said she was a freak?'

'Well…I'm pretty sure that I said *you* were the freak, CB.'

'She's the freak.'

'So what if she dresses weird?'

'She thinks everything has a consciousness.'

'What?'

'She reckons everything has a consciousness. Rocks and stones are in a trance, plants and trees are fast asleep, animals dream and humans are awake and have *self*-consciousness, which is why we say "I" and "you" and have morals and ethics and stuff.'

'Right.' Keek lifts one of his legs straight up in the air and stares at his shoe. His knee bends like a hinge and he lets the leg drop. 'What's that got to do with your conscience?'

'Not conscience. Consciousness. Trance is a sort of…I don't know. Trance. Sleep is kind of *un*consciousness I think. Dreaming – pictures and feelings and stuff. Dream consciousness. I dunno.' Why did I say anything about my mother's crazy ideas? It makes sense when she talks about it with Aunty Jean, but now, here, in the bowl, it sounds ridiculous.

Keek slaps his hand against the concrete. 'Is this concrete in a trance?'

It surprises me, that Keek doesn't just dismiss me. 'I guess so,' I say. 'Anything that's minerals. The mineral kingdom, Mum calls it.'

'That's a weird thought.'

And we lie there, with the sweep of the bowl blocking everything but the sky overhead, thinking it: the idea that the concrete is alive but in a trance. It's creepy. No wonder Mum feels so passionately about the earth, about *things*, if she thinks even dead stuff is alive.

'What if it wakes up. Out of its trance, I mean?' Keek says.

I imagine the bowl, shaking itself and getting up. Crushing us in the process. 'Maybe that's what earthquakes are. The mineral kingdom waking up.'

'It doesn't stay awake though.'

'No.' I feel his arm, warm against mine. 'If it did wake up, the planet I mean – and all the trees and animals, I don't think they'd be too happy with what we've done.'

Keek smiles at the sky. 'They should make a movie about that, like *The Day the Earth Got Revenge*.'

'Catchy title. Not.'

Keek punches me, but not too hard.

'Maybe that's why it's *not* awake.' I rub my arm and punch him back.

'What, so it doesn't have a revolution or something? Against humans?'

'Yeah.'

'Why are *people* awake then?'

'It's about being individual. Or individualised. But not individual*ism* – which makes you selfish. She thinks we're supposed to transform everything through art. By thinking with our hearts or some crap.' I suss out Keek for signs of ridicule, but he's listening. 'My mum is weird. She yells at the radio when they mention the economy. She doesn't think we're an economy.'

'What do you mean, she doesn't think we're an economy? How are we not an economy?'

'Well…we, society, put a monetary value on everything. I mean, *everything*, especially nature, so we exploit everything, anything, for profit, so there's like this mass destruction going on everywhere because globally we've gone crazy thinking everything is "the economy" – but it isn't, it's *life*; and Mum reckons it's made us all *personally* crazy because we have to be *doing* something all the time to make sure we're "economically viable" and we've forgotten how to value things that don't make money, or that you can't measure that way.'

'Like what things?'

'Nature. Artistic practice.' I yawn, and try to remember the things she goes on about. 'Peace and quiet.'

'What does she do?'

'Works as a temp, mostly. For publishers, and sometimes businesses. She has "ambitions" but mostly it's proofreading.'

'What's that?'

'Who cares. I'm sick of talking about her.'

'She makes good pancakes.'

'Yeah.'

What can I say to Keek about my mother? Just before Alison left for Canberra, she and I had a big fight because she said it was sad I didn't have a dad and I said everyone called *her* dad a God-botherer and she went red like she always does and said, 'Your dad could be *dead* and you wouldn't even know.' And then I realised: mums are supposed to keep dads for their kids.

I turn my head and take in Keek's profile. 'She doesn't fit in,' I say. 'You can't take her anywhere without being embarrassed.' Except maybe the Steiner School Fair.

'Righto, Clover, no need to froth at the mouth.'

'Now I have to meet *your* mother.'

Keek turns to me, then back to the sky. 'Maybe. It's weird that your mum went to school with my parents.'

I look back at the sky, too. 'Yeah.'

The wheel of a bike and a helmeted head stare down at us over the lip of the bowl. 'You right down there?'

'Mugzy.'

'Keeksie.'

Three guys and Cho, all on bikes like Keek's.

I can't help but admire the way Keek just lies there and finishes his cigarette. When he's ready, he manages to run his bike out of the bowl and give me a hand to run out too.

Then it's on: bikes crisscrossing the bowl in a chaos that resolves itself into an organic order, punctuated by gravity-defying moments of stillness. At first I am amazed by what they can do, especially flairs, where they flip right over, and the spills they're prepared to take, but it's like watching through perspex and after a while, I get bored.

'Hey Keek, I'm gonna walk home.'

'Nah, I'll dink you.'

Cho pulls up next to him and dismounts. 'Why don't you have a go?' She offers up the handlebars, her long fingers at the buckle of her helmet. Such beautiful hands. She swings the helmet towards me and gestures at the concrete. 'On the flat here, to start.'

I shake my head, almost a twitch. I'm not ready to mortify myself in front of Cho, who rides like the bike is an extension of her body, who rides with more grace and control than I can even walk with. I want to say thanks, though, for trying to include me. But all that comes out is, 'Nah, I'm cool.'

Cho's shoulder tells me that was her one and only offer as she reclips her helmet and races back into the bowl. I feel a lump of sadness.

'Keek, you stay and ride. Really, it's fine.'

But Keek won't let me go alone and we head off.

'Take me to your place,' I say.

When we get close to home, he stops the bike. 'I'm going to drop you off and then go home.'

'But—'

'That's what I'm doing, Clover.'

And that's what he does.

———

Keek never takes me to his house, he always comes to mine. Or he picks me up on the way through to the skate park, or school, or over to Mrs T's, who always has food. Or we hang out in my room talking and reading bits of books out to each other. Twice we've caught the bus down to Fernwood to watch a movie.

One Sunday morning, out of pure stubborn curiosity, even though I know he doesn't want me to, I turn up on his doorstep. The first thing I notice is that the blinds are half-closed. I knock. A blind moves and Keek comes out.

'What are you doing here?'

'Nice.'

'Sorry. But, what are you doing here?'

'I finished *The Chrysalids* and thought you might want it.' I hold up the book as evidence. 'You just turn up at my place and it isn't a drama. I'll go.'

'It isn't a drama.'

'Isn't it?'

'How come you came here though?'

'Forget it. I'm going.' I jump off the porch and Keek jumps down after me.

'No. Sorry. Hang on, I'll be out in a minute.' Keek takes the book, thanks me and disappears inside. When he comes back out, I can tell there are smokes wrapped up in his hoodie. The ache is back on his face. 'Mum's asleep.' He sniffs and spits.

'Charming.'

'Shall we go down to the bowl?'

'I can't. I have to be back by eleven-thirty. Barbecue at Aunty Jean's.'

Aunty Jean is my aunty in the same way Mrs T is my grandmother. 'Jeannie' and Mum went to school together and stayed friends ever since. I never know what the two of them might get up to. Some nights they sit around in candlelight reading aloud from Steiner books like the most boring witches ever spied on, but I'm as likely to get woken up by them dancing around the lounge room and drooling over Jimmy Page.

———

When I was nine, I showed Mrs T's real granddaughter Stephanie a photo of Jimmy with his electric guitar, his long curly hair and velvet dragon-suit – with a sense of ownership, as though the distant '70s rock star belonged to our family, to my mum.

'Is that really your dad?' Steph had asked, seeming more bewildered than impressed.

'Yeah,' I'd lied. 'That's my dad.'

'Led Zeppelin's so *ancient*,' I accused Mum and

Aunty Jean, as soon as I got old enough to realise. I was secretly glad, then, that Mrs T's married daughter had moved away to Sydney taking Stephanie with her, even though Yiayia had cried for a week.

'They were already old when we were your age,' Aunty Jean dismissed me. 'Who cares? Monster riff!' and they were off.

Aunty Jean doesn't have children and is always asking Mum to go overseas. 'For God's sake, Penny, you'll be a dried up old bag before long. It's only six weeks!' Mum always says no because of me. And because money isn't what you'd call plentiful. But Jean's all right. She makes Mum laugh and buys me clothes so I don't mind that she sort of wants to get rid of me.

───

'Let's go down to the willow,' says Keek.

'What's the willow?'

Keek laughs. 'It's a tree.'

───

The willow grows in an empty block a few houses down the road. The rest of the yard is dandelions and clumps of grass. Through the screen of delicate weeping willow fronds, the light changes and we're in some other, watery realm. But the lumpy bark is gnarled and comfortingly solid, the grass right up to its feet. There's no way Keek and I can reach around the trunk to touch hands, but it's nice to try, to press my cheek against the bark.

We sit, backs to the trunk. Time ticks past. I don't want to miss out on Aunty Jean's tempeh burgers with caramelised onion – 'tampon burgers' she calls them, but they're so good even that can be forgiven. But I do want to see in Keek's house. What's the big secret? His mother can't be more embarrassing than mine.

'Why don't you want your mother to meet me? Don't you think she'll like me?'

'It's not that.'

'What is it then?'

Keek fiddles with the cigarettes. Flicks the lighter a few times. 'Nothing.'

'Do you reckon I could come in then and wash my hands and rinse my mouth out with toothpaste?' I have my body spray, but am paranoid about Mum smelling smoke on me, although she seems oblivious so far. 'Please?'

I part the willow curtain and head off.

⸗——

Keek's place is even weirder than mine. A lot weirder. And it smells … odd. Lights are on, but they cast only a dim glow, as if electricity doesn't have the power to penetrate the gloom. When my eyes adjust, I see that the walls are hung with animal-print blankets: lions, tigers, elephants. Heaps of them. All different, but the same colours: brown and yellow and black. I feel like I'm walking into a cave. A cave crowded with furniture. The lounge is a corridor through cabinets and chairs.

'Mum buys and sells things,' Keek says. 'You know – eBay.'

I don't know, but I nod.

The large dining-room table at the end of the room is dominated by a statue of a bare-breasted black woman wielding a spear.

'Who's that?' I ask.

'Candace, warrior queen of the Kushite Empire. Fought the Romans in 350AD.'

Candace is dangerous, and ready to run – even though her feet are moulded into the platform she balances on. 'Did she win?'

Keek shrugs. 'For a while.'

There's a blanket-free wall dotted with hanging statues of Mother Mary and Jesus on the cross, and under them Keek's mother is asleep on the couch, her fair hair on the pillow.

'You don't have to sneak, she won't wake up.'

But I do sneak, fearful of disturbing her.

The hall is lined with photographs and I stop in the half-light to look more closely. A large framed Jesus with his bleeding heart is surrounded by family portraits, school photos and holiday snaps, all framed and arranged. Some enlarged. One face is in every photo. Like Keek, but not Keek. The same curly mass of hair, but more blonde. The same blue eyes. Before I can ask the question, Keek says, 'My brother, Matthew.'

'I didn't know you had a brother.'

Keek leans against the wall and a sigh comes out of him like he's tired enough to cry. He stares at the photos, takes a big breath as if he's going to launch into some long story, but all he says is, 'He died.'

The hallway shrinks, narrow and airless. That's what Keek's house smells of – more than dust and Jesus and toast – it smells of sad. The kind of sad that won't go away. I feel like hugging him, but he doesn't look like he wants to be hugged. He looks like he wants to escape.

Keek pushes himself off the wall and away from my sympathy. 'I was only seven when he died.'

'How old was he?'

'Seventeen.'

'That's young.'

'Yeah. Bathroom's through here.'

The bathroom is a shock, like a sudden loud noise: brightly lit with all white tiles.

'God,' I say.

'Sorry, should've warned you. You have to close your eyes and then let them adjust to the light. Dad's a fanatic for a clean bathroom.'

'And I thought *my* family was weird.'

Keek opens the medicine cabinet and reaches for the mouthwash. A stack of bottles and boxes meet my eyes. Pills, shoved in to fill the whole shelf space.

'What's all that?'

'It's Mum. She has – I don't know. Anxiety or some shit. All sorts of stuff.' Keek shuts the mirrored door and I rearrange the shocked face I see reflected there. He hands me the hyper-blue bottle. 'Use that.'

I rinse my mouth and wash my hands, pondering the strangeness of Keek's family. No wonder he's a loner at school. I'm dying to ask more about his mum, asleep out there on the couch that's made up like a bed. So fast asleep that we can walk through the house talking and she doesn't wake up. But I don't ask. I know how much Keek is already risking, just to show me.

'Come out the back,' he says.

The back garden is like nothing I've ever seen before: a network of creatures in cages. Dogs. Cats. Birds. Chickens. There's a concrete pond with a tortoise and the area around the pond is caged. Another caged pond has strange lizards crawling about underwater. Little monsters with giant grins. 'What are they?'

'Axolotl.'

He looks at me. I look back at him.

'Mexican salamanders,' he explains. 'Mexican walking fish?'

'Oh, right,' I say, as if they're not completely freaky.

Inside a cage with two huge cockatoos, three cats are fast asleep; others prowl. The cages are connected by wire tunnels. 'Don't the cats eat the birds?'

Keek seems surprised, as if this were a novel idea. 'No. Not that I know of. Check this out.' He shows me an above-ground pool with metal sides, filled to the brim with water and weeds and algae. Giant goldfish crisscross under the surface.

'Wow.' A weedy concrete path winds through the maze of wood and wire. 'Are your dogs always caged up?' I can't help but ask.

'Nah, hardly ever. Only when we're all out.'

I don't mention the fact that his mother is, technically, home. He lets the dogs out. They're old; two fat labs that ignore me, waddling off to the house. Keek points to the black. 'That's Cap, short for Captain Goodvibes, and the yellow one's Charlene. They're Dad's dogs, really.'

'Did he build all this?'

'No.' Keek's attention slides off the dogs to the drawn blinds. 'Mum.'

'Pretty handy.'

'Yeah. She spent a lot of time out here when I was growing up. I didn't know how weird it was until I started going to birthday parties and saw other people's backyards.'

'All these cages, aren't they sort of... cruel?'

'Mum hates the thought of anything being in

danger. That's what the cages are for. To keep everything safe.'

'What happened to your brother?'

Keek's fingers curl through chicken wire. 'He ...
We used to live at the beach.' A fat cockatoo unfurls
its crest and lays it flat again.

Keek is so ... stricken, I don't even want to know
any more. 'Keek—'

But he ploughs on, his forehead pressed against
the wire. 'He snuck off. Matt. Down to the surf beach.
Got pissed with his mate, Steadman. Rick Steadman.'
The cocky crests again and flaps its wings, making me
jump. Keek glances up at the bird. 'Just a bad rip.'

'Sorry.' It seems a stupid thing to say.

Keek lets go of the wire. 'Thanks. Mum and
Dad ...' but he trails off and changes the subject.
'Uncle Rob reckons I'm a lot like him. Matt. Anyway,
doesn't matter.'

The cocky spreads its wings again and squawks
a drawn-out raucous, 'Crack.'

We stand there for a while, leaning against the
wire, saying nothing. The cockatoo turns away to
preen, dragging his hooked beak down yellowing
feathers, and Keek says, 'Where's your dad?'

I stare at the big safe fish swimming in their pool.
'Promise you'll never tell anyone?'

'Okay.'

'Cross your heart?'

He crosses his heart. 'Cross my heart.'

'Mum doesn't know where he is. One-night stand.' I glance at Keek, to gauge his reaction. 'I've never met him.'

'That must be hard.'

'Yeah. His name's Michael Ellison and he lives in Sydney, or he used to. He went there before I was born. When I was little, Mum told me he was off on an adventure and I believed her. Aunty Jean told me the truth.' It still makes my throat ache to say it. 'He didn't want to know about me.'

Keek is offended on my behalf. 'Why did she tell you that?'

I bob down and stick my finger in the cage to stroke a cat. It shifts its ears. 'Cos.'

I don't want to tell him how I'd kept asking and yelling and blaming. I'd thought Mum was keeping him away on purpose. I was only thirteen. She was angry with Jean, for ages, but they're over it now.

'Mum reckons he was young. Panicked. Ran away. She's tried to find him but – anyway, no point, really.'

'That sucks.'

'I suppose so. If anyone asks, I say he lives in England.' The cat's fur is soft. Soft as a rabbit's. 'But sometimes I think he must be dead. Or that if we did find him, he still wouldn't want to know me.'

It feels strange to talk about my dad. Mum and I rarely do.

My voice drones on, almost as if it isn't connected to my body. 'I made up stories about him and did drawings, when I was little. He was sort of mixed up with Aslan from the Narnia Chronicles – appearing in the nick of time to rescue me.' I close my eyes, embarrassed to have blurted my childhood ridiculousness. No wonder my dad doesn't want to know me: I'm an idiot.

'Is that why you can't ride a bike?'

That opens my eyes again. 'What?'

'Is that why you can't ride a bike? Because your dad didn't teach you?'

The cat scares me by yawning and stretching. 'Trust you to relate every single thing to riding a stupid pushbike.' Keek's garden is freaking me out. I can't breathe. 'I've got to go.'

'I'll dink you home.'

'Nah, I'll walk. I'll see you tomorrow at school.' I picture Keek going inside, making himself a sandwich. Does he chat to his sleeping mother? When will she wake up? 'Thanks for ... you know. Showing me around.'

There's a swarm of Aunty Jean's chatty friends at the barbeque. Only a few have kids and they're all much younger than me. All the children have two parents of various genders; one little baby has two dads *and* two mothers. Everyone's normal except me. It puts me off my tampon burger.

'Cheer up, Shamrock,' says Aunty Jean, toasting me with a wave of her champagne. It sploshes out, sparkling to the grass.

I complain, a lot, and we leave early. As soon as we get home, I check our *people search* and *finders* accounts on the computer to see if anything has come up about my dad. Mum looks over my shoulder. 'Any luck?'

'No.'

'I'm sorry, love.'

'Doesn't matter.'

'I could try directory assistance again?'

'Maybe. It's probably a waste of time. Can I go on Facebook?'

'No. Jean keeps checking; he's not on Facebook. And you know how I feel about it, I—'

But I don't want to hear. I grab my sketchbook and a few greyleads, call for Lucille and go outside. Leaning against the old familiar trunk of the Golden Ash, I look out into the garden – Mum's jungle of vegetables mixed in with shrubs, herbs, flowers and weeds. Plenty of weeds. Dandelions with their clocks and forget-me-nots with their clinging seedy tendrils creep over the paths and through my memories. I try to capture them with the pencils, but without colour they seem bleak, and lonely, as though growing in the shadows of a forsaken place.

I look up. Bespeckling sunlight filters through the new spring leaves as if the whole canopy is lit from below; late sun, the kind of light that will soon disappear. I hoick myself up, but can't hang on and run up the tree like we used to – instead, I strain and clamber and almost give up, but once I'm on the old broad branch, it's worth it; the sweet smell, the quietness, the strange slow butterflies with their tiny brown lace wings.

But I could do with a cushion. I'd forgotten how uncomfortable it gets.

Mum calls me in for dinner, but I say I'm not hungry. Lucille, however, deserts her post at the foot of the tree and follows Mum inside, slowly. With a heart-lurch I see the dog's not sturdy anymore. Her back legs are thin and rickety.

<hr />

It's dark. I'm bored and starving and my bum's gone numb. I climb down (which isn't as easy as it used to be either) and go inside to make myself a toasted cheese sandwich. I don't want any big deep and meaningful about my absent father, but not talking has started to feel stupid, so I say, 'Mum, what was Keek's mum like at school?'

'Maria Yoxon? She was a spunk. Blonde hair. Cute little nose – like Keek's, actually. All the boys were crazy about her. Jean always called her Oxo. Only behind her back, mind you.'

I try to imagine the lump of snoring blankets I'd seen being the hottest girl at school, but it's impossible.

'Her dad was scary, though,' Mum says. 'They were staunch Catholics and she wasn't allowed do stuff that most kids took for granted.'

'Like what?'

'Oh, lots of things.'

'I know how she felt.'

Mum ignores my bait.

'Were you friends?' I ask.

It isn't like my mum to hedge, but her eyes slide away from me. 'Not especially. I was better friends with Dave.'

'Dave?'

'David McKenzie. Keek's dad.'

'You didn't go out with him, did you?'

'Have you had enough to eat? There's plenty of left over—'

'So you did go out with him?'

'We were friends. I thought maybe ... but then Oxo liked him and that was that.'

'Did you kiss him?'

'No.'

Is she blushing? 'You sure?'

'Have you kissed Keek?' she counters.

I'm not convinced, but do not want to get into a discussion about me and kissing. *Should* I kiss Keek?

'Have you?' Mum says.

'No. Shut up.'

'No need to be rude—'

'Keek's mum is strange. She—'

'Don't tell me about Keek's mum's private weirdnesses, Clover. I'd hate to think you'd tell anybody mine.'

Is she kidding? I'd rather die. Unfortunately, most of hers are right out there on the surface for anybody to see. But all I do is shrug. 'Sure.'

It's only later, in bed, that I think of Mum and Aunty Jean dissecting everybody they know and not only discussing private weirdnesses, but rolling around laughing about them. I feel annoyed. Mum is always encouraging me to open up to her about things but now that I want to discuss something, she shuts me down. I get up and pad down to the lounge where she has her CDs out for a change – Portishead. The shy, silky voice of Beth Gibbons laments softly from the stereo.

Mum's lying on her stomach flicking through an old photo album, feet in the air, a glass of red wine at her elbow. 'You should be in bed, Clover,' she says when she sees me.

'What are you doing?'

'Nothing important.' She closes the album and sits up. 'Anything I can do for you?'

'Mum, I need a mobile phone.' Because suddenly it burns how badly I do. 'It isn't fair that I'm the only person on the planet who doesn't have a mobile phone.'

'Where did that come from?'

'It comes from the fact that I need a phone.'

'Why?'

The right phone will give me unfettered access to Facebook, for a start. 'Everyone has one. You don't need to need one to *need* one. I'm not a little kid anymore.'

'Well, get yourself a part-time job to pay for the credit and I'll think about it. Now come on, go back to bed.'

'What were you looking at?'

'Photos.'

'Is Keek's mum in them?'

'Yes.'

'What about an iPod touch?'

'What do you mean?'

'Can I have an iPod touch then? If I can't have a phone?'

'Maybe for your birthday, Clover.'

'Is that her?'

Mum stares at the photos and disappears into her thoughts; back to school, I guess. Gently shaking herself, she points. 'That's Maria and that's Dave.'

I've seen Mum's school photos before and know where she and Aunty Jean are in every picture, but now I pore over the pages, trying to recognise Mr and Mrs McKenzie in the different years. 'And that's her?'

'Yep. That's her.' Mum drains her glass. 'Come on,

Poppet, I'm going to bed now.' She closes the album and tucks it into its slot on the bookshelf.

'You were prettier than her, Mum,' I lie.

Mum puts her arm around me and gives me a squeeze, shepherding me off to my bedroom. 'Thanks, Clover, but there was something about Oxo. We always thought she should've been a movie star.'

'They must have got married young, if Keek's brother was seventeen when Keek was only seven ...' I calculate.

'Yep, they were young. Now go on, off to bed!'

'It's horrible that Keek's brother died.'

'I can't think of anything worse, now go.'

In bed, I hear Mum take Lucille out for her before-bed toilet stop. It seems ages and they haven't come in again. I pull back my curtain and see Mum's outline through the window, another glass of wine in her hand, her other arm wrapped around herself, Lucille a dark lump leaning against her leg, and she's just standing there looking up at the stars.

———

As the need to smoke grows, Keek and I drift into the habit of going down the back during lunchtime. Before and after school too, depending on how many cigarettes Keek can pilfer. His mother is an excellent source because she buys them by the carton, but even so, he has to be careful and we have to make them last.

There's nothing worse than having no smokes. That makes your skin want to crawl off. In a way, I wish I'd never started. For one thing, I didn't realise it was going to be so time-consuming.

We sit on our customary logs. Keek blabs on about some bike comp he and Cho are training for, but I'm not listening. I'm thinking about my birthday. At twelve my body was like an outfit my mother bought without letting me try it on first. It looked like it *should* fit, but didn't; I avoided being alone with it. Thirteen is way cooler than twelve, but scary, like being transported to another planet. But fourteen sucked. Fourteen was nowhere. Fifteen's barely any better. I can't wait to be sixteen. As I light my smoke, it occurs to me that I'm sucking in gas fumes from the lighter as well. And the gas was probably smashed out of the planet by fracking – as if plain old polluting isn't enough, now they have to shatter the earth's heart to pieces. *They.* Who are they? The question sticks like a heavy lump under my ribs: I'm the one using the lighter.

'I wonder if I'm going to die soon?' I say out loud. 'With the gas fumes and everything.' I don't want to die being fifteen.

'What the hell?' says Keek.

At the same moment, Sutcliff comes over the hill and busts us. I burst into tears.

'Tears won't help you,' Sutcliff says, and marches us up the hill.

Because our 'disgrace' has taken up most of the afternoon and they've organised some special parent-teacher
meeting for tomorrow after school, we're allowed to
leave as usual at the end of the day. Most days it feels
like forever, walking home. Suddenly it isn't far enough.

'Walk me to my house,' I say.

'Your mum will kill us.'

'She'll kill me less if you're there.'

'My dad's going to spew.'

'I'll go with you to yours, if you like. If Mum'll
let me.'

But that plan is redundant. Mr McKenzie is standing
on my front porch, talking to my mother. It isn't hard
to tell that it's Keek's dad because he has the same red
hair, but cut short and practically shaved on the sides
with a trendy little peak on top. And there's something
about the way he stands that is exactly the way Keek
stands when he's at his locker and I watch him from
across the hall.

Besides all that, Keek says, 'Shit, it's my dad.'

Keek's dad and my mum. It's weird. She's looking
up at him and her face seems open and light. I catch a
glimpse of what she might've been like at high school.
Her face changes when she sees me.

Keek's dad says, 'Wow, Pen, she looks like you. Same cheerful expression.'

My mother hits him with the back of her hand. 'This is serious, Dave.'

Why is my mother being ... playful? She's supposed to be mad as hell. And that's not Aunty Jean or Yiayia she's casually belting and laughing with at my expense. That is Mr Married McKenzie. Keek's dad. Mrs McKenzie's husband. I think of Keek's mother asleep on the couch under her statues, and bristle.

Pretending to ignore Mr McKenzie, I notice his face is different to his son's. Longer, thinner, a different nose, but with the same blue eyes. 'Is there any food?' I ask my mother.

'Clover, don't be rude.'

I meet Mr McKenzie's eye. 'Hello.'

'Hello, Clover.'

Keek says, 'What's up, Dad?'

'Well, you tell me, Philip.'

I have the flywire half-open and am dragging Keek inside, but Mum stops us. 'Hang on. Dave and I have both had disturbing telephone calls from Mrs Sutcliff. It seems you two have been less than honest.'

Mr McKenzie takes up the slack. 'Cutting school, Phil? And that's not the worst of it.'

I have to sigh. I'd hardly consider missing PE to be 'cutting school'.

Mum out-sighs me. 'Smoking.'

What are they, a tag team?

'It was our first time,' Keek blurts. 'We just wanted to try it.'

I'm impressed.

Mum is deeply suspicious. 'Is that true, Clover?'

'Yes.'

'Dave' and 'Pen' raise their eyebrows at each other. 'Dave' says, 'Well, I'll take Phil home and we'll see what we can sort out. I'm sorry it had to be this way, but it's good to catch up, Pen. See you later, I hope.'

Inside, Mum's mood darkens considerably. 'What the hell is going on? Are you smoking?'

'No.'

'Tell me the truth.'

'I'm not smoking.'

'Then how is it that you're suspended for three days because you've been caught smoking? Show me your bag.'

'No way. That's invasion of privacy.'

'Yes, you're probably right. Open your bag.'

Luckily, Keek has the packet and she doesn't plunder my pencil case where tonight's smoke is stashed.

'Satisfied?' I say.

'No, Clover. Worried to death maybe, but not satisfied.' She marches into the kitchen. 'Help me with these vegies.'

While I'm peeling, she broods, chopping like a maniac. Finally, she says, 'You know love, if you do

63

smoke, there's no way I can help you. I won't be able to stop you from getting addicted.' She fries onion and garlic in butter and the smell fills the kitchen, making me love her even though her voice is driving me crazy. 'You do know that smoking is inexorably linked with lung cancer, premature ageing and a plethora of hideous diseases, don't you? And that once you start it's well nigh impossible to stop?'

Plethora: my mother is well nigh an alien. 'I only tried it once,' I lie. 'Sorry.' She looks ... lost. 'Sorry, Mum.'

Mum slides the vegetables off the chopping board into the pot and stirs them through the buttery onions. 'Three days off,' she muses with a heavy sigh. 'That's a good score.'

Later, while I'm watching *The Simpsons* on our stupid little television, the phone rings. Mum answers it, still holding a wooden spoon.

'Hello, Dave,' she says. 'This is a surprise. How did you go?' She turns her back on the lounge, drags the phone down the hall and shuts the door for privacy. I guess they're meant to be talking about us and the serious crime of smoking, but after a few minutes, she shrieks with laughter.

I've gotten away with nearly an hour of television without her complaining about the quality of the dialogue or the evils of ads before she gets off the phone and says, 'Oh, God, the soup'll be mush, and turn off that crap! It's appalling the way society ignores the detrimental impact of advertising, especially on attitudes to young women. Don't be a sheep, Clover. The sexism—'

'What were you talking to Mr McKenzie about for so long?'

'What's with the "Mr McKenzie"? His name's Dave.'

'What were you talking about?'

'Oh, lots of things. School, mostly.'

'Your school or my school?'

'Both. Here, put this bread on the table.'

'Is Keek in trouble?'

Mum comes out with two steaming bowls. 'You both are,' she says.

⸺

Keek can't be in too much trouble: while my mum forced me to help her in the garden for the three-day duration of my suspension, his dad took him and Cho to Bathurst for some big bike-nut event.

'Freestyle and flatlands,' he tells me, back at school on Tuesday with his burnt nose and multiple scrapes and bruises. 'And skate comps. And downhill.'

'Lucky you,' I say. 'I've been doing hard labour in Guiltsville.'

'They threatened not to let me go, but it was organised ages ago. Cho and I were both competing, remember?'

'Oh yeah,' I say, but I'm vague on the details. If I listen to everything Keek tells me about pushbikes, I'll have a brain haemorrhage. 'Anyway,' I ask, 'how was it?'

'Awesome. Bikes, skateboards and more bikes – and music on the mountain on Saturday night. It was so good.'

Beats dirt up your fingernails and being asked to admire the 'generosity of spinach'. I try to squash the jealousy out of my voice. 'That's great.'

'Even Dad had a go in the veterans' race – got knocked out in the second eight, but still, he was pretty pleased with himself for qualifying.'

'And Cho?'

'Thrashed me on time and points, every time,' he says ruefully. 'I came fifth in my freestyle comp, but she won hers.' He shakes his curls. 'Girls get a bit of a hard time, you know, and not all of them do flairs and that, but Cho is fearless: she was awesome.'

Yeah: awesome.

'By the way,' I shove a dog-eared paperback at him: Nick Cave's *And the Ass saw the Angel*. 'You can have this back. I hated it.' We've been on an Australian fiction binge since we had to read Margo Lanagan for English.

His forehead does a jig. 'But it's brilliant.'

'It's sick.'

'Yeah – but sick in a brilliant way.' A red flush creeps up his neck. 'You really didn't like it?'

'Yes, I really didn't like it.'

'It's better than *Sorry*.'

I'm insulted. 'Are you mad?'

'You're mad.'

My tirade about Gail Jones's book being a work of genius is surprised out of my mouth because Keek takes hold of my elbow and steps up close. 'Listen,' he says. 'Let me teach you how to ride.' His hand slides down my forearm to hold my hand. 'Just ordinary pushbike riding.'

I swallow and manage, 'Okay.'

'Awesome.' He lets go. 'Cho's right: it'll be so good for you.'

I punch him in the arm. 'Stop saying awesome.'

'Awesome.' He runs off, dodging and weaving up the crowding corridor, waggling the book over his head. 'Awesome!'

The next weekend Mum relents and lets me go down the bowl. 'Promise me, no smoking,' she says with her stern face on.

'I told you, I—'

'Promise.'

'I promise.'

While I'm getting ready to go, my old Steiner-doll Lucy (named by me, after the dog) stares down balefully from where, around Year Five, I stuffed her onto my bookshelf to live. 'It's Mum's own fault,' I mutter. 'She *makes* me lie to her.' Steiner dolls are made of cloth and stuffed with fleece – Mum made mine when I was about two – and they don't have fully formed faces: just little sewn eyes and a little sewn mouth. But that doesn't stop them from having plenty of expression. 'I have to,' I tell the disapproving Lucy. 'It's not my fault she can't handle the truth.'

I snatch Lucy down. Her face is grubby and worn with a hole at the temple, but her no-nonsense short brown woolly hair and blue-jean legs are as robust as ever, even if her red top is a bit faded. I wonder if Alison's still got Sallyann, the one Mum made for her because she loved Lucy so much. Probably not.

I chuck Lucy in the bottom of my wardrobe and go out to meet Keek on the footpath.

'New bike?'

'No, it's my mountain bike.'

'I'm not getting on that thing.'

'I'm going to teach you how to ride it, remember?'

'No, you're not.'

He holds up a hand to stop my protests. 'You said you'd try.'

'Yeah, but—'

'Come on, Clover, I can't dink you forever: trust me, it's not that hard.'

I size up the bike suspiciously. 'Right here?'

'I think we should get away from the road – on the reserve.'

We head off, Keek walking the bike as if it were a pet horse.

———

On a stretch of flat grass behind the footy oval, Keek tries his best to teach me. I'm hopeless. Every time he lets go, I wobble and tip off-balance, hopping along on one leg and bashing myself with the bike frame.

'Don't steer with your hands,' he says. 'Relax and sort of steer with your butt.'

I'm surprised by tears, creeping up on me. I'm not scared of his BMX anymore – it's like an old friend compared to this … beast. And it's nice to ride along feeling Keek's, literally, got my back. I try again, wobble, hop to the side and drop the bike on the grass, banging the inside of my ankle with the crossbar. 'Ow. I hate this bike.'

He gives up. 'You just don't want to.'

I sit on the grass to rub my ankle and wrestle back the sobs. 'You don't have to dink me. I can walk.'

'It sucks riding as slowly as you walk.'

'Well don't bother then.'

'I won't.' And he snatches up the bike and rides off, leaning forward, standing on the pedals.

It takes me about half an hour to realise he's not coming back.

———

Walking home past the oval, Robbo calls out, 'Had a fight with your boyfriend, Jones?' I'm so annoyed, I even feel pissed off with Rob Marcello.

'He's not my boyfriend,' I snap, but as Rob runs up to the boundary and leans on the metal piping fence it's as if all the angry air is sucked out of me and replaced with fairy floss.

'Is that right?' he says.

'That's right.'

Rob bounces on the spot, his knees as high as my waist.

'And how're things going with you and Rosemary?' I ask.

'Daniels?' Rob stops bouncing and stretches his thighs. 'Nothing going on with me and Daniels.'

Someone from his knot of friends calls, 'Come on you lazy prick,' and he winks at me and runs back to their social match. I watch for a while, but even though he looks my way a few times, he doesn't come and talk to me again.

I'm bored and as Mum's always telling me, life's too short for bad moods. I ring Keek.

'I'll walk faster.'

'Don't be stupid.'

'I'm not being stupid.'

There's a silence.

'Have a nice complain about me to your boyfriend?'

I feel my face heat up. 'What boyfriend?'

'Neanderthal man.'

'Don't be stupid.'

'I'm not being stupid.'

The space between us on the phone is like a vortex, sucking us into oblivion.

'You'd be independent,' he says. 'It would make your life heaps easier.'

'No, it would make *your* life heaps easier.'

'Why don't you want to learn to ride a bike?'

'I can't.'

'You can.'

'I have no balance.'

'You would if you didn't keep freaking out.'

'I'm going to freak out now if you don't shut up about it.'

There's another silence. Mum pokes her head into the hall. 'You okay?' she mouths. I nod and she disappears.

'What are you doing now?' he says.

'Nothing.'

'Want to come out?'

'Maybe.'

'I'll come and get you.'

'But—'

'I swear, I won't try and teach you anything.'

I stop to kiss Mum on my way out. 'Don't forget you've got exams coming up,' she says. 'A little study wouldn't go astray, so not too late.'

'Yes, Mother,' I groan.

When Keek arrives, he shows me the pegs he's fitted on either side of the front wheel. 'They should make it more comfortable,' he says.

I could kiss him, but settle for a hug. 'Thanks, Keek.'

'Yeah, well,' he embarrassedly wriggles out of my hug. 'Just until you get a bike of your own.'

⁓

It's only the beginning of November, but radiant heat from the hot concrete where we've been lying sends us down to the shady creek.

'I'll race you,' I yell, and run.

Without even working up a sweat, he and his bike are too quick for me.

A path runs through the trees. I think in the old days it led up through the grassy reserve, but now it's blocked by a fallen tree and a dismantled fence of old poles, like the one around the footy oval. A narrow track leads around the blockade into the dwindled forest: a stand of trees that stretches for about eight kilometres until the creek empties through a giant concrete pipe into the Yarra and, presumably, down to the sea. Mum and I followed it to the pipe a few times when Lucille was young and thrived on a long walk. I'd almost forgotten that the dog used to run everywhere at top speed and leap effortlessly into her chair; now she can barely manage it without a leg-up.

The path is overgrown with ivy and crisscrossed with peeling bark from the old gums – not old-growth forest, but venerable in their own way – sprinkled through with ferns, wattles, spiky native currant trees and blackberries.

We push through to the water's edge. It's another world, of tree ferns and mossy logs, the water over the rocks cold and daring us to drink. It's cool, though sunlight filters through the green, and quiet in a different way, like stepping into the past. We sit on a hoary long-ago fallen tree that juts almost to the other bank. Birds flit between branches and chorus in a strange jazz rhythm. The bubbling water sings too, swirling over rocks and stagnating in blackly shadowed pools dammed by bark, waterlogged sticks and an ugly smattering of rubbish. Upstream, an old kitchen chair looks surprised, as if it just tumbled in, its rusty legs angled skyward.

Keek slaps at a mosquito. 'Cho's grandparents used to live by a big river in Burma.' He claps at the mozzie, and seems thoughtful. 'Burma's called Myanmar now. Imagine that – you leave your country and they change the name while you're gone, so in a way, you can never go home.' He gets up to go poking further along the trunk. 'The river had dolphins in it.' He drags up a big stick to see if he can reach the other bank and, no doubt influenced by Cave's Euchrid Eucrow, thickens his voice into a Southern American accent. 'No dolphins in this here crick.' He amuses himself by repeating, 'Mah dolphin crick.'

I tell him to shush and, as my mum would whisper, just sit 'in its shadowy heart'. After a while, probably lulled by the peacefulness, I say, 'When I was little, Mum used to sing songs to the undines.'

'The what?'

I'm glad we're in shadow. 'Water-fairies. Undines in the water, sylphs in the air, gnomes deep in the earth, and fire fairies. I never liked the fire fairies' proper name.'

'Oh yeah?' Keek has his sceptical eyebrows on.

'Salamanders.'

'You can get axolotl called fire salamanders,' he concedes. 'People don't swim in this, do they?'

Alison and I used to paddle down here, when we were little: with Mum, of course. 'Probably not,' I say. 'It's not really deep enough for swimming, anyway.'

Keek points. 'Look.'

An echidna. We freeze and it scrabbles to dig its face into the dirt before freezing too, leaving only spines for us to admire. After a few minutes, Keek says, 'Bored,' and pushes me into the shallow water; I grab his shirt and pull him in after me. We wrestle, despite the rocks, and his skin against mine is warm even in the freezing water. He pushes past me to clamber out.

Did you want to kiss me? I want to say, but I never will. I mean, he would've already, wouldn't he, if he wanted to? And after all, I don't want to kiss him. I mean, I would've already, wouldn't I, if I wanted to?

'The anteater's gone,' he says.

Everyone was nervous about the end-of-year exams, even Mum, even Alison Larder, but I quite liked being sure there was at least some purpose to studying. Not that I studied much, but I think I did all right. I bet Alison gets all A-plusses. Lying under the Golden Ash, feeling the freedom of the school holidays lift me like a helium balloon to float up through the buttery leaves, it makes me feel happy to imagine she did.

Keek and I are supposed to be going to the movies at some stage, but he hasn't turned up. Perhaps his mum won't let him out. Sometimes she freaks out, or has 'episodes' that make him feel like he has to stay home.

'I can't go,' he says to me. 'She'll kill herself or something.'

But any time I go there – if she's awake – she's as nice as pie, if dishevelled, and a bit bloated, you know, in that unhealthy sort of way. But she's still beautiful and her hair is still blonde. I wonder if she dyes it. She must.

I've never seen anyone smoke so intensely. When she's not asleep on the couch, she sits on their back porch staring at the cages, chain-smoking.

'We grew up around here,' she's told me a few times now. 'I never wanted to move back here. I wanted to live in Queensland. Or Paris. But David ... when ...' She butts out her cigarette and reaches for another. 'He didn't work for nearly two years, you know. Hopeless. This is his uncle's house, you know. I never wanted to move back here.'

I find myself almost hypnotised, but Keek always drags me away. If he isn't allowed to go far, we hang out at the willow and read aloud to each other. Mum lent him *The Hitchhiker's Guide to the Galaxy* and he's obsessed. It *is* funny.

Whenever we do ride off, Mrs McKenzie shouts, 'Look after my boy, Clover,' and Keek says, 'Ignore her.'

My mother annoys me by being on the phone.

'See how I need a mobile?' I complain.

She cups the receiver and mouths, 'You'll have to wait.'

'Mum, I need to call Keek.'

She shakes her head and says, 'Sorry, I missed that.'

'I'll just walk there then.'

She nods and waves me away with a distracted air kiss.

———

Mrs McKenzie says hello and smiles, but her voice is croaky and she doesn't take off her sunglasses. Never a good sign.

'We're going to the willow,' Keek tells her.

'No.' She crosses her arms as if holding herself in. 'Not today. Stay on the property.'

He turns his back on her. 'I'm going to the shed.'

I follow. 'You all right?'

We hide behind the garage and light up. Keek keeps a lookout. 'Yeah, am now.'

'What happened?'

'Dad.'

'What'd he do?'

'Said he was leaving.'

'No shit?'

Keek scrapes mud off his shoe against an old brick. 'No shit.'

'Is he?'

'Nup.'

'Well, that's good. Isn't it?'

'He never does.' Keek kicks at the brick. It rolls over and there's a worm, squirming in the light.

Keek and I stare at the worm, now on his palm. Keek seems entranced but I don't find worms *that* fascinating.

'You right?' I say.

He grunts, softly, and the worm flips itself over.

I leave him to it and venture into the garage, pulling up the roller door to let in more light. The garage smells musty, oily. Keek's a million miles away: he's in the driveway now, watching the worm wriggle across the concrete, heading for the grass. I fossick around. There's gardening stuff, camping equipment covered in cobwebs, a stack of old wooden crates full of empty brown bottles with no labels, a wall of hanging tools that don't seem to have been used, a meccano-stack of old pushbike parts and – score! A whole box of aerosol paint, blue, red, black, green, gold, silver, white, never even used by the look of them. Keek squats next to me.

'Where's your worm?' I ask.

'It wasn't my worm,' he says.

I pull out a can – black. 'What's all this?'

'That's Dad's uncle's stuff. Uncle Andy. He restored pushbikes for a hobby, and Dad still goes on about his home-brew. He made wine, too – there are still a few bottles of Uncle Andy's Elderberry in the pantry, but I don't think anyone's game to open them.' He lifts a rusty crossbar from the stack and a big black spider scuttles off, scaring the crap out of both of us.

Keek says, 'Jesus' and drops the crossbar on a bunch of garbage bags filled with old clothes and shoes. 'I guess he spray-painted the bikes when he was finished fixing them up. He was pretty old. He died when I was about nine. That's why we got this house.'

'Do you remember Marilyn Lepace?' I say, peering into the paint-can box for spiders and hoping there aren't any.

'Who?'

'Marilyn Lepace.'

He picks up a handlebar to poke at a cobweb. 'Nup.'

————

Marilyn Lepace was a year above me and never so much as glanced in my direction until Sutcliff sent me to Berty for refusing to take off my beanie – and she was already outside the principal's office, lounging against the wall. She beckoned me to the window that looked out on the quadrangle.

'Check it out,' she said with a sneery curl to her lip. 'My farewell to Fernwood.'

I stared.

'Your mouth's open.'

I shut my mouth.

They'd tried to scrub it off, but in huge red lettering outlined in black on the drama studio wall, Marilyn Lepace's 'FKU BERTY' rose from a lumpy bed of skulls and refused to be denied. I was mesmerised: the chunkiness of it. The grunge. The pulpy-red blackness and the pale bone. The pretend flashes of light really worked. It was the coolest thing I'd ever seen.

The principal's door opened and he motioned me inside; then eyed Marilyn warily. 'Your mother is on the way.'

Marilyn held my eye. 'I'm expelled,' she said.

All I could do was nod, my blood racing with a strange, admiring thrill.

I pick up a can and flick off the lid. Adrenaline rushes up from the earth and into my body, my arm, my hand holding the paint. 'I want to spray this can.'

'Where?'

'Anywhere.'

'Not in my parents' garage.'

'What about the road?'

'Black paint on the road, it won't work. You're an idiot.'

I head out to the road. 'I don't care. I have to spray this can of paint as soon as possible.'

'An idiot with a spray can,' Keek says after me. 'Just what we need.'

An aerosol can is no pencil. No paintbrush, either. It's alive. I'm shocked by the force of the paint from the nozzle. By how wide it sprays. I've read that graff artists get special caps and now I know why. Keek's right, it does disappear on the road. But I don't care. It's intoxicating.

Keek hovers on the footpath. 'What are you writing?'

'My tag.'

'You have a tag?'

'I do now.'

He looks down at my scrawl. 'Kandas,' he says. 'What's that?'

'You know, Candace, warrior queen of the Kushite Empire.'

'That's not how you spell Candace.'

'It's a tag,' I say, mildly scornful. 'You can't spell it *right*.'

Keek yawns. 'I don't like it. No one will get it.'

I straighten and stretch my back, running a curious eye over the fence across the road. 'I'll get it,' I say.

Keek smiles when he sees me waiting on the footpath. His expression darkens when he spots my criminal backpack. 'What's in there?'

'Paint.'

He crosses his arms in a pretty good impersonation of Mrs Sutcliff.

'No one will care if I practise down there,' I reason.

It's taken days of sketching and mostly invisible road-scribbling to master 'Kandas', and how better to amuse myself at the bowl over the summer holidays?

'Or would you rather I hung out under the railway bridge?'

'Don't be an idiot.'

'Don't call me an idiot.'

'Don't act like an idiot and I won't call you an idiot.'

I hold it out to him. 'Are you going to carry the bag or not?'

***

At first I feel embarrassed, experimenting with Cho and the others being here, but they're busy practicing some new trick they've caught off the internet and barely pay attention to me. I feel sweaty and strange, as if the police might spring out from behind the bus stop. My first tags are horrible, but a flat section of the bowl falls prey to my freeform experiments and some of it doesn't look too bad, considering the dinosaur paints I'm using.

'Vandalism,' Keek calls it.

'Graff,' says Cho.

'Art,' I insist.

Well, it will be.

It's the dawn of Year Eleven and I groan as I drag my bag on my shoulder and head to the front door, half-dreading and half-excited to see what the new year will bring.

'What about we try homeschooling?' Mum asks, looking worried as hell about that idea.

'Bit late, Mum.'

'Oh, Clove, I don't want you to be ground into sausage meat.'

My mum might hate television, but she loves old DVDs and last night we watched Pink Floyd's *The Wall* – it's obviously had a lingering effect. I fell asleep before the end, but I saw the scene where the school kids get put through the meat-mincer. 'I don't want to be homeschooled,' I say, and give her a goodbye peck.

And that's true. God only knows what kind of

freak I'd end up being if my mother were the only person to have influence over me.

———

Looking down at school from the top of the hill is like witnessing an architectural crime scene. There's more art in a stop sign, in the necklace of mediocre tags strung around the art room portables. Asphalt, concrete and fibrocement; Mother Nature caged and dissected into squares of tanbark, nearly all the trees pushed to the edges. They'd rather we die of boredom than climb a tree.

Like a chink in my armour, Keek swings into step next to me.

'The Year Sevens look about ten,' I say. 'I want to tell them all to run home and stay there.'

'They'd get bored.'

I shoot him a look. 'Yeah? Well, Mum reckons boredom is the flip side of creativity.'

'Yeah? Well your mum's on the flip side of reality.'

'So you don't think school's priming us for neo-liberal servitude, like Mum says; having the creativity crushed out of us, shoving us into consumer boxes, little cogs in the economic machine?'

Keek gives me two thumbs up, saying, 'I don't think anything,' and splits off to catch up with Cho and head to their elective.

———

My VCE art teacher is brand new to the school as well as to me. Sutcliff introduced her at assembly as Ms Yamouni and that's all the class knows about her. We sit outside the art room waiting, tossing around the rumour that she's from Iraq.

Four girls slouch against the wall in the corridor and the rest of the class spills out from there.

'What? Like falafel?' Rosemary Daniels says, and laughs.

Presumably, Rosemary has given up SingStar. She has gorgeous blacker-than-black dyed hair that never grows out at the roots. Her posse of cool girls laugh at her joke, but they don't *have* to laugh and that gives them their edge. Their names are Natalie, Katie and Ellen, but Keek has secretly named them Parsley, Sage and Thyme: the Herbs. Ellen/Thyme's dress is so short, any movement flashes her cool undies – the brand Mum won't buy me because of some capitalist crime she reckons the company committed against their workers.

Pete Tsaparis laughs too loud and says, 'She's probably a terrorist.'

'Don't be a dickhead,' I tell him.

He gives me a shove. 'Shut your face.'

Rosemary says, 'She taught with a falafel in her hand,' like a voice-over, and people laugh. It's not that she or the other three are especially thin, or even beautiful. Not especially. Or even that funny. But they always manage to be in the same Home Group while the rest of us are shuffled around, and they never seem to need anybody or get excited about anything except each other. Everybody is in love with them – there are Herb-clones all over the school. It's the Asian girls who start trends, but somehow it's the Herbs who get crowned queens of style. Even Keek observes them from afar.

Rosemary wants to become a fashion designer, so I guess that's why they've elected to do VCE Art.

'Yes, like falafel.' The voice is rich and has a slight, warm accent. We turn collectively and there's Ms Yamouni with her incredibly thick dark hair tied in a knot on top of her head, and her oval face and her beauty spot. She's petite and rounded and when she walks past me, smells of acrylic paint and rose oil. I wonder how long she's been listening to us. She nods to Rosemary and says, 'What's your name?'

'Rosemary.'

Ms Yamouni's smile shows her big, square teeth. 'Ah! Like roast lamb?'

The class shifts uncomfortably. There is something scary about Rosemary Daniels and no one wants to get on the wrong side of her. But she laughs and says, 'Yeah. That's how my mum makes it,' and we all breathe out.

'Well, I'm a vegetarian, Rosemary, but I won't be forgetting your name. Not so sure about all the rest of you, so you'd better answer the roll and then we can get on with business.' She unlocks the art-room door and we pile in. Her voice rises up over our noise. 'And while I'm calling the roll, I want you to move all these tables into a circle. Do you think you can manage that?'

Just as well every art class is a double because it takes about fifteen minutes for us not to manage it well at all. I groan. First amateur theatre, now furniture removal. When she's given us a lecture about respecting the space, equipment and art supplies, she makes us put on our smocks, roll up our sleeves and sets out a dozen bottles of acrylic paint – all blue – and lays out a slab of butcher's paper.

'Just one colour?' asks Rosemary.

'Just one.' Yamouni wipes her hands. 'Prussian blue was created by a Swiss paint-maker called Diesbach. Funnily enough, he was trying to make red, mixing plant ashes that had been soaked in water, called potash, and iron sulphate, which he would have called *copperas* and might have been made from blood.' There's a collective squeamish lament.

'Blood?' I ask.

'Blood,' she replies. 'It's only been a relatively short time that artists have had the privilege of going to a shop and buying pre-mixed paint off the shelf. In the past, many artists were scientists, too: chemists, creating new pigments in their search to express adoration, beauty, pain, the human condition, our aspirations.' She takes a deep breath, as if standing by the ocean. 'Blood, animal fat, all sorts of things. Luckily for us, when Diesbach tried to improve his pale red gone wrong because of his cheap ingredients, he heated it to concentrate the colour and accidentally discovered this stunning blue instead. At the other end of the blue spectrum, ultramarine was made from precious stone, lapis lazuli – quite rare and at times, in some places, more valuable than gold.'

Yamouni instructs us to pour a blob of our colour wherever we like on our paper. 'This is acrylic paint, of course – all synthetic. Not too much,' she says. 'But don't be stingy, either.'

Pete Tsaparis makes a gross phallic gesture with the bottle, then squeezes so hard it slurps onto the floor.

Yamouni says, 'No.' She takes it off him and hands him a roll of paper towel. 'Clean that up and go and sit down. I meant what I said. If you can't respect the art supplies, you can't participate. But there's plenty to be learned by observing: sit over there and watch.'

I can tell Pete wants to arc up, but he obviously thinks better of it and deflates. Everyone knows he's on a behaviour card after almost getting expelled for punching Lisa Dalboni's younger brother Mike after the cross-country run.

While Yamouni ladles paint back into the bottle with a palette knife, he wipes the worst of it from the floor and slouches off to take a seat at the back of the room. He acts like he doesn't care about getting into trouble, but we've all seen his dad go off at the footy and no one would want to cross that guy – always gripping Pete by the back of the neck; I think it's meant to be affection, but it looks more like intimidation to me.

Alison puts up her hand. 'Are we doing finger painting?'

'Yes, but not like when you were in kindergarten,' says Yamouni. 'This is a meditative exploration of colour.'

I sigh: meditative finger painting. I don't suppose da Vinci ever had to put up with crap like this.

Yamouni instructs us in a low, lulling voice. 'The object isn't to make an image, but to experience the colour – just move it around the paper and see what it has to say to you.'

Laughter mixed with groans of disgust swells as our fingers come in contact with the paint's sticky smoothness.

'Shh, that's it, well done. Work slowly, slow as you can. Shh, no talking.' She walks around, standing near the Herbs, who are laughing the most. 'Take a deep breath,' she says. 'That's right. Breathing in, breathing out. Long slow breaths. Keep working. Colour is far more valuable than gold. If you take the time to get to know it, to listen to its secrets. Some of humanity's greatest artists have loved this colour – Van Gogh, Monet, Picasso ...'

It's deep, the blue – and as I work it slowly over the page and the smattering of sniggers settles into quiet, I follow Yamouni's instructions to listen to my breathing: in and out. Moving the blue, there's a sense of expanding space, like a dark ocean or an evening sky. Or even what's behind the sky – the swirling cosmos that has no edges, no end. There's something fearful about the thought of a blue infinity, like you could fall into it and disappear; or be swept into it like the blue of great waves engulfing a ship.

Yamouni says, 'The palette is breath to the artist. Shh, that's right,' and the fear passes into a feeling of freedom, like flying, and the blue is serene.

At last she says, 'Bring what you're doing to a close and wash up.' Noise erupts and kids threaten each other with sticky blue hands. Over the bustle she says, 'Next week, I want to have a quick warm-up and get into our bodies before we start the class.'

Up the back, big Mark swears quite loudly, but Yamouni ignores it.

'If you can do the tables and get the paper set up in less than five minutes, everyone who participates gets a handmade chocolate.'

'Is that safe?' The class stares at Alison, who rarely says anything, ever. Red falls over her face like a mottled shadow. Trust Al to be worried about safety in the face of chocolate – she's more like her mother than I thought.

'Guaranteed nut-wheat-egg-free and not made on any machinery at all. Anyone allergic to sugar? Lactose?

I don't have any medical forms for those, so as long as I don't lace them with arsenic, I think we'll be fine. Now off you go and as they say in the classics: Be careful out there.'

'What classic is that?'

'*Hill Street Blues*.'

Alison blushes into her beetroot hues and looks worried, as if her Year Twelve ENTER score might depend on knowing the reference. Trung pats her arm and says, 'I've never heard of it either.'

Yamouni breathes a light laugh. 'Don't worry. You weren't meant to get it. It was my dad's favourite cop show in the '80s. He used to say it and I say it now for my own amusement.'

It gives me a shock, to think of a teacher having a 'dad' and private amusements. I try to picture Sutcliff as a child with parents, but it's not possible.

⁓

Keek comes around for dinner and to play 500 with me against Mum and Mrs T. Yiayia is passionate about 500. All her children and most of their partners play, they pull out card tables and turn her lounge room into a 500 frenzy. When we were little, Alison and I had lined up with Mrs T's grandchildren, running through the maze as fast as we could without bumping the flimsy tables. Being yelled at by the Theopopolouses wasn't anything like being yelled at by my mum.

'Did you like school, Yiayia?' I follow Mum's lead with my only trump, the Jack of Hearts.

Yiayia makes a smug face, says, 'Beat that!' and lays down the Joker. 'I love school.' She leans back to fold her card-hand on her belly and stare into space. 'I love it with all my heart and soul. And my shoes – oh my God, such beautiful school shoes.' She sits up and examines her cards. 'But they made me leave at the end of Grade Six.'

'Who made you leave?' says Mum, collecting the trick for their growing pile.

'Everybody. In my village, no girls went past Grade Six. I was lucky my father sent me to school at all.'

'What did you do when you left?'

'I work for Mr Andreadis in his bakery.' A smile creeps over her. 'And then I met my Theo. Now, come on – take that!' and she leads the 7 of Clubs. She must be sure Mum can win it with a trump.

She's right. They flog us.

'Don't worry,' says Yiayia, happy to win, nodding toward Keek, 'he still has his training wheels.'

After the game we walk down to the local kiddies park. Keek is against slaving for a handmade chocolate. 'It's weird,' he says.

'She's ...' What can I say to Keek about a teacher who talks about paint as if it were as valuable as gold, or air. 'I dunno.'

We sit on a strange seesaw-bugs-on-a-spring installation at the park. 'I've got Ratshit for Home Group,' Keek complains.

Good old Mr Radshaw. Every year at assembly he tells the same 'how does a mathematician pick his nose?' joke.

'You told me that already,' I say. 'However, I feel sorry for you and accept that it's worth complaining about twice. How are his hairs going?'

'Still tufting out of every orifice, thank you.'

'Who else is in your Home Group?'

'It's full of footy heroes like Jason Eldrich and that stupid Robbo. Robbo, ug ug. Lisa Dalboni's all right. And Cho is cool.'

I bounce. 'Cho has so got the hots for you.'

Keek stubs out his smoke and flicks it into the bushes. 'She does not. You're just jealous because she's a good rider and you're completely hopeless.'

I point to his abandoned cigarette butt. 'Some little kid could find that and eat it and die.'

'Right, Mum.'

'It's poisoning the earth. Pick it up and put it in the bin.'

'Thanks for that, Mum.'

I have to get off the springy bug and punch him before he'll do what I tell him.

We sit there for a while, seesawing.

'Rob Marcello's a good footballer,' I say.

'I can't believe you like football, Clover. It's something I've always found very disappointing about you.'

'And he's very good-looking.'

Keek reacts like I've offered him snot to eat. 'Robbo? If you like the hairy Neanderthal look.'

'Just because someone has reached puberty doesn't mean they're Neanderthal.'

'Are you serious? That's not puberty – the guy has to shave his *neck*.'

'Unlike some boys who don't have to shave at all.'

'I don't want to be hairy. I don't want to shave, either. Rob Marcello has to shave his forehead.'

'His nose.'

'His eyelids.'

'Behind his knees.'

'His gums.'

We roll about at this hilarity.

'Anyway,' I say. 'I think he's going out with Sage, or it might be Parsley.'

'So you *do* like him?' Keek practically throws himself off the seesaw in disgust, which makes my bug hit the ground hard. I'm bounced off, half-annoyed and half-laughing.

'Good one.' I reach out a hand to demand help. He takes it and I pull myself up and brush off the tanbark. 'We'd better get back. School tomorrow and we don't want mother freaking out.'

'Yeah – wanna make sure you get your beauty sleep for Robbo.'

'Don't be a dick.'

'Robbo.'

'I'll kill you.'

'Robbo. Robbo. Robbo.'

I give up trying to catch him long before he peels off to his place.

———— ⁓ ————

Chocolate is good bait but it takes us seven minutes and twenty-three seconds to arrange the tables in the art room because stubborn and obese Mark Creswell sits on a table and refuses to budge. He has a bag of mini Mars Bars and offers to share them with those who join his rebellion. In the end, we band together and move him and his table, protest and all. We get our chocolates for teamwork. They're good.

Mark burrows in and says, 'I'm not getting up.'

Yamouni leaves him there, but throws him encouraging glances while she gathers us into a circle. I feel sorry for Trung Nguyên and Alison Larder; the dickiest pair in class, shoved along by the pecking order to stand next to the teacher. Trung's second-generation Vietnamese Australian, but whenever he says anything, idiots like Pete Tsaparis act surprised that he's got an Australian accent.

'Right,' says Yamouni. 'Time to get into our bodies and wake up, ready for the class. We're going to play the clap-your-name game.'

'Are you serious?' It's Thyme, her eyes sliding their challenge between Yamouni and Rosemary Daniels. Rosemary's eyes slide to Pete, who sneers.

Yamouni says, 'Not in the slightest bit.'

Thyme is crusty with scorn. 'What?'

'I mean I'm not in the slightest bit serious, Ellen – it's just a thing.' Yamouni shrugs. 'It's just a thing I want you to do.'

Thyme looks to Rosemary, who crosses her arms and says, 'Why should we?'

Yamouni smiles as if Rosemary's challenge makes her happy. 'Well, if you don't, you'll never know.'

'Know what?' asks Mark Creswell. I'm not even sure he meant to, because he looks surprised to have spoken.

Yamouni glances over to him and nods. 'Where it might lead us.' She looks around the circle. 'What are you afraid of? You know, if you want to make art, real art, you have to learn to know fear and make it your friend. Anyone heard of the saying "Feel the fear and do it anyway"?'

I feel hot tears, but won't let them out.

Pete and a couple of the boys swell as if menace can prove they aren't scared of anything.

'This is crap,' says Thyme. She stares at Rosemary, daring her to do something.

Yamouni gestures as if she's offering something invisible. 'Thanks, Ellen,' she says. 'I forget how odd I seem to most people.' She turns to the group. 'It's my way, a bit of not-schoolishness and not intended to make you angry or waste your time.' Her eyes rest on each of us briefly but calmly, taking us in. 'For a group of people to make art in one room, to truly explore what art is and where art can take us, there has to be trust. But trust doesn't necessarily exist in the world. The older we get, the more it's got to be built up. Won. My way works for me, but perhaps not for you, so I'm sorry about that.'

There is nothing mocking in her voice. It's as if she means it.

'I would like you to have a go, though,' she says. 'So at least you know what you're rejecting.'

Thyme seems shocked. 'Rosemary,' she says. Like a password. Or a charm.

Everyone is looking between Yamouni, Rosemary and Thyme – except Pete, who says, 'I only chose this subject cos it's slack as,' and gets out his mobile phone. Alison's eyes are shut; the Larder has been red-faced for a while, simmering with whatever strange passions possess her. But Yamouni keeps her kind eyes on Thyme, who flickers between the teacher and Rosemary.

Rosemary Daniels has a way of treating people as if they're an experiment she's conducting. Mostly she seems only mildly curious about the outcome.

She observes her friend and the new teacher. 'Chill out, Ellen,' she says.

I think I see a cloud form over Yamouni's head, but she says, 'Repeat after me,' and claps twice. We repeat. She claps again and says, 'Laila.'

'Now: everyone.'

Clap, clap, 'Laila,' we say, her first name strange in my mouth, like some sort of transgression, and she gestures to Alison who claps twice and says, 'Alison'.

We clap twice and repeat Alison's name. If Yamouni is relieved, it doesn't show. She nods to the next kid as if all is as it should be and we clap and name our way around the circle. By the time we get back to the beginning, a rhythm has taken over and the sting has gone out of it.

She makes us do it again, quicker this time, and instead of our names, any old sound at all. Whatever comes. 'Don't think: clap,' she says. She doesn't raise an eyebrow when Pete says 'motherfucker' for his sound and Thyme says 'Piss.' She just says it with the rest of us and moves on. When it comes to me, a freaky little squeak comes out and I think I might die, but everyone makes my freaky little squeak and by the second round, even Alison's boring 'hello' has a laugh attached.

'Now, bring the chairs around. You'll need a pen and your notebooks.'

In the shuffle, Trung accidentally bumps Pete with the leg of his chair.

'Watch it, boat-boy.'

'Boat-boy?' Trung looks confused. 'I was born in Nunawading.'

Yamouni slams a heavy hardback art book on the table and I'm not the only one who jumps. 'How dare you?' she says, her eyes levelled squarely at Pete.

Pete is embarrassed. 'What? My dad reckons all—'

'Wake up,' she snaps. 'You'd better learn some respect. I won't have racism in this room.' She sweeps her fiery eyes over us. 'Do you understand me?' She turns back to Pete. 'Apologise.'

'Sorry.'

'Sorry, who?'

Pete tenses his reddening jaw and I hope this doesn't have an ugly backlash. 'Sorry, Trung.'

———

By the end of the week, she has us doing the hokey-pokey. The Herbs roll their eyes and Pete flat out refuses, but it's hysterical, and dangerous when we hold hands and surge into the centre shouting 'Whoa, the hokey-pokey' but Yamouni manages to keep going and people pull each other up from being crushed and no one dies.

And that is that. Every art class starts with stupidity. Mark sits and watches us do weirder and weirder things: standing in a circle as close to each other as we can be, and shuffling in closer and closer until we can sit on each other's knees, balanced. All crossing the circle at the same time with our eyes closed and not sticking our elbows out. Playing crazy games with lots of clapping and making eye contact and yelling things like 'peepo' at each other. We have to mark ourselves off on the roll and not cheat. The Herbs are her pets. Even Thyme, who doesn't like anybody.

I love Yamouni. But it's not just because she talks about trust and truth and beauty and art and nature and humanity and purpose and transformation as if they actually matter in the universe. And it isn't her enthusiasm for doing weird stuff that makes her the best art teacher I've ever had – I've had spectacularly enthusiastic teachers before and they mostly make you want to chuck. It's because on that second day she never even considered confiscating Mark's Mars Bars, or charging him with premeditated disruption, or sending him off to be punished.

And she looks at him, right at him – Mark Creswell – which few humans ever do, and she smiles. Genuinely. Repeatedly. It's compelling. When Pete bails to Woodwork, Mark gets up and joins our 'warm ups'. He moves his body and no one laughs. I think we all feel the miracle.

As the year goes on, she shows us how to create depth with light and shade, and master the drawn line with texture and dimension – and she helps me turn the darkness that pours from my soul into form and colour and shape. She patiently explains how to get the perspective right, making us practise how the masters did it. Michelangelo, da Vinci – taking elements of their work, just small studies, and helping us replicate them, encouraging us to interpret and adapt them in our own time, if we want to.

'Why do we have to do all this old shit?' asks Parsley in a fit of frustration.

'Because they've already found answers to the problems you can't yet even conceive, my dear.'

'So?'

'So, when you discover what the problems are, you'll also discover you have the solutions.'

Parsley drops her brush on her tray and says, 'I'm going to the toilet.'

Yamouni looks over my shoulder. 'May I?' she says and, when I nod, with the smallest flick of the brush, tames the shape and brings it closer to where it needs to go. 'More shade, here.'

I spend most of my lunchtimes in her art room, sometimes alone, but often with Alison Larder. We rarely speak. Alison's painting a to-scale reproduction of Van Gogh's sunflowers that she's working out with maths. It's getting so good, I'm convinced she's going to be a forger.

Yamouni has managed to organise us a couple of couches for the art room and when it rains, Keek comes and reads. I like it when he sits there, reading, but today he closes his book and comes over to my painting. 'I liked it better before you did all that stuff.' He waves vaguely at the canvas.

'Gee, thanks.'

Yamouni arrives to do something at her desk and he disappears.

I've chosen Hieronymus Bosch for my major art-history assignment and I've been leafing through a giant book on him that I borrowed from the library, full of colour plates of his work depicting medieval life, and darker things. It's rubbing off. The background of my painting is a watercolour experiment of the primary-colour work we've continued in class, but I've fallen in love with the storytelling in Bosch's paintings, the macabre yet beautiful little details – he might have been a religious nut who believed in eternal damnation, but at least he was *saying* something. What do *I* want to say? At the moment it's a bunch of vaguely medieval characters falling into or climbing out of a fiery abyss that's less hell and more red splodge. Keek's right, it's not working: it's a mess. A heavy sigh escapes me, embarrassingly audible.

Yamouni pauses on her way past. 'Oh, this wonderful moment, this little happening here! I love this.' She reaches around me, her hand hovering over a place where the colour washes have combined and bled into a shape that's morphed, with my help, into a character. 'I see what you're trying to do here – keep going. Don't be afraid to scrub that back and rework the colours, if you need to, and follow this impulse.' She pats me. 'It's all right to make a mess, Clover. It's part of it.'

Once when I was down at the creek, a small brown bird landed so close to me I could've touched it, if it would've let me. It opened its beak and a warbling of joy came flooding from its feathery throat – and that's how my heart feels now, like that little singing bird.

'Thanks,' I mumble.

'And I like this willow. Who's the onion man?'

It's not possible to lie to her. 'My father.'

'He turns up a lot.'

'I like onions.'

'And the lion? Lovely use of the yellow, by the way.'

'My father.'

'I'd like to meet this father of yours.'

I shrug. So would I.

⁓

Winter's over, but it's still too cold and wet to go outside. I'm at my desk in my bedroom and Keek's sprawled on the bed reading from *The Phantom Tollbooth*; another old treasure from Mum's bookshelf. 'Genius!' according to Keek. I was sure it was a kids' book, but he is convincing me otherwise.

Mum pushes the door open, flourishing the local newspaper. 'Look!' she demands.

We look. The headline reads: FREEWAY LINK GETS GREEN LIGHT.

'And?' Keek asks.

Mum nearly wriggles out of her skin with outrage at our apathy. 'That's your creek. That's Fernwood. If this goes through, they'll put the creek underground.'

My heart twitches with tears. 'But they can't,' I say. 'It's a wildlife corridor.'

Keek sits up. 'What's a wildlife corridor?'

'Bushland connecting wildlife habitats,' I say.

Mum's voice is shaky. 'My gardening group has a plant co-op so people can put the right kind of native plants in their gardens, to add to the corridors. We're mentioned in this article, for what it's worth.' She slaps the newspaper. 'For years the council has been fighting the proposal and now they've lost and say there's no budget to fight any more. I bet it's because they've given the go-ahead for that bloody new housing estate. The bulldozers are moving in.'

'My dad reckons that freeway will be great,' says Keek. 'He works in the city and – don't look at me like that Clover. I dunno.'

Mum bristles. 'Well, nobody's denying roads are convenient. But at the expense of old trees? Of biodiversity? Of wildlife that's already reduced to using corridors because most of the natural habitat has been destroyed? Your father knows better than that – or maybe he's changed more than I thought.'

'I dunno,' says Keek.

She stares at us. We stare back.

'The trees will be chopped down,' she says.

———

On Monday morning, the Friends of Fernwood picket the council offices. I take the day off and wave my homemade picket sign: Save the Creek! People in cars ignore us, not even the occasional beep. Passers-by sign our petition, but it's clear most of them feel that a road linking to the freeway will be great for Fernwood and make it quick to drive to the city.

'I haven't been down to the creek for years,' is the general response.

The library is part of the council buildings and the librarian stops to read the signs on his way to work. 'Last time I was down there, those kids had filled it full of shopping trolleys,' he says.

'Surely not full, Tom?' Mum has her best smile on, though I know she's seething inside.

'Well, you know what I mean.' He waves dismissively in the direction of the reserve. 'It's full of rubbish.'

'I think that's been deliberate.' Mum gestures to the council building. 'The developers have been submitting for approval to do this for ten years. Purposeful degradation of the creek is all part of it. Are you really happy to let them destroy the oldest sliver of forest left in this area for the sake of a bit of rubbish in the creek?'

'I'm not one for conspiracy theories.' Tom nods and strides away. 'Good luck to you.' He flinches away from me as if I might bite before unlocking the library door and disappearing inside; I think the skaters have made him allergic to teenagers. I imagine him sitting in there with a cup of tea, reading something intensely tedious and educational.

Heading off to protest with Mum was exciting. Actually being here with our petition is boring. And disappointing because there are a total of nine Friends of Fernwood and only six of them could take the day off work. There are a few people from some orchid society and a small handful of locals who live near the proposed development site. Looking around, I reckon the average age is sixty-five.

Things get a little more exciting after lunch when Diane Martin, our local member, comes out to speak to us, and a journalist from the local paper turns up.

'Thanks for doing this, Jeff,' Mum says to him – they must be friends; she sometimes works for the *Fernwood Mail*.

D Martin MP stands on the step. 'It's really wonderful that, like the Fernwood council, you are also passionate about the environment,' she says brightly. 'We commend you. The council has thoroughly examined this issue and weighed up the advantages for the local economy and our responsibilities to the wider community who will benefit from the completion of this freeway link and bypass. There were several public meetings that were well-attended and the feedback from those meetings has been duly considered. We are all very proud of this beautiful Shire and there are still wonderful parkland areas.'

'What about the function of the creek as a wildlife corridor?' Mum calls out.

'An environmental impact study has been completed and after assessing its findings, we are happy for the project to proceed.'

But Mum is ready, backed up by shouts and murmurs from the rest of the Friends and from the orchid society. She waves papers in the air. 'Environmental studies have been done in previous years and dire consequences reported, including the destruction of marsupial rats, birds and native orchids, now endangered in Victoria because of developments like this freeway. For ten years the plans have been knocked back. With dwindling land for wildlife and an increase in threats to our native flora and fauna thanks to the granting of land for the new housing estate, how can the feasibility of the area have suddenly changed for the better?'

D Martin MP is uncomfortable. 'I am not an expert on the environment, but the impact study was undertaken by an independent body.'

Mum practically jumps on the spot. 'Independent? It was commissioned by the State government, paid for by the developers and refused to take into account data from previous environmental reports including that of the Australasian Native Orchid Society, an organisation dedicated to the conservation and preservation of native orchids in their natural habitat, who have registered a threatened species in the Fernwood creek area.'

'Hear, hear,' shout the orchid people.

'Fernwood council has registered your concerns and once again we congratulate you on your community spirit, but this development is part of the Victorian government's vision for the future. Our hands are tied. But, really, it is fantastic to see the community motivated by concern for our environment. Thank you.' And that's it. She turns and disappears inside.

'Can you all bunch together?' Jeff says, ready to take our photo. 'Let's put Clover out the front, environmentally aware young people and all that. Yeah, that's good – and hold up those signs.'

The article in the local paper is disappointing. It makes me sound like an earnest Rotary exchange candidate and it's supportive of our protest and the picture came out well, if highly embarrassing, but it's clear nothing's going to change: people want the freeway link and don't see much value in the forest and none in the creek, which 'isn't going away' because it will 'still be underground'.

No one is listening. The corridor is doomed.

Keek takes a break from riding and comes to inspect my latest aerosol masterpiece. 'What's that bit meant to be?'

'The nose.'

'It looks like a bum.'

'Go ride your bike.'

'Face it, CB, you're a vandal.'

I appraise the piece he's bagging. My suit guy is more like a failed Manga-Simpson hybrid and I can't spray a decent 's' to save myself, let alone save the creek.

Keek waves across the reserve. 'Bit late now.'

'It's not too late – the trees are still standing and your dad's helping Mum and the Friends submit their appeal.'

'He's a property solicitor,' Keek says scathingly. 'Not an environmental rights lawyer.' He shrugs. 'He doesn't even reckon it's going to work.'

'Don't say that.'

'He told your mum it was just postponing the inevitable. He doesn't think it'll make any difference.'

I bristle. 'At least they're trying. It's not fair. I used to play there. Mum walks Lucille down there.'

'What are you talking about? I've never seen that dog get out of her chair.'

'Don't be a dick, Philip.'

'Don't call me Philip, dick. How old *is* Lucille, anyway?'

'She's old.'

Cho walks around to have a look. 'Laro the Geek? Is that what that thing's name is?'

'It's meant to say Save the Creek.'

Cho pats my shoulder and says, 'Practice makes perfect,' then zips off into the bowl to prove it.

⸺

I'm meant to be painting a colour wheel – Yamouni's getting strict about everything we have to hand in – but I'm well on my way to painting the whole page black instead.

Yamouni says, 'What's up?'

'They're going to turn Fernwood creek into a road,' I say. 'They're going to chop down the trees and turn it into a road.'

'Who gives a crap?' says Rosemary and gets a laugh.

And then it begins. Climate change. Melting polar caps and homeless polar bears. Rainforests chopped down. Indigenous people being screwed over – still. Oil spills. Fracking. The Middle East. Palestine. China. North Korea going nuts with nuclear testing. Americans going nuts with guns in schools. Drones. Police going crazy. Tsunamis. Oceans dying, rivers dying, everything dying.

And the fracture yawns and opens like a chasm. I feel old. Like I'm being buried under a mountain but expected to stand up and keep moving with the whole mountain weight pushing down. Pushing me into the darkness.

Yamouni's hand on my arm is cool and dry. I love the oily, acrylic smell of her. 'Paint it out, Clover,' she says. She rolls back the paper to reveal the painting board underneath. 'Make beauty from pain – there's a kind of joy in that; and maybe that's what art is for?'

We're working on a study of da Vinci's boots that we have to hand in for assessment and it's nearly impossible. Rosemary comes and stands by my easel. 'You're good at this stuff, aren't you?'

God, I think my face has done a Larder.

She points. 'How did you do that?'

'A hint of light, along there. Makes all the difference.'

'Show me on mine.'

Rosemary's canvas makes me feel like maybe I am talented after all. 'Try not looking at the line itself,' I suggest, echoing Yamouni. 'It's not like working with a pencil – you don't *draw* the line. Put dark where it's dark and light where it's light. Then the line appears.' I fiddle. 'See?'

'Yeah. That's better.' Rosemary's eyebrows do a jig. 'Want to do the rest of it?'

I smile, but I'm not sure she isn't serious.

'You going to Jason's party?' she says.

Jason Eldrich, football star. As if I'd be invited. I shrug as if I don't care.

Rosemary shrugs back. 'Come with us.'

'Rosie – ?' says Thyme.

'Shut up. Jason told me I could bring people. I'm bringing Clover. Anyone got a problem with that?'

The Herbs have been the standard against which I have rebelled: wearing my uniform in perfect opposition. I've hemmed my skirt so it was half a centimetre above my knee and longer at the back than the front. I've worn large jumpers and long socks and as their fashion changed, I was forced to adapt to a tiny shrunk jumper with a big shirt and tights instead of socks. Not that I think they ever noticed. But still, despite despising them for the past three years, I can't control the thrill that rolls over me to be invited to a party by Rosemary Daniels.

Mum made me help her with the shopping this morning before she'd drop me off at the bowl. It's busy today, a rhythmic flurry of bikes and skaters, and Keek is being difficult.

'I've already cancelled our 500 game and dinner at Mrs T's,' I tell him. 'Come to Jason's party with me.'

'With roast lamb Rosemary?' The front wheel of his bike rears up and then bounces on the concrete. 'Suppose your mate Robbo will be going.'

'Yes, with roast lamb Rosemary.' I step back. I'm probably in no real danger of having the bike hit me, but it feels like it's right in my face. 'I don't know about Rob. I suppose so.'

'Go and get roasty-toasty with the Herbs.' He laughs derisively. 'Clover and the Herbs.'

'Why are you being such a knob? I hang around with your friends.'

'Oh yeah, your *friends* now are they?' Keek swings his bike around. 'Whatever.' He pulls his hood up over his helmet and pedals off like a maniac.

I walk off, up to the oval, feeling a whole lot better about not really wanting him to come.

———

My mother wears suspicion like a coat. 'You sure there won't be alcohol?'

'I don't think so, Mum. Jason's like, fit and everything, and strict about training and all that. He wants to play AFL and his parents are totally into it so I don't reckon they'd let him have alcohol.'

'Yeah, well, you'd never imagine a footy player drinking, would you. I'd better speak to his mum.'

'Could you not embarrass me? Please? No one else's parents are ringing up Jason's parents. Mum, I haven't had girlfriends since Alison. Please let me go. Please?'

Mum searches my face for clues. 'What's the address?' she says at last.

'Why?'

'So I can pick you up.'

———⌇———

Mum pulls up at Rosemary's and susses out the Herbs huddled on the front step. From the outside, Rosemary's house isn't very different from my house – an older brick suburban box – but it's naked: there are no buddhas in the garden. No native bushes and bells. No funny little mosaic paths snaking off to long-abandoned cubbies. Rosemary waves. Mum fake smiles with a return wave and the girls disappear inside.

'All right, then,' she says, as if she's about to dive off a cliff. 'Have fun tonight, but be sensible, for God's sake. I'll pick you up at, what? Ten-thirty?'

'One.'

'Forget it.'

'Twelve-thirty.'

'Midnight.'

'But—'

She stops me with a hand. 'Unless you don't want to go at all?'

That shuts me up.

She kisses me goodbye through the window. 'Be careful, Clover. Midnight, and *don't drink*!'

I walk up a neatly paved path dissecting two even squares of closely mown grass, edged by pristine rose beds. I have dressed conservatively: hoodie, jeans, connies – entirely in black. Rob Marcello opens Rosemary's door and says, 'It's emo-girl.'

I don't know what I'd expected, but despite the thrill of being this close to Rob out of school, I feel let down by Rosemary's house: brown, beige and boring, a plastic basket-load of unfolded washing in the corner. I was expecting a huge flat-screen TV and glass-topped tables, something sharper, less ... tawdry.

'So, Jones is coming to the party.' Rob gives me a friendly bump with his hip.

'Shut up, Robbo.' Rosemary shoves him onto the couch, where Sage climbs on his knee.

The Herbs and their boys give me their casual hellos. Both sexes are wearing stripes and pastel. It amuses me that footy boys like Pete are such complete homophobes, but wear hoodies that wouldn't be out of place in the girls' section of Kmart – except for the price tags. For a strange moment, I imagine them all rocking up to Aunty Jean's for a barbeque. She wouldn't like them.

I'm not sure that I like them, either. I certainly don't like Pete. But I'm hypnotised by how entirely happy they seem to be in their shallow selves – not freaky or strange or lonely or worried about existential questions of art and the death of the planet. Keek loves me like a sister, but Cho can only barely stand me, and the others are indifferent. I'm not a rider. I'm not one of them. But with footy, anybody can belong. Really belong. Is it wrong to want to belong?

'Your mum's a milf.' Rob jiggles his eyebrows at me suggestively.

Sage punches him. 'That's rank.'

Rob stands up with Sage in his arms and spins her around. She squeals, laughing, until he dumps her on a chair and virtually skips away. 'Come on.'

The boys detach themselves and stand, adjusting their hair.

'Seeyas all in ten,' says Rob.

Rosemary's eyes narrow. 'Where are you going?'

He winks at her. 'Got to pick something up.'

Rob Marcello takes up a lot of space. It's easier to breathe when he and his mates have gone.

Thyme says, 'I'm definitely hooking up with Robbo tonight.' She lays back and crosses her ankles, using Sage's thighs as a footrest.

Sage flings the feet off. 'I'm getting a drink of water.'

Sage disappears, to the kitchen, I guess. Rosemary throws Thyme the hair straightener. 'Hook up with this,' she says. She turns to me. 'Do you want to borrow a dress?'

'No, I'm good, thanks.' My black hoodie and jeans feel like the only real friends I have.

It's nearly half an hour before the boys come barrelling back in.

'Come on,' says Rob. 'Party time. Hurry up. Can't expect us to wait all day.'

There's a flurry of girls and phones and we spill out onto the footpath. I have no idea how the girls walk in their shoes. Rob is next to me, his arm jostling mine.

'Carry my Cruisers, Robbo?' says Thyme, tottering over to us and glaring.

'Sure.' Rob takes the four-pack, but keeps walking with me.

'Clover's mummy says she has to go home at midnight,' says Rosemary, supporting Thyme, I guess. They laugh.

'That's a shame,' says Rob. 'The party will hardly have started.' But when we get there, he hangs with his mates and forgets I even exist.

———

Thyme finds me and says, 'Jones,' as if I'm her lifesaver, which, scary as it seems, is a relief, as since we arrived I've been standing alone in the corner like a dork. She's drunk her Cruisers, lost her shoes and hangs all over me, pulling me into the house, through the laundry and out to the back deck. It's dark because everybody who's having a good time is around the other side in the partied-up garage.

'I really, really love Robbo,' she confesses to me, as

if I've asked. 'We did it three weeks ago at Pete's house when his parents went to Sydney for the weekend and he said he loved me. He did. He said, "I love you El." Like that: "El."' She's all dreamy for a second, then shakes her head like a wet dog, but in slow motion. 'But now he reckons it was just a hook-up.' She breathes in my face. 'If I'd known, I wouldn't have done it and he'd still be trying to get into my pants.'

'Did you use a condom?' I ask.

'Nup,' she says and vomits in my lap.

In the car, it takes forever to convince Mum that the vomit she can smell is not my vomit.

'But there was obviously alcohol there.'

'Yeah, someone sneaked it in. But I didn't drink any of it, did I?'

'No, you're right. You didn't. Well done.'

'Yeah, hurrah for me.'

'You'd better have a shower and put your clothes straight in the washing machine when we get home. You reek. Have you been smoking?'

I'm glad it's dark. 'No way.'

When she tucks me in bed she says, 'Apart from the vomit-girl, did you have a good time, Clover?'

'I think so.' I spent most of the party outside, with wet jeans, helping Thyme keep the chuck out of her hair. 'Anyway, it was nice to be asked to go.'

'Mm.' Mum kisses my head and turns off the light. 'It is nice to be asked.'

❧ ⌒ —

On Monday morning at school, I drag Keek over to where I'm hanging with the Herbs. 'Guys, this is Keek.'

The four of them give him a weak hello. He grunts and rides off.

'He's such a weird guy,' says Sage.

Rosemary smooths her fringe. 'What's the hardest thing about being a BMX rider?'

'Dunno, what?' says Parsley.

'Telling your parents that you're gay.'

❧ ⌒ —

On the way home, to try and make myself feel better about having laughed, I tell the joke to Keek.

'Hilarious,' he says. 'Not. And there's about a million versions of that joke on Facebook, anyway. Why do you hang around with them? They're such backstabbers. All of them, footy knobs included.'

What is his problem? It was funny when they told it. Sort of. The Herbs and their footy-club crew are small-minded, it's true, and a bit snarky about anyone who isn't them, though it wouldn't surprise me if Jason Eldrich is genuinely gay: he's obsessed with the idea, just in a negative way. But they're not that bad, not really – it's not their fault they're so ... it's the way they've been brought up. Eventually, when we know each other better, I might be able to broaden their minds. And I hang around with Keek's friends often enough, even though they ride their freakin' bikes all the time and practically ignore me. And unlike Cho, Rosemary at least likes me. I think she does, anyway.

'Well, I guess that makes me a backstabber too, then?' I say.

'No,' says Keek. 'It makes you a *homophobic* backstabber,' and he rides off.

———

Wire fences festooned with Keep Out signs have been erected at the bottom of the reserve to keep us away from the new roadworks. I stare from behind the wire. From here, the creek is concealed, like a secret. Soon it'll be hidden forever. It's as if the trees are holding their breath.

Keek rides up, stops a few feet away and stares, too. 'Nothing's happened yet,' he says.

We're joined by a big invisible rubber band – stretched tight – that's going to bounce us back towards each other, or snap altogether and send us flying off into the ether.

I feel his eyes on me. 'So, I didn't get to ask, how was your party?'

His face is mercifully free of mockery. 'It was all right.' I look back to the pensive trees. 'Would've been better if you were there.'

'Why's that?'

'Coz then Thyme might've spewed on you instead of on me.'

Keek moves towards me with a suitable mixture of repulsion and delight. 'What happened?'

We turn our backs to the fence and I tell him all about it. Well, not all; nothing about Rob.

⁓

Mum stands in my bedroom with a tin in each hand.

'It's a collection,' I say.

'A collection of aerosol cans. Do you think I'm a fool?'

I've gradually transferred the ones from the musty old cardboard boxes in Keek's garage to my bedroom and I have a whole drawer full, though a few are empty, and there are more hidden under my bed; my prize possessions: Monstercolour classics with the proper caps that Keek helped me buy.

'You get a discount if you order them online but pick them up from the shop in the city,' he told me, but I was too chicken to go down there, so he had them delivered. But I love the look of Uncle Andy's cans too. They're like works of art themselves.

Mum doesn't agree with this point of view. 'Criminal damage – that's what they call it,' she yells.

'They, *they*? You crap on about freedom and resistance, but when it comes down to it, you're just as conservative as everyone else,' I yell back. 'Is Banksy a criminal?'

Mum shakes the tin at me. 'So they *are* for street graffiti?'

'That's not what I said.'

She plops on my bed and stares at the cans. 'Darling, it's not as simple as you think. I agree that graffiti is possibly the last peaceful challenge to notions of property and ownership – especially since they crushed the Occupy movement – and I absolutely do believe we are here on earth to transform the world and ourselves through art,' she takes a breath, 'but down at the community house I've met kids who've not only been fined a fortune but *locked up* for criminal damage – just for graffiti. Good kids.' She looks up at me, stricken. 'I couldn't bear for that to happen to you.'

'Mum, stop panicking. No one's going to lock me up.'

'You have so many other beautiful ways of expressing yourself, Clover.'

'Drive me to the bowl?' I say. 'Please?'

~

Mum stares at the stretch of painted concrete. I think for a horrible moment she's going to cry.

'It's not hurting anybody,' I say.

'God,' she says at last. 'Please don't get yourself into trouble. You won't do anything stupid will you?'

She grabs me and hugs me. 'I can't stand the thought of you being crushed by a train.'

'Nah. I'm not that hardcore, Mum. It's safe down here. Nobody cares.'

Mum doesn't mention it again, but gives me Banksy's *Wall and Piece* for my sixteenth birthday.

'I love it Mum, thanks.'

'Penny Jones!' says Aunty Jean. 'That's monstrous. Do you support vandalism?'

'She's not scrawling "I love Michael Hutchence" over every available surface like *some* people I know might have done, Jeannie. She's an artist, aren't you, Clover?'

'Con artist, more like it,' says Aunty Jean. 'But here you go: knock yourself out,' and gives me an iPod and a rude birthday card.

I stifle my disappointment that it's not an iPod touch and give her a hug. Turning sixteen isn't as big a deal as I thought it was going to be. Eighteen is better. Everyone does everything when they turn eighteen.

I open *Wall and Piece* and am taken to another world. I think it's love.

Yamouni is leaving.

'This is my last day,' she says as we sit in our circle, outraged and depressed.

'It's not fair,' says Mark.

Rosemary reaches out and squeezes his giant shoulder with her manicured, fake-tanned hand and that, more than anything, makes the fracture rumble and spit like it's full of lava.

Yamouni uncrosses her legs and stretches them out in front, leaning back on her chair. 'You know what? It isn't fair. But your VCE work is up-to-date and we'd be moving on to another unit anyway. And I think, for me, it's meant to be. I'm not cut out to be a teacher.' She wriggles her feet.

There's a swell of discontent at that, but she waves us down. 'No, I mean, it's not the *teaching*, it's the whole "being a teacher" thing. You guys don't know the nonsense we're put through – and that's before we even set foot in the classroom. And the meetings!' She's exhausted, just remembering them. 'I'm an artist and I've already been teaching for eleven years. I thought maybe a change of school – but it's no good. It's time I *did* something.'

'Like what?'

'I've saved some money. I'm going overseas.'

'To Iraq?' Mark's chins wobble with worry.

'Well ... maybe on the way home. No, I've got the opportunity of a residency, at a place called the *Goetheanum*, in Switzerland, to study and to sculpt.'

I know the place she's talking about. 'That's a Steiner thing,' I blurt. 'That's where my mum reckons I should go when I leave school. To study art.'

Yamouni smiles at me. 'Maybe I'll see you there, Clover? I'd love that.'

I want to tell her that I'd love that too. More than anything. But I can't.

I can't speak at all.

A week later, Sutcliff introduces our new art teacher at school assembly. He's got short, silvery hair and wears jeans, heavy bike boots and a black leather jacket.

'He's got a Harley,' Trung whispers to Alison.

'What's that?' she whispers back.

Kids around them laugh, and Jason says, 'What a dweeb.'

I feel the sting of unfairness: everyone knows Alison Larder's the smartest kid in our year level.

Trung doesn't laugh either, and when he smiles gently and says, 'A motorbike,' the red subsides from Al's face.

She smiles back at him and says, 'Oh, yeah.'

Sutcliff glowers towards the noise and her eyes land on me.

It's Sutcliff who lets us into the art room. 'Mr Jardine won't be long.' She pulls the key from the lock and bestows one of her admonishing glares. 'I expect you to respect the room as if Ms Yamouni were in it.'

We haphazardly gravitate to our customary circle and suddenly Jardine's there, between Thyme and Rosemary.

'Hello everyone,' he says. His voice is friendly, but I feel a resistance well up, a hatred towards him, as if somehow that will bring Yamouni back – or punish her for leaving us. By the look of Thyme, she feels it too.

'So ... what's going on?' he asks.

There's a bleak pause and then Mark claps twice and says, 'Mark'. We teeter on the brink of apathy, then join in. Jardine looks surprised, or maybe it's confused, but follows along – his name is Craig.

When we've gone twice around the circle with 'whatever comes', Thyme says, 'It's just this thing.' She almost smiles. 'This thing that we do.'

Jardine is slightly bewildered. 'Well, fine,' he says. 'Now take a seat.'

He takes off his jacket and hangs it over the back of Yamouni's chair, then surprises us by taking off his boots and socks as well. He pulls a pair of crocs from his backpack and puts them on.

'Ah,' he says. 'That's better,' and turns to us as if he's just remembered we're there. 'Righto, attention please.'

People stop talking and stare. Craig gestures to the walls, where prints of the masters hang along with our studies. 'I agree with Mrs Sutcliff that you've done terrific work in this class and there's plenty of talent, but to be frank, you lot probably know more about the old masters than I do, so hold on to your hats because we're in for a change of pace.'

After Yamouni it seems scandalous that a teacher should admit to knowing less than us, and it's hard to imagine Sutcliff singing our praises, but my interest quickens as he outlines his plans for the module. A silhouette first, and then screen-printing, and we can make our own simple stencil design for a garment.

'What kind of garment, Mr Jardine?' asks Thyme sceptically.

'I think your clappity-clap has established that you can all call me Craig,' he says. 'A T-shirt.'

She huffs, disappointed.

Rosemary says, 'Can we, you know, like, alter it?'

'After you've printed it and I've assessed it ...' he stretches his shoulders back and cracks his neck from side to side, 'you can, you know, like, do whatever you want to it.'

I'm paired with Mark for the silhouettes. We're allowed to go outside to find walls to tape up our paper. I position Mark so his shadow casts in the right place, ready for tracing.

'Are you sure the paper's big enough?' he says.

I don't know if it's wrong or not, but I shave a chin or two off Mark's silhouette.

By the next week the silhouettes are done, mounted and pinned on the walls. It's fascinating to pick who's who. How quirky and different we all are, even the Herbs, who often strike me as similar. Craig asks us to drag the tables into one big central table and half-a-dozen kids help him lump in the wooden frames with their screen-printing mesh from the storage room.

'Keep to simple geometric shapes for now and later we'll introduce text. And careful with the art knives – any mucking around and you're out,' he tells us sternly. 'Each colour is a separate process.' He puts bottles of screen-printing ink on his desk. 'We'll only use these.'

We're back to the primaries: yellow, red and blue – and a fourth colour Yamouni never encouraged: black.

Over the next weeks we design our stencils and practise with paper and paint before Craig hands out the white T-shirts and stiff T-shirt-shaped cardboard to stick them to. We use a hair dryer to dry the ink between printing – 'flashing off', Craig calls it, which makes us snigger. It takes weeks to finish them all and it's fun, like a factory, with various groups going in turns and everyone helping each other.

I'm glad I chose text – the plain geometric shapes look a bit clunky and arbitrary to me. With Craig's help to nut out the black-on-orange, I've managed to make a sort of word-search puzzle:

H	I	E	R	O
N	Y	M	U	S

I overhear Rosemary and Thyme snarking over how they don't get it.

After the last screen-printing class, a few of us stay behind to wipe down the tables with citrus cleaner.

'You've got a good eye, Clover. Good balance,' Craig says, giving us a hand. 'When it comes to registering the colours, you can just see it – you could have some fun with print design, if you wanted to.'

Encouraged, I ask, 'How do you stencil on walls?'

Craig wipes his hands on a rag. 'It's just a different application. For a vertical surface you'd need a flop stencil – exactly like it sounds: you flop it up against the wall and roller it, or spray it. Airbrush templates are just another kind of stencil.' He chucks the cloth at the sink. 'The stencil is simply a tool. It's the vision of where you want to be, how you use the tool, that's where the artistry comes into it.' Craig pulls his jacket off the back of his chair. 'Deconstructing images can be a good place to start. Anyway, I'm off.'

He passes Keek coming through the art room door. 'Can I help you?'

'I'm looking for Clover.'

'Righto.' He turns to me. 'Make sure the lock's snibbed when you go, won't you?'

'Sure, Craig.'

'Craig?' says Keek, when he's gone. 'Righto. You want a dink to the reserve?'

'Thanks,' I say. 'But I think I'll go straight home.'

He shakes out his curls, suspicious. 'Are you all right?'

'Yeah,' I reassure him. 'But I feel an obsession with flop stencils coming on.'

Keek says, 'God,' and backs away. 'See ya later, CB,' he calls from the corridor.

❧ ～

At the end of our next class, Craig gives us back our artwork from Yamouni's last module.

Mum is chuffed with my A+ and shows off my folio to Aunty Jean, who's uncharacteristically serious while she sifts through my work, spreading it out over the dining-room table.

'It's beautiful, Clover,' she says at last and gives me a big squeeze. 'What a clever clogs!'

Yamouni has left messages in my art journal and I keep going back to them, but it's hard to believe that *nothing is a highlight unless there's the dark to make it shine* when on Saturday morning the roar of destruction drags me outside to find my mother standing in the street in her pyjamas, shouting at the neighbours across the road.

Intensely embarrassing she may be, but I'm right there, at her shoulder. The old gum they're chopping down shudders as another branch rattles to earth, guided by men with ropes. The tree-loppers ignore us. The neighbour across the road tells my mother to calm down.

'It's this or eventually restump our house,' he yells over the scream of the chainsaw.

'Not good enough,' Mum yells back.

'Piss off,' he says, and disappears inside, slamming the door.

Mum rings the council, but the tree is within thirty metres of their house and there's nothing she can do.

It's horrible. A murder. The noise is like torture. To get away, we head into Fernwood, but the tree haunts us. Everything around me is smothered in concrete and asphalt. The poor trees down Main Street poisoned by traffic. There are gardens in Fernwood, but every one is trapped and tamed; the planters outside the shops are littered with cigarette butts.

I take in the ugly buildings, the signs – who decides it's okay to turn the earth into instructions, into concrete squares? Into poison? Why is everyone walking around as if nothing is happening? As if the planet isn't groaning and shrieking. As if, like the tree, it's too inconvenient to save.

When we get back, the stump is surrounded by sawdust and debris and a great unruly pile of trunk-rounds, like giant checker pieces. Branches are bundled up, ready for green rubbish collection, and there's a mountain of mulch.

Mum bursts into tears.

***

Sitting up in bed later that night, I pull a sketchbook and my art journal out of my bag. Yamouni wrote *transform your love into art and let art transform the world*; but how is my art going to transform the world if I'm the only one who ever sees it? I can't just go out scrawling 'Save the Creek' everywhere. Or can I? No: I'd rather tell a story that somehow shows what's really happening to the corridor, if I can. Craig told me I've got a good eye: if I use freestyle colour and make smart stencils, maybe I can do something quick enough not to get caught, but good enough to at least make people think.

At least I'll have tried.

I make rough sketches of the key players in the drama: the trees, of course, and the birds, the echidna and the orchids. The creek remains passive, the source from which they draw their sustenance. And how to represent the enemy? I start off with a caricature of whatshername, the MP, but it's not her fault – she's just the patsy who had to come out and say something reasonable for the local paper. It's more sinister; the real reason the planet is covered in tar and pollution. Politicians big and small are puppets, their strings pulled by corporations with investments in everything bad: war, oil and, Mum's pet hate, consumerism. A guy in a suit emerges, a dollar sign where his heart should be.

Somewhere along the line we seem to have let ourselves forget that nature is necessary for its own sake, not just for what we can get out of it. We've forgotten what's real, *our* source. We can't get rid of everything beautiful and living and free. Can we?

Mum knocks softly and I close the sketchpad. 'Come in.'

'You've been crying.'

She hugs me, and Lucille shocks us from our wallowing by making a jump for the bed, chaotically scrabbling at the bedclothes and scratching my leg. Her anxious face is so pathetically adorable, we laugh. Mum helps her up.

'Ouch,' I complain, rubbing the welts. 'Look what you've done.'

Lucille collapses into comfort, puts her head on my thigh and stares up at me with raised eyebrows.

'You silly old lunatic,' I say.

***

Banksy wasn't kidding when he said mindless vandalism takes some thought. A few weeks after the death of the tree, I show Keek the stencils I've slaved over, carefully slide them into my art folio, put it next to my loaded backpack, and float the idea of a midnight trip to Fernwood.

'Don't be an idiot.'

I swear he's Sutcliff's illegitimate love-child.

I match his folded arms. 'I'm doing it Tuesday night, whether you come with me or not.'

'Bullshit.'

***

It's Tuesday night.

I've been lying in bed for hours, sweating, crushed between a heavyweight blanket of guilt and fear and the adrenaline of an unstoppable vision. And I've told Keek that I'm doing it, so I have to go through with it. The tension drives me out of bed.

Getting dressed sounds unbearably loud. Lucille, deaf as a post the rest of the time, scares the crap out of me by jumping off Mum's bed and coming to investigate. I pray she won't bark when I leave. 'Good girl,' I whisper, give her a kiss and sneak out the door.

The street is quiet, dark. I'm cold. Scared to leave the porch. The thought of walking on my own even to the end of the block seems impossible. Keek riding up out of the dark makes me startle, but I could cry with relief.

'You're really doing it?' he asks.

'I really am,' I say, and feel a different kind of fear.

He offers up his handlebars. 'Come on then.'

Keek shoulders my backpack. I didn't kiss him when he fitted these footrests, so I suppose I shouldn't kiss him now. I climb on and lean back, the wax cardboard folio across my knees. It's good to feel him there. He's warm.

'Where?' he says.

'Supermarket.'

'We'll get caught.'

'No we won't.'

I feel sick, riding there, and the folio is an aero-dynamic disaster. Finally, Keek pulls up in the shadow of a shop doorway across the road from the supermarket. I get off and he passes me the backpack.

The supermarket is on the corner, and it's the Main Street wall I've been dreaming about. With stencilling of any kind, whether it's for screen-printing or a wall, the smoother the surface, the cleaner the line. The supermarket wall is perfect – I've felt it. It's beautifully smooth, softly lit and calling to me.

Keek shakes his head. 'It's too visible.'

'I'll be fast.'

'Start somewhere more private.'

'Private doesn't count. They—' Anger rises like bile, choking me. 'They think they own everything, but they don't. They don't own anything.' A wild thrill rolls over me.

'Who's they?' says Keek. 'The dudes who own the IGA?'

'Stay here.' I run across the road. My hands are shaking and I can hardly get the stuff out of my bag. I'm glad I stole mum's window squeegee to help stick the thin cardboard jigsaw of A3 stencils to the wall; I hope they're as easy to peel off when I'm done. Stencilling SAVE THE CREEK steadies me. It looks good but the A4 letter-stencils are too small and messy around the outside. I'll have to do something about that.

Keek rides up. 'That'll do,' he says.

'Wait, I haven't done it yet.'

I work as fast as I can, running up and down the footpath, jumping up, wishing I had a stepladder. I strip off a stencil. Keek helps by putting it in the folio.

'You've got to wait till they're dry, it doesn't take long,' I say. 'Or you may as well just chuck them in the bin.'

He waves one around. 'Just hurry up.'

The tree is all right, covering its eyes with one twiggy hand – it's faint at the top, but hardly any bleed. Soon enough the other stencils are down and the image makes sense: the tree cowering from a suit with a dollar-sign head, axe in hand. Not quite as I'd imagined it, but I don't have time to fret. I spray a few highlights on the tree in green and purple, and blood on the axe, but before I can begin on my plan of painting in the creek freehand, a car turns the corner into Main Street. I make an ineffective grab for my gear and a can rolls away.

Keek hisses, 'Leave it, run,' and disappears. I bolt and hide behind the St Vinnies donation bin in the car park round the corner. The car drives on, followed by another one a few seconds later.

After a minute or two, I spot Keek looking for me and wave.

'Let's go,' he says.

'It's not finished.'

'It's too risky. Two a.m. would be better.'

'You promise you'll come again? At two?'

'Look at you,' he says. 'You're a mess. Is that dry? I don't want it all over my—'

'Promise?'

'Not tonight.'

'Another night?'

'For fuck's sake, yes, whatever.' He wipes his hands on my paint-peppered hoodie and hoists my backpack onto his shoulder. 'I'm tired, let's go.'

'I've got to sign it.'

Keek's practically busting out of his skin with wanting to go, but he waits. Tagging 'Kandas' feels so good, the marker so fat and compliant and smooth, I want to do it again and again. But I need to be cool, and Keek is waiting.

———

I'm in the car with no chance of escape and Mum says, 'So …' in that particular way that lets me know that she's about to say something I don't want to hear.

'Alison Larder won a national maths prize,' I say, in a desperate attempt to distract her into a nostalgic 'remember when' about Alison. As an added bonus, Mum has a maths phobia. The mere mention of the word usually sends her into a cold sweat and off on some story about when she was at school and the follies of the mainstream education system.

'I'm not blind, Clover.'

'That's good, Mum, considering you're driving.'

'It's not funny.'

'Well, excuse me for being amusing.'

'I want it to stop.'

'Okay, I'll never make a joke again.'

'You know what I'm talking about. I get what you're doing and why you're doing it. But it's too dangerous. I want you to stop it.'

I stare out the window. 'Mum, what are you even talking about?'

She pulls up outside the IGA. 'That's what I'm talking about.' She nods to my piece, surrounded by tags now.

I want her to shut up about it. She hasn't even said if she thinks it's any good or not. It's none of her business. 'You've lost it,' I say. 'I don't even know what you're talking about.' Lucky for me, there's a beep and she has to move on.

'So that isn't your work?' she says, pulling into a car park.

'Shut up about it.' I shove the door open and slam it behind me.

'Where are you going?' Mum calls after me, slamming her own door.

'Walking to Keek's.'

'I mean it, Clover – it's enough. And be home by dinner.'

I am home by dinner, but Mum is acting as though we're in an angst-ridden SBS film and she's the psychiatric patient.

I say, 'Have you seen my hairbrush?'

She blurts, 'It has to stop.'

I slam off to my room.

———◦———

We sneak out whenever I can talk Keek into it. It doesn't take much. I reckon he secretly loves zooming through the empty streets.

One night a bunch of scary local 'lads', all graffers, chase us down the street throwing stones and shouting, 'Art fag'.

'Congratulations,' Keek hisses when they drop back, laughing. 'Your peers.'

'I'm not like them!'

'Aren't you?'

I have a vague stirring of excitement. 'You want me to tag a train?'

Keek pulls up, traumatised.

'Don't worry. I haven't got the guts.' The street behind us is empty when I glance back. 'And they know it.'

Apart from the lads and the occasional furtive weirdo, Fernwood is dead in the early hours. Mondays and Tuesdays are the quietest. I've never loved the moon so much before; never realised how bright it is, never missed it when it wanes. I can't imagine getting caught, but the possibility fuels my pieces – which are getting tighter and smarter because Craig is full of good ideas about stencil design.

Each piece requires concentration, commitment and speed. I disappear into the act, into the strokes, into the wall. I guess it's the same for Keek with his riding. Once he drops in over the lip of the bowl, there's no turning back. Maybe that's why he puts up with me. He understands the adrenaline. The whole-body flow. The art of it.

Periodic car-beeping from the local footy crowd is usually the only reminder the bowl-dwellers have that the rest of the world exists, but today is the first Saturday of the local footy finals and there's a swarm of riders, skateboarders and rugged-up people everywhere. Excitement wafts from the oval and the roar is rhythmic, and passionate.

I hope Fernwood make it through. I'd love to watch Rob play in a grand final, but we'd have to play at another ground – to avoid the home-ground advantage – and I probably wouldn't have the guts to make my way to another suburb to watch him. Not alone. I'm not game to get the tins out, either, with all these people about, so I play with chalk pastels. A landscape.

Cho takes off her helmet. 'That's actually good.'

'Thanks, Cho.'

She runs her fingers through her hair then reties her ponytail. 'Don't get Keek into trouble, Clover.'

'I—'

'Just, don't.' She flips her helmet on and clips it. Even wearing a bike lid she still manages to look supercilious.

Keek rides over. 'What's up?'

'Nothing.' Cho smiles at him. 'I was just admiring Clover's picture. It's good, isn't it.'

'See,' says Keek when she's ridden away. 'She does like you.'

'Awesome,' I say.

It's the wee hours of the morning and I'm transforming a perfect factory wall, wonderfully smooth and ugly as sin; and there's a good view of it from the train.

Keek sits on his bike and watches me; pausing his tuneless iPod-humming to say, 'Hustle, CB.' He fiddles with the iPod. 'I'm cold.'

Keek had to manhandle his bike through a gap in the fencing so I'm freaked in case we have to get out in a hurry. Still, it's the best piece I've done; a beautiful orchid, the evil suit snipping it off with a pair of scissors, a snatch of road in his other hand like money.

I'm almost done when Keek yells, 'Fuck!' and blinding lights are on us.

We freeze like rabbits.

From behind the light, a gravelly voice says, 'Police. You, put that down, step away and face me. You on the bike, get off. Turn off that torch.'

We obey.

Stepping back, I accidentally kick a bunch of tins that crash, rolling around on the concrete. For a mad moment, I imagine running off.

'My name is Senior Constable Boyd and this is Constable Ramidge.' Big and square, Senior Constable Boyd steps over the last rolling tin to inspect my piece.

Constable Ramidge reminds me of Mrs Fitzpatrick, but Fitzy never wears a gun. 'State your names,' she says, and we do, like little robots. She jots them down in her notebook, double-checking the spelling.

Boyd runs his superior torchlight over my gleaming, dripping handiwork, unsatisfactorily unfinished. Ramidge gives it a cursory glance and says, 'What a bloody pain in the arse.'

My fractured soul yawns open and fury rushes up to eclipse how small and stupid and scared I feel. 'Visual art is a legitimate form of protest,' I demand. 'Picasso painted *Guernica* to wake people up to the horrors of the Spanish civil war. Banksy—'

'Shut up, Clover,' says Keek.

'Car's up there.' Boyd points up the hill. 'Go on.'

'Where are we going?' I ask.

Keek won't look at me. I can feel how mad he is.

'To the station where you can have a nice cup of tea and wait for your parents,' says Boyd.

'What about my bike?'

'Fuck your bike, you little shit,' says Ramidge.

'Philip never did anything,' I blurt. 'He came so I wouldn't have to be on my own. He thinks it's a dumb thing to do.'

'No, I don't, Clover.'

'Yes, you do.'

'I—'

'Keep your mouths shut and do what you're told.' Ramidge shoves Keek towards the car.

'Hang on,' interrupts Boyd. 'Did you do any graffiti, Philip?'

I get the feeling Boyd doesn't like Ramidge any more than I do.

'No.' Keek hunches his shoulders and says under his breath, 'She won't let me.'

'What was that you little smartarse?'

What is Ramidge's problem? Nobody's being rude to *her*. Boyd sighs and says, 'Bring the bike along, son.'

The cops have opened the gate, but to fit Keek's bike in their boot, they have to take out a bunch of orange traffic cones that they jam in the back seat with us. Ramidge is not happy.

We sit there like stunned mullets, divided by witch's hats. I stare out my window and concentrate on not crying. When I turn his way, Keek is staring out his window too.

A stack of the traffic cones, heavy, chewed-looking and dirty, digs into my leg. I move them and Keek adjusts them back. I wriggle. He wriggles.

Ramidge says, 'Been a busy little pain in the arse, haven't you? My son's quite a fan.'

Keek turns further away from me and I stare harder out my window.

———

Our parents arrive at the police station together. Mum's wearing jeans and a plain black jumper. No pearls. Mr McKenzie is wearing jeans and a hoodie. Weird; they look young. Mum isn't as visibly shocked as Mr McKenzie. Just worried. She has her hand on his arm when they walk in, sharing vibes of parental distress and for a flash of a second, I wonder what it would be like for my mum to walk in like that with my dad.

Mr McKenzie hands Keek a mobile. 'She's waiting for you to call.'

On the phone to his mum, Keek says 'sorry' and 'fine'. A lot. While they talk, Mum keeps patting and hugging me as though I've been lost in the bush overnight. It's claustrophobic, but I don't mind, even when she kisses my paint-stained fingers and says, 'Oh Clover, you've been smoking.'

Constable Ramidge, who suddenly doesn't seem so keen on abusing us every ten seconds, goes off 'to organise the rooms'.

They separate us. Keek disappears with his dad. He doesn't look back. Mum and I are led into a bleak little room. Boyd sits on one side of the table, us on the other; Mum's protective arm around me. Boyd shakes his head. 'There's a five-hundred-and-fifty dollar on-the-spot fine.'

Mum is angry, but relieved. 'Can I pay by credit card?'

'Yes. Yes, you can. Look, you realise Clover will be charged with criminal damage?'

Mum bristles. 'What does that mean?'

'It probably means another hefty fine and definitely means a summons to front up to a magistrate at the children's court. We don't take kindly to vandalism in Fernwood.'

'It isn't vandalism.'

Mum grabs my arm.

'I don't want to hear that, young lady,' says Boyd. 'I want to hear that you're very sorry and that you'll never do it again. Do you understand? If you want me to have a chat with my senior and deal leniently with you because this is a first offence,' he sizes me up squarely, 'you'd better be smartening up your attitude.'

I feel my bravado draining like the colour from my mother's face and start to cry.

'So let me ask you again,' says Boyd with mock patience. 'Have you done the wrong thing?'

'Yes.'

'That's right.'

Mum's voice is tight with tears. 'Can I take her home?'

'Not yet,' he says.

As we leave the interview room, other cops are manhandling a bunch of drunk boys, handcuffed, struggling and protesting loudly.

When they see us, one yells, 'They fucken arrested us for no reason.'

Boyd ushers us out to a couple of benches in the dingy foyer where we meet up with Keek and his dad. Keek puts his hood up.

His dad flicks it down. 'Stand up straight,' he says.

'It's not his fault,' I say.

There's an uproar behind the darkened window: boys shouting, cops talking and phones ringing. After a while it quietens down, with only occasional yells of complaint from the boys, and laughter from the cops.

I lean on Mum, reading over her shoulder while she flicks through *Blue Light,* the police magazine. It's trying hard to advertise their community spirit – every cop in it is a young person's best friend. 'Hmmm,' she says and tosses it down. A minute later she picks it up again. It's the only magazine available.

Mr McKenzie wanders around, reading and re-reading the community service posters on the walls. Keek jiggles his knee, stares at the floor and doesn't say a thing. The only bearable moment is when Mum lets loose a small but audible fart and we laugh.

'Just when I thought things couldn't get worse,' she says.

It's hours before Boyd appears again at the counter. 'You've been damn lucky tonight; we're going to let you go with a warning. Both of you. And we're not going to see you again, are we, Clover?' He clicks the end of his pen. 'Are we?'

'No,' I say.

'And Philip,' Boyd shifts his attention, leaning in to point the finger. 'I don't want to see you in here again either, do you understand? You're not helping Clover by encouraging her to break the law.' He glances at our parents. 'Take a seat, there's paperwork to sort out.'

Another hour later, they finally let us leave. In the back of the car on the way home, I flop over and rest my head on Keek's lap, watching street lights out the window flicker by. He doesn't shove me off.

'Thanks for driving, Dave,' Mum says.

Mr McKenzie taps his thumbs against the steering wheel. 'I think we're lucky they brought in that bunch of drunken louts.'

'Poor kids,' Mum murmurs.

A mobile phone buzzes. Mr McKenzie throws it over the back to Keek. 'Tell her we're on the way.'

Keek answers and between bouts of silence, says 'yes' and 'no' and 'sorry' and 'I promise'. He also strokes my hair, which is nice.

It's getting light by the time Mr McKenzie drops us off. Mum leans in the driver's window and kisses his cheek. 'Thank you, David.' She blows a kiss to Keek, who gets in the front. 'And thank you Kee— Philip. I know you were trying to look after her. I'm so relieved it wasn't anything worse than a warning.'

Keek mumbles, 'Thanks,' then looks up at me, standing by the passenger window. 'Sorry, Clover.'

'No, I'm sorry.'

Keek's dad says, 'Spare me,' and drives away.

'Mr McKenzie hates me.'

Mrs T appears in her fuzzy purple dressing-gown and Snoopy slippers. 'Tsk. You know how scary it is to get a call from the police in the middle of the night? Your poor mother, she thought for a moment you were dead. Do you know how long such a moment can be?' Then she hugs me, hard.

'See, Mum, it could've been worse, at least I'm not dead,' I squeeze out. 'But I might be in a minute, Yiayia.'

I feel her 'tsk tsk' run through my body. 'Clover, it's no good, sneaking off in the midnight. Anything could happen to you!'

She lets go, but Mum takes my chin in her palm and meets my eyes. 'No more graffiti.'

———

Two hours sleep is not enough. I can't bear the thought of going to school. When Mum finally forces me out of bed, I slump at the kitchen table. 'I'm not going.'

Mum reties the cord of her dressing-gown as if she's strangling something. 'You bloody are.'

'You can't make me.'

Something flips in Mum's head and she tries to wrestle me into the bathroom. We struggle in the hallway for a minute before she lets go and shoves me. 'Get ready for school.'

'No.'

She screams, 'Go to school!' red-faced and strange, like some other person's mother. I run into my room, slam the door and won't let her in. With my shoulder to the door, it takes all my storming strength to keep her out.

Finally, she stops yelling, says, 'Oh, fuck this,' and there's silence.

When I dare to come out to investigate, she's gone to work. When she gets home, she won't speak to me even though I've done the dishes without even being asked. She shuffles off to an early night as though she's a thousand years old.

———

Two days of silent treatment and the fact that it's nearly the weekend anyway forces me back to school. Thanks to Constable Ramidge's son, Martin, who's a year below me, everybody knows. Keek points him out as one of the 'art fag' crew. So much for him being my 'fan'. But I am the tiniest bit cheered by the fact that Ramidge's precious little boy is a rampant station-rat graffer called Catfood.

Cho bails me up in the corridor. 'Why don't you just leave Keek alone?'

'Keek makes his own decisions.' I've never punched anyone, but I'm wondering right now what it would be like. 'Tell him off, if you've got a problem.'

'He feels sorry for you ...'

I'm rescued by Sutcliff, who orders me to follow her to the principal's office.

'You've tarnished the good name of Fernwood Secondary College,' Berty tells me.

As if I care.

The Herbs, on the other hand, are so excited about me and Keek getting arrested that Rosemary Daniels decides to throw a party.

'I knew it was you,' she says. 'And I think you're cool.'

—⁓—

I endure a lengthy Saturday afternoon lecture from Aunty Jean along the lines of, 'Your mother has sacrificed her whole life for you, Clover. She doesn't need this crap.' She grabs me for a rough hug. 'Come on, it's all too horrible, let's go to the movies.'

We invite Keek, but he's not allowed.

When we get back, Yiayia is huddled with my mother over cups of comforting tea. I feel instantly guilty. 'What's happened?' I search around in panic for the dog, but Lucille's under the table at Mum's feet, as usual. She wags her tail and comes out to nose me for a pat.

Mum offers me a small, worn-out reassuring smile, but her voice is flat. 'Dave rang. The creek—' She stops, to swallow her tears. 'Our appeal's been rejected. Construction starts as scheduled, on Monday.' She pushes the *Fernwood Mail* across the table. 'And Jeff's immortalised your shenanigans in a charming little piece reporting the decision.'

<hr />

We can't see what's going on at the roadworks from the fence at the bottom of the reserve, but the sound is unendurable. It's a particular agony, the creak and crash of a felled tree; discernible even over the roar of the chainsaw and rumble of machinery.

'I'll catch up with you later,' I tell Keek when Cho and the others ride up, and wander off home.

I've been driven along roads like the one they're building behind the reserve; where the remaining treetops peep over the noise barriers. Roads that aren't essential – roads that only get us to where we can already go, faster. Scuffing along the footpath, I wonder about all the concrete and tar we've poured over everything. It's a crime we've committed against nature, but nobody thinks of suburbs and cities as 'criminal damage'. But when I put *paint* on that concrete, those buildings, that's exactly what they call it. Shouldn't we be *planting* trees, not chopping them down? Shouldn't we be nurturing the green belts that still exist? And not just in Australia, but everywhere. I don't want the earth to shrivel like a dried apricot, or sink under salt water.

'Hello, Clover.'

Her voice makes me jump.

'Hello, Mrs Sutcliff.'

It's bizarre seeing her out of school. She seems small and scruffy, her clothes have the familiar grubby dishevelment of a woman who's been gardening.

'Just out to get milk,' she says, lifting her empty green shopping bag as if she has to explain. She peers at me. 'Are you crying?'

'I'm fine.' I pathetically sniffle up my sleeve. 'Thanks.'

'Righto.' She strides off and pauses to turn back. 'Laila Yamouni spoke highly of you in the staffroom. I was very happy to hear it.' She spears me with one of her sharp looks. 'I always knew you had terrific potential.'

I sit on the nature strip to watch her disappear around the corner into Main Street.

Keek rocks up. 'What are you doing?' he says.

'I think I've just had a hallucination.'

He steps off his bike and crouches, suddenly pale and worried. 'Serious?'

'No.'

He sits next to me on the grass and looks so relieved, I have to wonder what the heck goes on in Keek's house.

I thought the trouble with the cops was all over, but at half-past-seven on Sunday morning, John Archer turns up on our doorstep to complain to my mother and give me a serve for the piece I stencilled on the footpath outside his pharmacy. He waggles a rolled-up copy of the *Fernwood Mail*. 'It doesn't take a genius to figure out who's the culprit.' He seems disappointed they haven't locked me up and insists we go with him to 'examine the damage'. Mum rolls her eyes behind his back, but says, 'Come on, Clover, get in the car.'

The shop has been crappily tagged by 'nobitz' and 'gutz'. I have to agree, it's awful. With a stab, I see nobitz has also tagged my footpath piece – a direct insult to the quality of my work. Or maybe he's just a dickhead. I can't look at the pharmacist: how I feel about nobitz must be how he feels about me.

'I'm sorry,' I manage, and turn to Mum. 'I only chose this spot because you can see it from both ends of the street.'

Archer crosses his arms. 'Well, what are you going to do about it?'

'Clover and I could repaint the outside of your shop?' my mother suggests weakly.

'I'm getting it done professionally,' he says. 'I'm sorry, Penny, but I'll be forwarding the bill to you.' He doesn't look sorry.

Mum says, 'Yes, of course,' with that embarrassed, pinched face she gets when the EFTPOS machine comes up 'insufficient funds'. It's unbearable.

'I understand why you hate tags,' I blurt. 'And I'm sorry they messed up your shop. But I didn't *touch* your shop. And anyway, those kids just want to be heard too, you know. They want someone to know they exist. And what about what's happening to the creek? And all these ugly buildings. Aren't *they* acts of vandalism?'

Archer dismisses me with the shake of his head. 'I don't know what's happened to young people,' he says to my mother.

'They woke up,' she flashes at him. 'Send me your bill, John, if it will make you feel better about yourself,' and she stalks away.

I practically have to run to catch up with her.

But when we get home, she goes into my room

with a rubbish bag and confiscates my paint. 'Not my Monstercolours!' I beg and cry, but she's made of stone. Then she crawls into bed with Lucille, a pen and a writing pad, and won't come out.

My beautiful tins! I throw myself on my own bed and ache with loss. After a few hours, I recover enough to complain about being starving.

'What am I supposed to eat?'

'There's eggs. You can make me some too, while you're at it.'

'What?'

'And feed the dog.'

'It's tonight,' I tell Keek on my front porch, ready to head to the bowl. 'The party. Rosemary's parents have gone to Tasmania for the weekend.'

'I'm not going.'

'Why not?'

'Mum won't let me. She's hardly stopped crying since the cops called in the middle of the night. I'm only here because she's asleep and doesn't know.'

'But it's for you.'

Keek's face floods red and he shouts, 'No it's not, Clover. It's for you.'

I shout back. 'It's for *us*.'

'It's for you.'

And he rides off, without me.

'At least leave me a smoke,' I yell.

'Get your own.' And he's gone.

⁓

I stand in Mum's bedroom doorway. She's propped up in bed reading, even though it's almost eleven o'clock. Lucille sits up and wags her tail. I pat her bony old head, her once-black face almost completely white, her eyes cloudy, and smell the familiar doggy smell of her.

'You stink,' I say, and kiss her nose. 'Aren't you getting up?'

'It's Saturday.'

'It's nearly lunchtime.'

She twitches an indifferent shoulder and turns her attention back to her book. Lucille treads a few circles, collapses into comfort and lets out a big sigh.

'Everybody's mad with me.'

'You mean Keek?'

'You heard?'

'I heard the shouting. Sounds like you'd better get yourself a job.'

'What do you mean?'

'To pay for your cigarettes.'

Mum looks at me. I look away. There's no use denying it. She goes back to reading, but disappointment wafts off her like yesterday's garlic.

'Rosemary Daniels has invited me for a sleepover.'

'I don't want to drive anywhere today, Clover.'

'I'll walk.'

'Is her mother going to be home?'

'Yeah. It's a sleepover.'

'Okay then.'

'Thanks.' I sit next to her and give her a hug. She hugs me back, but it's lukewarm and when I turn at the door to say, 'I'll come and say goodbye before I head off,' she has already rolled over and is staring out the window.

'Yes. Please do.' She doesn't even look around, let alone offer to get up and help me pack a bag, or change her mind about driving.

Her purse is on the kitchen bench where she always leaves it, near her car keys. Checking over my shoulder, I open it. A ten and a twenty dollar note stare back at me.

'You sure you don't want to drive me?' I wheedle when I kiss her goodbye.

'Quite sure,' she says. 'Now I'm trusting you, so be good.'

'I am good, Mum,' I lie.

———

'Do you know Robbo's nearly eighteen?' Thyme asks me.

On Rosemary's instructions, we're moving the couch to make room for dancing. 'He had to stay down a year in primary school because he had bad appendix-itis and got really sick and spent nearly the whole year home from school.'

'Appendicitis,' I correct her.

'Yeah,' she says. 'It's when your appendix gets swollen, or something.'

'How's it going for you two?'

'Me and Robbo?' Thyme looks mildly shocked, as if she'd never considered them a couple. 'Nah, I'm hooking up with Jason Eldrich tonight if it kills me.'

'Doesn't Parsley like Jase? They've been hanging out at school.'

Thyme stops like she's been donged on the head. 'Parsley?'

'What?'

'You said parsley.'

'Parsley? No. Natalie.'

Thyme gives me a confused, suspicious look then jiggles her shoulders. 'She had her chance. Guys like Jason don't want frigit girls.'

'Isn't it frigid?'

'That's what I said.'

'Maybe Jason's not like that? Maybe he likes Natalie for who she is?'

'Don't be a dickhead, Clover. Pete Tsaparis already told me that Jason told all the guys that Natalie's frigit. So—'

'So—?'

'So, that's why *I'm* hooking up with him tonight.'

'What about Natalie?'

She tosses her hair. 'Like I said, she had her chance. Anyway, what do you care?'

'I don't know.' I tidy couch cushions like a grandma. 'Won't she … I don't know. Be upset?'

'Life's tough, she'll have to get used to it.' Thyme plucks up the cushions and tosses them into the corner. 'Maybe the next time she's got the guy she likes where she wants him, she'll know what to do to keep him.'

'It didn't make any difference with you and Robbo.'

Thyme looks hurt. 'Jeez, you can be a bitch,' she says.

I'm relieved when the other two Herbs roll in.

Watching Thyme act like Parsley's best friend, I decide the best thing for me to do is to stay as far away from Rob Marcello and his footy mates as possible.

But I don't feel like that when he plonks down his little esky and sits next to me on the back porch where I've gone to smoke as soon as everybody starts arriving. 'Do you want a beer?' he asks me.

'No thanks. I hate beer.' Aunty Jean's favourite drink. Yuck.

'Cruiser then? Sherbet one?'

'Thanks.'

I try to settle my breathing. Being near Robbo is like having stood up too quickly.

161

'You're famous then, eh Jones?' Rob teases as he hands me a bottle. He puts on a stupid voice-over voice. 'The Fernwood greenie vandal strikes again.'

'I didn't mean to be a vandal.'

'What did you mean to be?'

'An activist.'

'What, like Che Guevara with a spray can?'

'You know about Che Guevara?'

'Just because I play football doesn't mean I don't have a brain. I've seen *The Motorcycle Diaries*.' He grins at me with those perfect teeth. 'Besides, everybody knows the T-shirts.'

'I guess so.'

'Though I gotta admit, it wasn't what I was expecting when Mum got out the DVD.'

'What were you expecting?'

'Something more like *The Dukes of Hazzard*.' He laughs.

I laugh too and the sherbet Cruiser zings on my tongue and frees it from its awkward tangling. I tell Rob about Banksy and how my aunt gave me the DVD of his movie, *Exit Through the Gift Shop*. 'The film is weird, and wonderful, and I think I'm in love with his hands,' I say.

'You're the weird one.' He hands me another Cruiser. 'But everyone reckons you're a champion, Jones.' Rob sculls his beer and reaches for another.

This second Cruiser is so yummy I've nearly

finished it already. Rob leans back and crosses his ankles. He has a broad chest and square shoulders. Nothing like Keek's wiry body.

'So what was gonna happen to the chopper dude in the suit?' he asks.

'In my pieces?'

'Yeah.'

'You saw them?'

'Yeah.'

It is as if he's kissed me, smack on the lips.

'The echidna was going to put him and his road six feet under and plant a tree on him,' I say. 'The bulldozing of the orchids was going to send the echidna over the edge, and then later the orchids would bloom from under the tree.'

'Ha! But what if he came back as a zombie?'

'Look around. I think he already did.'

Rosemary appears at the back door. 'Are you two coming in or what?'

'Or what,' says Rob, then he grabs my hand, pulls me up and half-carries me off into the dark. When he puts my feet to the ground, I run with him. We get to the next street down from Rosemary's house and fall laughing to the footpath on the corner. After the laughter, there's a stillness. 'You left your beer behind,' I say to break it, though I can hardly breathe.

'Doesn't matter.' He pulls a crumpled rollie from his top pocket. 'I've got this.'

I know what it is. At least, I think I know what it is. Rob puts it to his lips and lights up, the twisted end bursts into brief flame before the tip glows. The feeling of being a rabbit in the headlights is back, but I don't say a word and when Rob hands me the joint, I take a drag as though it were something I do every day. I manage the drawback twice before I choke.

After I've coughed my lungs up, it seems natural to go from sitting up smoking to laying down on the concrete smoking, comfortable in the arms of Rob Marcello. A couple of cars drive by and that makes us laugh. The sky is cloudy, but then a few stars come out and that makes us laugh, too.

We lie there for ages. Just lying there, periodically chortling at anything that occurs – a bat flies overhead; the wind blows; there are more cars. It's peaceful.

I could stay forever, but Rob says, 'We'd better get going.'

We walk back, Rob with his arm across my shoulders and me with my arm around his waist, but when we get to the front door, he disengages. 'You should come to the oval sometime,' he says.

The door opens, there's a footy-roar of 'Robbo' and he's dragged in by the tide. Rosemary pulls me into the kitchen.

'Did you hook up with Robbo?' she demands.

'Not really.'

She screams and hands me a Cruiser. 'That would be hilarious.'

'What would?'

'You and Robbo.'

I guess it would be, so I laugh.

<hr />

Rob has disappeared. I can't find him anywhere. But the kitchen has filled up with kids shouting and laughing. It's fun. The whole upper school seems to have been invited, even the superbrain. I feel special because the party is for me, even though half of the people here don't even know I've been into graffiti, let alone got caught. It's strange, but good, to be at the heart of things.

I'm stopped in my tracks when Thyme practically shoves her drink in my face and says, 'It's wrong to vandalise stuff.'

'It isn't vandalism.'

'Oh bullshit it isn't. You're full of shit, Clover. You'd do anything to get attention.'

For a hideous moment, I think I'm going to cry.

'Harsh,' says Rosemary and punches Thyme in the arm, hard. A couple of boys laugh.

Thyme says, 'I'm changing the music,' and we peel off in opposite directions, her to the computer and me outside, grabbing another Cruiser from the fridge on the way.

I find Parsley sitting on the porch.

'Hi, Natalie. Mind if I sit here?'

'It's a free country. Got any smokes?'

I hand her the packet and she shakes one out.

Parsley blows her smoke out in a novice's puff. 'Your friend was here.'

'Who?'

'That McKenzie kid. He turned up a while ago.'

I jump up. 'Where is he?'

'He's gone.'

I sit. Jumping up made my head spin. 'I didn't see him.'

'You were off up the road with Robbo.'

'You didn't tell him that, did you?'

'I didn't tell him anything.'

I breathe a sigh of relief. Though actually, it's no one's business who I spend my time with.

Parsley puffs. 'But Ellen did.'

'Bloody Thyme, she hates me.'

'Thyme? Ha! Rosemary and Thyme – that's funny. Don't take it personally. She hates everyone.'

We sit there for a while. I toss up whether to ask Rosemary if I can call Keek's house. But it's too late.

'Don't cry, Natalie.'

'I'm not.'

She sniffs and sits up, but her not-crying is worse.

'Do you want to talk about it?' I ask.

'I don't think I can.'

'Is it Jason?'

'He's so different away from the rest of them.'

'So's Rob.'

'Robbo. Jason. They're weak as piss.'

'What do you mean?'

'You'll find out, if you hang around with Robbo long enough.'

'Where are they, anyway?'

'They've gone off in Josh's ute with Katie and some of those other girls. There's about ten of them, all piled in the back.'

Josh Eldrich is Jason's older brother and their footy coach. He's twenty-one, but hardly seems any different from the Under 18s he coaches.

'Rob too?'

'Robbo too.' Parsley picks up my Cruiser, polishes it off, throws the empty in a bush and heads inside.

Sitting alone in the dark, the sounds from the house feel sinister. Someone's cranked up the music and I hear thumping from the lounge room with shouts and giggles and I'm suddenly convinced everyone in there is laughing at me, stupid enough to be sucked in by Rob Marcello.

I sidle up to the kitchen door and peer in. It's empty except for Trung and – oh God, Al – macking-on in the corner. I'd noticed she was finally wearing a bra – I guess she's more grown up than I thought. A bubble of loneliness swells in my throat, making it ache. I don't know what's wrong with me: it's not like

I want to be friends with Alison Larder. There are no Cruisers left in the fridge so I grab two beers, stuff them in my bag and sneak off.

❧

It's eerie, walking in the dark. Everything has tipped to the left and my knees are marshmallow. It takes me over half a scary hour to get to Keek's place and by then, my head has detached.

The thought of creeping through Keek's freaky back garden by moonlight is more than I can cope with. As it is, I manage to get lost in the smaller front garden, attacked by a random tree that wants to imprison me. I thrash about in a panic. When it lets me go, I fall in a fuchsia bush and sit drinking beer until I'm pretty sure I know which window is Keek's bedroom, and clamber out to knock on the glass with a stick. His face appears, pale and scared. I scream, then laugh.

Keek hurries out wearing a hoodie pulled on over his pyjamas and crocs with socks. I point to his feet and snigger.

'Shh!' he hisses at me. 'What are you doing?'

'Do you want a smoke?'

'Sure,' he says with a sigh. 'But shut up will you? My parents will freak. Come down the back.'

'Want some beer?' I say. 'It's disgusting.'

'Shut up.'

Down the back means following him through the

gate and along the path between the cages. I hold on to him with one hand and finish my beer with the other.

The cages open out into a play area near the back fence where a big cactus looms out at me like a teenage mutant ninja aloe vera. 'Whoa there, Leonardo,' I say, laughing.

Next to it, Keek's old cubby is a cube of peeling blue weatherboards with a gabled roof, red-painted doorway and a funny round window with a blue curtain. A Shrek torch hangs from the ceiling. I think of Alison and our cubbies made of tree branches and sheets. Mum used to bring a basket out to us, laden with home-baked goodies, fruit, dog crunchies, and candles in jars for the dark and we'd winch it up the Golden Ash. We loved that tree. I lived inside the pictures I drew up there. So did my dad.

'Are you all right, Clove?'

'Yes. No. I'm going to be sick.'

'Are you really going to be sick?'

'No.'

But I collapse at the foot of Leonardo and chuck my guts up.

Keek brings me water. Then a camping mattress, pillow and blanket. He makes me a nest in the cubby and once I'm settled, hangs a towel for the door.

'Thanks.' The word lurches out of me on a wave of nausea. I pull down the towel when I lunge outside and Keek uses it to wipe my face and mouth. I lay out there for ages, breathing and heaving, certain I'm going to vomit up my stomach lining and die.

Eventually I let him tuck me into the nest with an empty ice-cream container for a bucket. He wraps a blanket around his own shoulders and sits with me.

'I'll have to go in soon,' he says.

<hr />

But we are both shocked awake by his father in the morning. His mother stands behind him in her dressing-gown, her crumpled face under hair ghostly with fear. Mr McKenzie bundles me into his car to take me home. He won't let Keek come.

'Get in to your mother,' he yells.

It seems a long, silent car ride and when we arrive, Lucille barks. Mum opens the door and, bleary, hurries down the stairs, almost tripping over Lucille. 'Oh shit, God, is everything all right?'

Mr McKenzie crosses his arms. 'No, it's not all right, Penny. I'm sorry, but Phil won't be allowed to come around to your place until your daughter cleans up her act.'

Mum steps back like she's been slapped.

'Clover turned up at our place in the middle of the night, drunk, if the smell of her is any indication, not to mention the vomit in my garden. And the two of them spent the night in Phil's old cubby.'

'Is this true, Clove?'

I nod. 'Can I go in? I'm sick.'

Mum opens the flywire and almost pushes me inside. 'I'll be there in a minute.'

I crawl onto the couch. They're arguing. Lucille ramps up her short, incessant, old-lady barks.

Mum yells, 'What the hell is wrong with you?'

Mr McKenzie's voice cracks with anger. 'You don't know what Maria's like.' Mum retaliates with, 'But none of *that* is the kids' fault—' He says, 'Get some bloody control of your daughter—'

And then they're shouting over the top of each other until Mum, shoving Lucille ahead of her, storms inside and slams the door so hard a painting falls off the wall. One of hers, called 'Crucifixion of the Feminine'. The dog shares a few joyous parting remarks and trots to me, wagging her tail.

I would probably feel less guilty if Mum stayed angry, but instead she's terribly, terribly disappointed. It envelops her like a depression-scented mist. She puts a pillow under my head, throws a doona over me, feels my head for temperature and puts a glass of water on a table by the couch. 'Drink that. In sips.'

'Sorry, Mum.'

She rubs calendula cream into my visible cuts and scratches. 'What happened at Rosemary's?'

'She had a party.'

'Did you know she was going to when you went there?'

'No.'

'Did something happen at the party? Why did you go to Keek's?'

'I got … I dunno. No, nothing. I was sick.'

'You should've come home.' She rubs the last of the cream into her own hands.

'I wish I had've.'

Mum half-heartedly pats me on the shoulder. 'Well, if there has to be a next time, at least you know you can come home. Drink. You're dehydrated. Do you need a bucket?'

She doesn't go back to bed, but is still slouching around in her pyjamas and dressing-gown at three in the afternoon when Keek turns up.

'Come in,' she says wearily.

'I'm not allowed,' he says, coming in.

'I know.'

He fiddles with his bike helmet. 'Mum's freaking out and Dad's being a dickhead.'

'Isn't the first time,' my mother says, and shuffles off to her bedroom. She sticks her head back out to say, 'You know you're welcome here any time, Keek,' and shuts the door.

Keek stays near the front door and pats the dog. 'Are you all right?'

'Yeah. Pretty much. Thanks.' I feel full of tears. 'And thanks for—'

His face tightens. 'Are you going out with Robbo?'

'No.'

'But you hooked up with him last night?'

'No. Well … sort of.'

Keek's face crumples as if he's found out I'd been torturing kittens or something. It isn't fair.

'He treats girls like—'

'Like what?' I shout.

He practically spits the word, 'Whatever,' and stomps out.

'Keek? Keek, don't go. Where are you going? Don't be a dick.' But by the time I've disentangled myself from my sickbed, he's on his bike, heading off. 'Get back here,' I scream down the street. 'Or I'll never speak to you again.'

He doesn't even turn his head.

I crawl into Mum's bed, Lucille following, and Mum pats me while I cry. I settle down and it's comforting to lie here for a while.

She disturbs the peace by saying, 'You didn't sleep with anyone, did you Clover?'

'Anyone?'

'Well, Robbo.'

'Robbo?'

'It's a small house, Clove. Tell me you didn't sleep with Robbo.'

'I didn't sleep with Robbo.'

'Now I don't know if I can believe you.'

'Trust me, Mum. I did not, could not and will not have sex with Rob Marcello.'

'Hmm.' My mother's face is a mixture of scrutiny and compassion. 'Well, I hope you've learned your lesson. Have you learned your lesson?'

'Yes, Mum.'

She stares at me. I try to stare back, but opt for snuggling in, instead.

'Well ...' she says at last. 'I can't be bothered cooking. Set the computer up in here.' She gets up and throws on her clothes. 'I'm getting pizza and DVDs.'

'And orange juice.'

'And orange juice. And ring Rosemary and tell her you're all right. She's probably worried to death and afraid to call in case she gets you in trouble. And, Clover ...' She seems suspended, staring.

'What?'

'You didn't sleep with Keek, did you?'

'Mum!'

'Well, David thinks you did. You spent the night together.'

'We've spent heaps of nights together.'

'Yes, but here. In separate beds. It's different.'

'Mr McKenzie hates me.'

'David is ...' Mum wriggles as though shaking him off. 'And that doesn't answer my question.'

'I'm a virgin, Mum. All right?'

'Good.' She throws a laugh at me. 'So am I.' She

disappears out the door, then pops her head back in. 'I'm saving myself for Jimmy Page.'

'Yeah, right!' I yell as she runs off down the hall-way. 'He's the biggest slut ever!'

'Don't talk about God like that!' she yells and the front door slams.

While Mum's gone, I set up the computer then have a shower. It feels good to be in clean pyjamas. When I phone Rosemary, she cracks the shits.

'Thanks for helping clean up.'

'Sorry.'

'Doesn't matter,' she says, though obviously it does. 'Heaps of people crashed and helped so it wasn't too bad when my folks got home. Except for the smell. Where did you go?'

'I'm sick. I came home. Sorry.'

'You can make it up to me by doing my art homework. That stupid Andy Warthog thing Sardine's making us do. Just don't make it too good.'

'Warhol.'

'See, you're the right man for the job. By Tuesday.'

'Okay. Thanks. It was a good party.'

'It surely was. Everyone was slaughtered.'

'Got to go, my Mum's back.'

'Is she angry with me?'

'You? No, I don't think so.'

'Cool. I like your mum.'

'You do?'

'Yeah, she's hilarious.'

I put the phone down suspecting my family has just been insulted.

Lucille is all over Mum like she's been gone for a week. 'I must've lost twenty dollars somewhere,' Mum says, half-patting the dog and half-fending her off. 'I've searched my bag and the car. I can't find it anywhere.' She pushes Lucille aside. 'Come on old girl, give me a break.'

She dumps the DVDs, fossicking around where she keeps her purse. 'I have no idea what I've done with that money, but it was food or movies and I got movies. It will have to be left-overs after all. But I managed the orange juice. Hey! You're not crying over pizza are you? You should be thinking yourself lucky you're not on bread and water.'

I hug her. 'I love you,' I say.

'I love you, too.' She kisses the top of my head. 'But for God's sake, Clover – behave yourself, okay?'

———

Heading to school on Monday morning, I still feel queasy, but I'm not game to ask Mum for the day off. I figure all I have to do to avoid Keek is hang out with the Herbs. They have their own circle of logs down the back and I am all set to ignore him, but he doesn't turn up.

We stroll to the quadrangle. Keek calls it 'Herb

Headquarters' and avoids it like the plague. Two close shaves have convinced me I'd better stop thinking of them by their herb names.

Rob bounces up to me, full of beans. 'Hey,' he says accusingly. 'We went off the other night to get beers and when we got back, you'd gone.'

'Is that what you went for? Beers?'

He tickles my ribs and jiggles his eyebrows. 'What else?'

I don't reply. Rob's beautiful, grinning face begs to be kissed, if I had the guts. What if Pars— Natalie has it all wrong?

'So where'd you go?' he asks. 'I thought you were crashing at Rosie's?'

In the distance, Keek zooms in on his bike. I watch him chain it to the bike rack. Cho bounds over to him across the asphalt and they speak for a minute. Seeing them together, I realise he's tall. As tall as Robbo, probably, but a third of his width. Then she hugs him. I can hardly believe it when he lifts his dangling arms and puts them around her. They just stand there.

'Hello?' Rob knocks gently on my head. 'Anyone at home?'

'Sorry.'

'What is it with you and good old Phil, anyway?'

'Nothing.'

Rob is sceptical.

'We've known each other since primary school, but now his parents don't want him to have anything to do with me.'

'Bad vandal-girl. And he cares what his parents think?'

'His mother's – not well.'

'Well, the little BMX Bandit's loss is Captain Robbo's gain. I want you to go to Josh Eldrich's with me on Saturday night. That'll be a *real* party.'

A giant Fruit Tingle is melting in every part of my body. I can hardly breathe. The footy crowd is moving off and calling for Rob to go. Another party so soon after my last effort? And at *Josh* Eldrich's, who doesn't even live with his parents? But I can't quell the Fruit Tingle and the pressure makes me want to scream.

'I don't think my mum will let me,' I manage, against my will.

'C'mon, Jones. It's finals. Come down and watch me play Saturday and we'll go from there. Then we'll send her a text message. I gotta go.'

'She doesn't have a mobile phone.'

He's running towards the oval but flashes me a grin. 'Even better!' he calls. 'She won't know *where* we are.'

Rosemary scoops me up to sit with her on a bench, pushing off the three kids already there. They leave without even complaining. 'You gonna go?' she says.

'There's no way my mum will let me.'

'Well I reckon you better go.'

'Why?'

'Katie told me she's going.'

Sage! 'So?'

'They hooked up after you left. Katie and Robbo. Practically did it in Josh's ute, but Katie had her rags. That's what Ellen told me, anyway.'

'Maybe he should take Katie then.'

'But he didn't *ask* Katie. He asked *you*. And you know Ellen. She's jealous as hell when it comes to Robbo. She could've made it up.'

'Why are you telling me then?'

Rosemary shrugs. 'You're so weird, no wonder your name's Clover. C'mon, it's maths time.'

How am I supposed to think about maths? Mr Ratshit's ear hairs make me vomitus. And where has Keek disappeared to? He's supposed to be in maths. I'd forgotten all about him because of Robbo and Katie and bloody Ellen and don't know if he's gone off with Cho or what.

'. . . Clover?' says Radshaw.

'What?'

'Why are you not writing down the problems?' Mr Radshaw is looking at me as though I'm supposed to know what the hell he's talking about.

'What problems?' The fracture opens and spews out lava in triangles. 'What do I need more problems for? Why are you loading us up with problems? Who gives a shit about the size of triangles? What the hell

179

difference does it make, Mr Radshaw? The world's going down the toilet and you can't trust anyone.'

'You can't swear at me like that. It's not on.'

'Jesus, Mr Radshaw, is that all you've got to offer? Pythagoras was a philosopher for God's sake. He changed the world – why don't you stand up for his bloody triangles?'

'Sit down and write the homework equations. If you don't, you'll be staying in after school until it's done.'

'Fuck off,' I say.

———

Rob comes to see me while I'm waiting on the vinyl bench for Mum. Keek still hasn't shown up.

'I hate Berty,' I say, under my breath.

Rob yawns. 'Do the crime, you do the time.'

'Ratshit's an idiot.'

'So what? Just get on with it. That's what I reckon.'

'I'm suspended again.'

'I heard. How long?'

'A week.'

'A week?' He lowers his voice. 'What did you do? Tell Berty to fuck off, too?'

I snap off a thread hanging from the hem of my school uniform, modified by Rosemary and short as any Herb's.

'Jesus, Jones. What's your problem?'

'School.' My voice is all croaky with tears. 'School is my problem.'

Rob shakes his head. 'I don't get it: it's just school.' He stretches. 'Well, I guess I'll see you at the game then, on Saturday?'

'Will Katie be there?'

'Katie? Maybe. Why?'

'I thought you two were ... you know.'

'What makes you think that?'

But my courage fails me. I sniff and tug on my skirt – it really is too short.

'Jealous? That's a good sign.'

'Is it?'

At the appearance of a couple of mates, Rob is off again, up the corridor. 'Means you want me, Jones,' he calls. 'You want me *bad*.' He disappears in a rowdy knot of sniggering testosterone and is replaced by Ellen, hurrying along the corridor out of breath.

'I wanted to catch you before you left,' she pants. 'Did you know that Philip McKenzie is going out with Cho?'

Three nights into my suspension, Aunty Jean arrives on the doorstep after nine, unannounced. Months ago my mother agreed to go with her to Queensland for the weekend, but she's cancelled because of 'everything that's going on' and Jean's here to insist Mum 'honour her commitment'. I'm packed off to bed as soon as possible, but creep back up the hall, listening through the partially open door.

'Come on, Pen. Clover will be all right. She'll be with Mrs Tzatziki next door and she can always invite her sexy little side-Keek to come and keep her company.'

'Jean!'

'What? The kid's cute, what can I say?'

'You're shocking.'

'No, I am not. You've just lost all sense of perspective. Relax, you know perfectly well that I'm not interested in premature ejaculators – but he's a little hottie, Penelope, like his dad. Anyway, are you coming?'

'I don't know if it's fair on Yiayia, she's getting old. And Clover's been arrested, Jean. And now she's suspended from school again.'

'See? She's killing you. You need a break.'

'I don't think it's the right time—'

'It's nearly seventeen years since "the right time". This is bullshit. You just don't want to spend time with me. With yourself.'

'Don't say that, Jeannie.'

'Well? Come! I know it's cheesy Gold Coast corporate nonsense, but who cares? It's all paid for and there's massage … and karaoke …'

'Karaoke?'

'Okay, fair enough. But come on, Henny Penny. Massage. Beach. No dickhead Dave. Free food. No bills … and it's a fabulously kitsch Surfers Paradise hotel by the looks. And it's been booked for months.'

'I've got nothing to wear.'

'I've got clothes enough for both of us.'

'It would be fun to get away.'

'Mrs T can cope with Clover for one weekend, surely?'

'I suppose it might even be good for her.'

'That's it Penny: do it for Clove. God forbid you do it for yourself.'

'Stop making me out to be a masochist.'

'It's your fault.'

'It's my fault that you're making me out to be a masochist?'

'No, I mean Clover.'

'What do you mean?'

'She's a chip off the old block, that's what I mean. You were an angst-ridden drama queen always telling teachers to stick it up their jumpers.'

'I was not.'

'Mr Farquharson?'

'Well, the man was practically a fascist – what kind of subject is *consumer economics*? Brainwashing into the same neoliberal values that are currently wrecking the planet. Cooperating with him would have been tantamount to appeasement.'

'What about Mrs Thompson? All she did was try to get you to run, you lazy little cow.'

'Shut up, you.'

'Poor woman. She had a nervous breakdown in the end.'

'That wasn't completely my fault.'

'It was a group effort, true, but still: she probably still has nightmares about you.'

Mum scares the crap out of me by getting up to shut the door. 'Shh. She's enough trouble as it is without—'

But I'm gone, back to bed, half-thrilled and half-terrified at the idea of maybe being able to talk

Yiayia into letting me go to Josh's party after all, and totally pissed off with Mum and Aunty Jean for talking about me behind my back.

———— ⸱⌒ ————

Mum gives me the third degree while I sit on the bed and she packs to go away. 'Do you swear on your grandparents' graves that you won't do anything to upset Yiayia while I'm away?'

'Like, what?'

'Like run around spray-painting the neighbourhood.'

'I swear it.'

'Lucille's grave.'

'Mum.'

'Swear.'

'I swear.'

'Have you seen Keek?'

'No.'

Mum tuts and picks fluff off the cardigan she's folding into the suitcase. 'He probably doesn't want to upset his mother.'

'Or his girlfriend.'

She turns to me. 'Keek has a girlfriend?'

'Apparently.'

Mum's packing slows and becomes careful. 'Who?'

'Cho.'

'The one that beat him in that bike comp thing?'

'Yes, the one that beat him in that bike comp thing. She's liked him for ages.'

'And he likes her?'

'Apparently.'

She sits next to me, clutching a pair of socks. 'How do you feel about that?'

I could fall into her lap and cry my head off, but I'm still mad with her for bagging me to Aunty Jean. 'I don't care,' I say.

'Well, you've had him all to yourself ...'

'I don't care, Mum. Good for him. His parents hate me anyway and he's obviously decided they're right about me so good luck to him.' I push away her comforting arm. 'Don't.'

Mum purses her lips and returns to her packing.

'She's an even bigger and more boring bike-head than him, anyway,' I say.

Mum nods unconvincingly. She seems sad. Why won't she believe me? Why should I care what Keek does? He's not my boyfriend.

In a rush of fury I want to slap the worried, knowing look from her face. 'I said I don't care, all right?' I yell, and leave. Or, as Mum describes it later when she's 'having a talk' with me about my attitude: flounce out of the room.

On Friday afternoon Aunty Jean arrives to pick Mum up and it's as though they've already stepped into another realm where I don't exist, talking over the top of each other and joking about having sex with strangers. I hover between not being able to wait to get rid of them and latching on to my mother like a monkey, never to let go. When she finally leaves, half-dragged away by Aunty Jean, it's a shock.

Mrs T is babysitting in Oakleigh until half-past eleven. A sense of freedom thrills through me. I bring the portable CD player from my bedroom, plug in the iPod and crank up my music.

Free, at last!

But when it gets dark, the creeps scuttle up my spine to the base of my neck and nestle there, freaking me out. I have to go to the toilet, but the hall is full of shadowed doorways.

'Is there anyone there?'

Nothing.

The silence gets louder. Someone or something is watching me. Waiting. I take a few steps into the hall. 'Lucille?'

A shadow looms. I scream.

'Bloody hell, dog, are you trying to kill me?' I grab her collar and make her go with me. It isn't far, but as soon as the first doorway is behind me, I have to run the rest of the way because something absolutely *is* going to grab me from behind.

Rushing Lucille back to the lounge, I pick up the phone to call Keek – but don't dial. He's Cho's boyfriend. His parents hate me. It's impossible. Half my heart's been chopped away. I slide down the wall and cry. The dog settles against me with a sigh.

There's only so long one can sob on the carpet. I pull myself up, turn on more lights and try to make Lucille snuggle with me on the couch, but she keeps jumping off and going into Mum's room. No doubt because, on account of her general hairy smelliness, I'm usually shoving her *off* the couch. In the end, I leave the TV on, crank up the music and get out my pencils. Drawing helps the creeps to slink off back into the night, until Lucille comes out to bug me with her extremely bad breath and full bladder and makes me take her outside, where they come scuttling back. I'm almost relieved when Mrs T arrives and makes me turn off the stereo.

'You make your ears deaf as posts,' she says, wagging a finger. 'Bad as your mother with that Von Zeppelin rubbish of hers.'

Even though she's making me mental, I take hold of her fingers and kiss her hand. 'That was *not* Von Zeppelin, Yiayia.' I've loved her hands ever since I was little; worn and weathered and brown with slightly paler palms. She works in the garden, but her nails are always whitish and clean. 'I want to paint your hands one day, Mrs Theopopolous.'

'Darling, you're going to be a great artist.'

'Thanks. Can I paint your hands?'

'Of course. But do I have to sit still for long times? I don't think I'll be fun at that, Clover.'

'I'll take a photo.'

'Okay, Michelangelo.' She laughs, her enormous bosom rocking. 'Come on.'

I haven't slept over at Yiayia's for years. She still makes the bed with crispy sheets and woollen blankets, her palm so firm on my forehead while she says a prayer over me in Greek.

Saturday morning at the Theopopolous's has always been about food, but the spread on the kitchen table is daunting. 'Is the family coming over?' I ask, hopefully.

'No, no, just us. Why?'

I'm saved from having to answer by the telephone. I'd forgotten that Mrs T yells into the receiver, as if the person is in the other room, or on another planet.

'No!' she shouts, and almost dances on the spot. 'Of course, I come immediately!'

She hangs up and rushes around the kitchen.

'Is everything all right?'

'No. Yes. My Olivia, her baby is coming early. I have to go.' Her hand flies to her forehead. 'Ach!'

'What's wrong?'

'I fly to Sydney!'

'Don't worry about me. I'll call my friend ...'
I cast about for a name she won't think is trouble.
'... Alison Larder, and stay at her house.'

'You sure?'

'Yes. She's always asking me. Quick, I'll help you pack. Do you have to book?'

'Theo, he all arranged.'

When the taxi arrives, she hugs me tight and hands me a slip of paper with numbers in her fine scrawl. 'I can't wait any more. You sure it's all right for Mrs Larder?'

'Yeah, I'm sure. I'll get her to call Mum, anyway, so you don't have to worry.'

'Okay. Well, here's Theo, his mobile phone. He's not far. He says he will be our back-up man. Or you can go to his place now. What do you think?'

I think my brain is going to burst out of my heart because the universe clearly wants me to go out with Rob Marcello. 'Alison's will be fine, I'm sure of it,' I say reassuringly, glad she's handing her bag to the taxi driver and not looking at me. 'Give my love to Olivia and say hello to Stephanie for me. I'll call you if I need you. Thanks, Yiayia. Have a safe trip.'

Mrs T settles herself into the passenger seat. 'Be a good girl!' she calls as the taxi pulls away, and the bright, nervous, hopeful kiss she blows me makes me want to cry.

I feel like a criminal, heading home after waving her off, but it's time to take Rob up on his offer. I haven't seen or heard from him all week, so I can only assume I'm still invited.

But I feel like a complete knob when it comes to fronting up at the oval so I turn off and walk down to the bowl instead, then end up halfway to nowhere. I sit on a rock and have a smoke, courtesy of the emergency money Mum left me. Trung works part-time at his parents' run-down milk bar and he sold them to me without even raising a fine black eyebrow.

'Might want to stock up,' he tells me. 'Mum and Dad are selling. It's going to be a 7-Eleven with a petrol station.'

There's a new wooden fence dividing Fernwood Reserve from the almost-completed roadworks. There are still trees up to where the new wall blocks out the future traffic noise and the creek disappears under tonnes of tar and concrete. I itch to set to work on that pale wood, unadorned except for a few familiar tags, which are slowly developing style. People don't understand tags. A good tag is calligraphy and calligraphy is a meditative art. The fracture shifts like a shark under water. Maybe I'll paint the Nguyêns' milk bar on there so it won't disappear without a trace.

But all I feel like writing is 'CHO' in mile-high letters, and then burning them.

'You all right, Clover? You look like you're about to kill something.'

Cho. On bike, naturally. Have I called her with my thoughts? Aunty Jean told me that whatever you think about passionately, good or bad, you bring into your life. I said at the time that I guessed in my mother's case either Rudolf Steiner or Jimmy Page were bound to turn up soon then, and how amusing if they arrived together. Now I wonder if she's on to something.

Cho sits back and crosses her arms. 'Aren't you talking to me?'

'Sorry. I was miles away.'

'Are you coming to the bowl?'

'Maybe.'

She's pretty, even with a helmet on. And smart. And a champion bike rider. Why am I being such an idiot about Keek? He has the right to have a girlfriend if he wants. Doesn't he? And why wouldn't he go out with Cho? It doesn't mean there's anything wrong with me. Does it? But I still don't feel like seeing him. 'Is your boyfriend down there?' I try to make my smile genuine.

'Yes.'

'Congratulations, by the way.'

'Thanks. Are you gonna come down?'

'Yep. Later. I said I'd meet someone over at the oval first.'

'Right. Seeya then.'

Cho rides off, smooth as cream.

———— ❦ ————

It's packed at the footy oval, but Katie's still the first person I recognise, leaning on the fence with Natalie and Ellen, all rugged up against the cold, cheering. They have their backs to me. I could leave. But then the pack rumbles up close and I'm distracted.

The superbrain blocks my view. 'Clover. What are you doing here?'

'Alison, hi.' It crosses my mind to ask her to corroborate my alibi. Maybe she could pretend to be her mother? But then I remember who it is I'm talking to: the girl who blushes from head to toe even when she tells the truth. I don't think lying to parents is in her repertoire. 'What are *you* doing here?' I ask.

'My cousin plays in the juniors and he wanted to hang around for the Under 18s. My aunty asked me to watch him.'

'Fun for you.'

'Oh, I don't mind.' Alison shifts sideways to shout, 'Stay in the reserve!' at a knot of twelve-year-old boys running by in fits of devilish laughter. 'Trung's coming after work,' she adds, airily.

'Oh, right.' Alison Larder with a boyfriend is strange. In a weird way, I feel almost jealous. 'You and Trung. That's ...' Bloody hell, what am I trying to say? *Gee Alison, and I thought you were a lesbian.* 'Great,' I finish, lamely.

'Well,' she meets my eye steadily, though her face has gone its signature beetroot. 'You know what Oscar Wilde said.'

'No, I don't.' Who the hell knows what Oscar Wilde said?

She closes her eyes to recite. 'Keep love in your heart. A life without it is like a sunless garden where the flowers are dead.' As if that explains everything. Or anything.

God, she's weird. So is Oscar Wilde.

'Right.'

'Are you going to jail?' she asks me.

'I hope not.'

'Ellen said you were.'

'Yeah, well, Ellen says lots of things.'

'Are you here to see Robbo?'

I spot Rosemary near the scoreboard and trudge toward her. 'Gotta go, Alison.'

Rob runs by on the footy field, face gritted with determination and legs splattered with mud. My pulse races as he picks up the ball and the pack thunders towards him. Jase shepherds him brilliantly, a few others collide and Rob manages to kick it on, long and accurate. A bunch of them swerve off, chasing the play with Rob hard on the ball. He's there in time to receive a short pass and just escapes a mighty tackle that makes me scream with the tension. He kicks towards goal. Yes! The exhilarating roar carries my voice into the buzz. Rob's swamped by teammates. I imagine him as a real AFL player and my heart swells with hope that he'll make it to the Essendon Reserves next year.

Rosemary is all smiles. 'So you came?'

'Looks like it.'

'Does Robbo know you're here?'

'Don't think so. He looks pretty occupied to me.'

'See ball. Kick. Run. Punch. Ug.' Rosemary laughs and steals the smokes from my pocket. 'Want one of your cigarettes?'

'Don't you like footy?'

'God no. Do you like bikes?'

'Not that much, I suppose. But I do like football, actually. Mum thinks it's a seething cesspit of violent male chauvinism, so I have to go watch it with my old-lady neighbour.'

'Yeah, right,' she says, thinly disguising her dis-interest in the details of my football appreciation sagas. 'Are you going to Josh Eldrich's tonight?' Rosemary adjusts her fringe and regards me sideways.

'Mum's gone away, so I might. Are you?'

'After last weekend? No way. My dad's freaking out. He found a used condom in the garden.'

'You're kidding?'

'Thought it might be yours.'

'What?'

'Well, you and Robbo were gone for a while . . . there's a rumour going around. Katie's mad as hell.'

'A rumour going around? About me?'

'You make it sound like no one ever talks about you, vandal girl.' Rosemary takes a swig on her water bottle. 'I hate smoking,' she says. 'It tastes like – hey, where are you going?'

But I can't answer. The Herbs and everybody in the world are staring at me. I walk as fast as I can without running, my throat aching with tears. It's a long horrible way home and when I get there, Lucille has pissed on the rug. I ring Aunty Jean's mobile, but she won't get my mother.

'What's wrong?' she wants to know.

'Nothing. I just want to talk to her.'

'Listen Clove, I can hear you're in the throes of one of your dramaramas, but your mum deserves a break, don't you think? Talk to me. What's wrong?'

I hate Aunty Jean. 'Nothing's wrong.'

'You better be telling me the truth. Is there something wrong?'

'There's nothing wrong, I just want to talk to her.'

'Well, she's not here.'

'Where is she?'

'Having her hair done courtesy of my company. Then we're going out. Is Mrs T all right?'

'Yes, she's fine.'

'Is the dog all right?'

'Yes.'

'Are you all right?'

Hate her guts.

'Are *you* all right, Clover?'

'Yes.'

'Shall I get her to call you at the Larders'?'

'No.' God, I hope I don't sound as desperate as I feel. 'We're going out. Some church thing.'

'Lucky you. Well, be good, stay safe and keep out of trouble. I'll tell her you called and you're fine. Unless there *is* something wrong?'

'Thanks a lot,' I say.

***

The television is in my room and Lucille has figured out that's where the food is too. I curl up in my pyjamas. What if Mum calls the Larders? What if she never comes back from Queensland? What if Aunty Jean has opened her eyes to everything she's been missing, stuck with stupid, criminal, idiot me? Lucille sits up and stares, no doubt hoping this latest bout of tears will mean she gets the handful of Cheezels I'm sobbing into. I hand them over.

'One of us may as well be happy,' I say.

Then I hear a knock, and I scream. Lucille barks and falls off the bed in her race to the front door. I creep to the lounge room. Whoever it is knocks again.

'Who is it?'

'Me.'

I startle, then open the door a crack. 'Rob?'

'Cute pyjamas,' he says. 'Who's that again?'

'Snoopy.'

'That's right. Snoopy. And who's this?'

'That's Lucille.'

'You and Snoops and Lucille going to let me in or what?'

I open the flywire. Rob Marcello. In my house.

'Far out, how cool is this?' He makes a beeline for my mother's record collection. 'Zeppelin. No way.'

'My mother thinks Jimmy Page is her boyfriend.'

'Mmm, milf.'

'Robbo!'

'Don't call me Robbo, Jones. You're the only one who doesn't.'

'Don't you like it?'

'At home they call me Roberto.' His grin is almost shy. 'I don't like that much either.'

'Roberto.'

'It's my real name. Roberto Ercole Marcello.' He gives it an Italian flourish.

'Ercole?'

'After Hercules.' He shows me his muscles and

they flex under his skin and it's as though they're turning in my stomach. He reddens, as if he's afraid of his secret name. 'But don't tell anyone.'

'I won't. Do you speak Italian?'

He turns back to the albums. 'My dad thought it would be better for us if we spoke English. Mum and Dad speak it to each other sometimes. I know a little, from my Nonna. I wouldn't mind going there one day though. Italy.' His hands rest on Mum's records, but he looks up at me. 'You wearing Snoopy to the party?'

'I'm not going.'

'Yes you are.'

'Say something in Italian.'

'*A buon intenditor poche parole*,' he says. 'Nonna's favourite saying.'

I am enchanted. 'What does it mean?'

'Sort of ... don't talk too much. I dunno. It's more about listening than talking. I'm hopeless at translating. Can I put a record on while you get changed?'

'I guess so. Be careful.'

'Are you kidding? These are like gold.'

'Have you ever used a turntable before?'

'No, but how hard can it be?'

So here I am, madly throwing on clothes in my bedroom while Rob Marcello scratches my mother's fourth-favourite vinyl album in the lounge room.

I opt for the safety of black.

'It's emo-girl, returned,' says Rob. 'I love this song.'

Yep, good old *Stairway to Heaven*. But with Rob sitting there surrounded by album covers and Lucille waving her legs in the air in a back-scratch of ecstasy, it doesn't sound so bad. Mum's right – it is a monster guitar solo.

'Do you want a drink or something?' I ask.

'I have beer and Cruisers,' he says.

My stomach turns in a different direction. 'I don't think so.' ,

'How about a joint, then?'

And before long, it doesn't seem weird at all to be playing air guitar and falling onto the couch for an acoustic *Going to California* cuddle. The kiss comes as a surprise and I clam up like a snail poked with a stick.

'Relax, Jones. I won't hurt you.'

'I . . .' Embarrassment rolls over me like nausea. 'I've gotta go to the bathroom.'

'When the levee breaks, heh heh.' Rob laughs at his own joke, but I'm a blank.

'It's the name of this song,' he explains.

Sitting on the toilet, the room spins. In the bathroom, I hunch over the handbasin for a few minutes, wash my face with cold water and have a long drink straight from the tap. Mum's record is clunking away and I stagger out to rescue the needle.

'It's not like a CD player,' I explain before collapsing into the armchair. I can't move.

Rob puts the album back in its sleeve.

'I'm starving,' I manage. 'If I don't eat something right now, I'm going to chuck.'

'Where's the kitchen?'

I can hardly raise my arm, but manage to point. 'Through there.'

He returns with a thick, badly cut piece of bread that's more gouged than spread with butter. 'Not very exciting,' he says. 'But it's all I could find.'

I feel better when I've eaten it.

'I think we should get going,' Rob says. 'They'll be getting started.'

'How are we going to get there?'

Rob brandishes his phone. 'Taxi.'

I've only been in a taxi a few times in my life and in the arms of Rob Marcello, the trip is a perfect forever until it's over and we're stepping over bodies strewn on Josh Eldrich's lounge room floor. Thrash music blares, but everyone seems half in a coma.

In the kitchen things are more lively and, though I'm wary, I say yes to a Cruiser, but ask for water as well. It goes down quite nicely and I accept another. Rob talks cars and footy with his mates and a bunch of older people I don't know.

I'm bored.

But at least Rob has his arm around me.

A guy called Arvo says, 'Never seen an umpire with tits before.'

'What difference does that make?' I say.

'Oops, look out,' says Arvo, nudging me with his tattooed arm. 'The little lady's getting riled.' His forearm tattoo reads 'Levington' in big ugly letters; in case he forgets his surname, I guess.

I wave my water at him. 'Men umpire women's sport, don't they? Why not the other way around? What's the big deal?'

Arvo snorts, 'Women's sport,' and there's a general snigger.

Rob says, 'How about those bloody Magpies?' and they turn their shoulders to me, ever so slightly.

Idiots.

I lean into Rob and ask, 'Where's the loo?'

'Just down there.' Rob kisses me. 'Don't get lost.'

On my way, I see Katie coming in from the backyard. I can hardly push the pee out quickly enough, and sure enough, by the time I get back Katie's sitting on the kitchen bench next to Rob, flirting for all she's worth.

'Hi, Katie,' I say.

She looks embarrassed. I probably do too. Rob kisses her cheek, then grabs me by the hand. 'Come on, Jones, let's see what's happening up here.'

Leaving Katie behind, I let myself be led up the dingy hallway and into a bedroom with spectacularly ugly brown-and-orange curtains. Sagging boxes stacked by the window leak clothes across the grotty carpet. Rob kicks them out of the way. A sports bag has been dumped on a chest of drawers, the fake-woodgrain veneer peeling off the chipboard.

'Spare room.' Rob grins wickedly, patting the double bed. He switches on a lamp and turns off the main light and the room is instantly nicer.

We smoke a joint, but after a few puffs, I have to lie down. I watch him, then he lays next to me, half on top of me, and we kiss.

It starts off with the giant Fruit Tingle effect, but when he moves his hand down the front of my jeans, I push his hand away. He kisses me again and I relax. Then he puts his hand up my top and I panic. He'll think I'm a fool. I try not to tense up, to relax into the kissing, but it's like my body acts independently and before I can stop myself, I scrabble backwards up the bedhead and shove his hand away as if it were a spider.

'Sorry,' I say.

'Are you frigid, Jones?'

Am I? How am I supposed to know?

'No,' I say. But what if there *is* something wrong with me?

'Good.' And he kisses my neck. His hand on my skin, cupping my waist, feels good. He pushes at the waistband of my jeans, but they're tight, so he undoes the button and the zip slides down. I am relieved and disappointed when his hand goes back up under my top.

'I saw you today, playing footy.'

'Yeah, I know.'

'You saw me?'

'For a second. Then Nat told me you'd gone home and ...' he grins, '... that you told Rosemary your mum wouldn't be home.'

'Did she tell you about the condom?'

'Yeah, I heard.' He props himself on an elbow and smiles at me. His hand slides down my body and he runs his finger under the elastic of my undies. I suck in my breath, my stomach shuddering of its own accord.

'Everyone thinks I've popped vandal-girl.'

'You didn't tell them it wasn't us?'

Rob acts like telling the truth had never occurred to him. 'Nup.' He kisses my collarbone. 'So we may as well do it now – seeing as everyone already thinks we have.' And tugs down my jeans.

I sit up, pull up my jeans, zip them and cross my arms. 'I can't believe you didn't say it wasn't us?'

'What are you getting pissed off for?'

'Are you kidding?'

'Heaps of girls would kill to have everyone think they'd been with me.'

'What? Like Katie?'

'Katie is a cocktease.'

'Don't say that.'

'As if you like Katie Marshall?'

I roll away and sit on the edge of the bed. 'That's not what I mean.'

'If you're frigid, Jones, just say so.'

'I'm not. I mean—'

'Mean what?'

'Don't you think we should ... you know.'

Rob's eyes light up. 'Use a condom?'

'No. I mean ... I mean go out for a while. First.'

'Sure, we could go out. Why not? I like you, Jones.' He reaches over and undoes my jeans again. 'But come on. You can't say no now. My balls are going to drop off.'

I push his hand away. 'Say no? You haven't even asked me.'

'Asked you?' He grabs my hand. 'Feel that.'

I hear scuffling, like rats in the wall. 'There's someone in the hall. At the door.'

Rob gets up. He almost loses his balance getting to the door to check and I realise how drunk he is. 'Nah,' he says. Fall-sitting back down, he puts his arm around me. 'I do like you, Jones.'

He pulls me down and pushes up my top, rubbing himself against me while I babble on about, of all things, my mum. Could I be any more embarrassing? 'Mum reckons at our age we should go out for at least a year before ...' Oh yes, good one. Shut up. Shut up.

But I can't shut up. I don't want to do it with Rob. Not here. Not with Katie sitting out in the kitchen. It's too weird. Not without being his girlfriend. I mean, I've heard how they talk about the girls they've slept with at parties. But I don't say any of that. I continue to blather on about my mother, instead. 'After a year of "going together", as she calls it – pathetic, I know – she'd let me go on the pill if I wanted to.' A year? What am I even talking about?

Rob takes my hand again and rubs it against the bulging crotch of his jeans. 'I can't wait that long, Jones, I'll explode.'

I pull away.

'Come on. It'll be good. Please.'

'No.'

Rob reaches out and strokes my fingers. I think he's going to say something nice, but he tries to guide my hand to his trousers.

'I don't want to, Rob.' I pull away. 'Don't.'

Rob jerks, like he's been burnt. 'Then what did you come in here for?'

He's right – what *had* I expected? I'd expected – well, not this. But I've heard it's painful for guys if girls are cockteasers.

'Come on, Clover ...'

Rob has never called me by my first name, ever. I melt. Maybe if I can relax? If I don't stay now, that will be the end of it, I'm sure. He'll go off with Katie and everyone will know there's something wrong with me. And I love him. Don't I?

'Give me a hand job then.'

I shove him. 'Keek's right about you. You treat girls like shit.'

'Yeah right – Saint Phil. As if he can talk.'

'Keek wouldn't hurt anyone. Not on purpose.' I want Keek, now. Wish we could jump on his bike and disappear.

'Yeah, right. After what he said about your mother.' Rob sculls the last of his beer.

'I'm going.'

'Didn't wait a year with your dad, did she?' Rob's mean laugh scares me. He opens a new stubby and takes a slug.

I want Mum. Or better still, Aunty Jean – she'd rip his stupid balls off and chuck them out the window. I don't owe Rob Marcello anything. Poor Ellen. What would I have done if he'd said he loved me? I get off the bed to do up my jeans, but my fingers are like sausages.

'You're talking shit,' I say, shaking with rising anger. 'I thought you were ... But you're a loser dickhead like the rest of your dickhead mates. I bet your Nonna is ashamed of you, *Hercules*.'

Rob jolts upright and clenches his fist. I've seen his face like that once before, when Pete Tsaparis called him a wanker and they almost had a punch-on. 'Yeah?

It's your slutty mother that should be ashamed. Up for the good old one-night stand according to Sanda.'

'What do you know,' I say, my vision blurring with tears. 'Who's Sanda?'

'You know – Cho's brother?' Rob sits back and toasts me with his empty beer. 'So much for your friend Phil.'

'I hate you.'

Rob rubs his face. 'Shit, Jones—'

I stumble to the door and wrench it open. Half-a-dozen drunken blokes clogging the hall suppress their laughter. When I push through, it roars out. I run, and crash into Katie.

'What the hell?' she says. 'Are you all right?'

'Leave me alone.'

Behind me, I hear Rob tell the boys to fuck off.

I half-turn to see Katie put her hand on Rob's arm. 'Hang on – Robbo, what's going on, babe?'

He laughs. 'Come on Katie, I need a smoke,' and, putting his arm around her, lurches to the kitchen.

I run outside, hide behind an old shed, and cry.

———

I've stopped sobbing and sit, staring.

'Clover?'

I peek.

Katie's standing on the step, peering into the garden. 'Where are you? I've got your bag.'

I want my bag. It has my smokes in it.

'Clover?'

I wipe my nose on my sleeve. 'I'm over here.'

Katie sits next to me on the rotted railway sleeper. 'Are you all right?'

I shake my head.

'I'll be back in a minute.' She disappears inside and comes back with a roll of toilet paper. Grateful, I blow my nose.

'Want to talk about it?' she says.

'No.'

'I won't tell anyone. Seriously. It doesn't matter, but you can tell me if you want and I promise I won't tell anyone.'

'What about Rosemary?'

'Especially not her. She and Ellen have spread so many rumours about me. I hate it. Seriously. I promise.'

'I can't. Anyway, aren't you going to get with Robbo now? He's all yours.'

Katie stands – though how she balances on those shoes, I have no idea – brushes bark off her pink miniskirt, and frowns at the dirt. She sits on her bag – it's big enough; there's probably a small make-up department in there. 'I don't like him anymore,' she says. 'He's been horrible to me the whole time anyway. And he—' But she doesn't finish.

'What did he do?'

'He didn't do anything.'

'What did he say?'

'Don't—'

She doesn't say what her 'don't' is supposed to mean and I don't ask. We're stuck in a weird, untrusting silence.

'Oh, well,' she says after a while. 'Know any jokes?'

'Jokes?'

'You know – like: How did the sultana drown?'

'I dunno.'

'Dragged down by a strong currant.' Katie laughs at her own stupid pun, then proceeds to reel off a string of bad jokes including the one about the interrupting sheep. The next thing I know, I'm telling her about Rob and then Keek and Cho, but I lie and say Keek lied about my mum and dad, while she repeats, 'You're freaking kidding me?' and creates the most insulting swearing combinations I've ever heard, winding up with, 'Rob Marcello is a toe-sucking dickweed with his nose right up Cho Roberts's butt-cheeks.'

I laugh.

It's getting cold. We snuggle up for warmth and sit there, Cock-tease Katie and Vandal-girl, daughter of Slut.

After a while, I ask, 'How are you getting home?'

'I don't know. I was going to crash here. I thought with Robbo, to tell you the truth. Mum thinks I'm at Rosemary's, but I'm not going there, even if I knew how to get there. She convinced me to come. I was so pissed off when he turned up with you.'

'She told me I should come because you were coming,' I say.

Katie stares at her shoes. 'Rosemary did?'

'Sorry, Katie.'

'No way. You did me a favour. I was thinking about doing it with that pig.'

'He didn't seem like a pig. He's ...' I don't know what he is. 'I want to go home.'

'Why don't you then?'

'I'll have to walk and I don't know where I am.'

'Where do you live?'

I tell her and she says, 'That's miles away. You can't walk that far in the middle of the night, you'll be killed or something.'

With a rush of inspiration like the smell of freshly baked baklava, I say, 'Katie, can I use your mobile phone?'

⚬━━⁓━━

If Theo Theopopolous isn't that thrilled about getting a call at one in the morning, he never lets on. 'Here I am,' he says. 'Your back-up man.'

Sitting with Katie in the warm safety of his car, I can't thank him enough.

'Keep out of trouble, Clover.' Theo smiles, but his eyes are sad. 'And I won't even tell your mother.'

'What about *your* mother?' I manage a smile.

'Definitely not!' He laughs a big Theopopolous laugh and I burst into tears.

'Ah, sweetheart,' he says, reaching back to pat my knee. 'You think you're a big prickly cactus, but you're a little clover-blossom after all.'

I'm so glad to be home, I don't even care that Lucille has peed on the rug again. I hug and kiss her like I haven't done since I was little.

'That dog's tail is going to wag off,' says Katie. 'What a weird house.'

Suddenly it seems kinda cool. 'My mum's an artist,' I say, soaking up dog pee with paper towel. 'Like me.'

It's fun, being alone in the house with a girlfriend. We watch children's DVDs from my unmistakeably dweebish collection, drink Milo and eat homemade 'pizza subs' and Greek shortbreads made by Mrs T.

'These are the best biscuits I've ever eaten,' says Katie, icing sugar cascading down the front of her top.

I point next door and say, 'Mrs T lives over there. She bakes.'

Katie makes a few theatrical bows. 'I worship thee, Mrs T,' she says, cracking herself up.

Underneath the blonde hair and make-up, Katie Marshall isn't what I had imagined. 'You're different at school,' I say.

'Yeah. So are you.'

It's nearly dawn when I give Katie my bed and crawl into Mum's with Lucille, who snores almost immediately. Lying in the dark, I can't believe Keek told Cho about my dad. Or that Cho blabbed on to her stupid brother. Is my mum a slut for sleeping with someone she hardly knew? And obviously 'safe sex' hadn't come into it. Only last week she gave me a box of condoms, saying, 'I do believe you, but just in case.' What a hypocrite.

Aunty Jean reckons Mum had a few boyfriends when I was little, but nothing worked out. Except for Yiayia's 'blind dates', the only men I know of that Mum's ever shown any interest in are actors and musicians she'll never meet. Would she sleep with them, if she *did* meet them? I have a vision of her saying, 'You bet I would,' and leaping around the lounge room with her air guitar. A big laugh bursts out of me and wakes the dog.

Laughter. It does shake the black stuff off your soul.

'I hope my dad's not dead,' I whisper to Lucille, who snorts and tucks her nose under her foreleg.

⁘ ⌒ ▬

I'm up making toast when Katie shambles out of my bedroom wearing my Elmo pyjamas. My blood is thumping because there's something about hanging out with Katie that reminds me of hanging out with Alison all those years ago. Something fragile and if I hold on too tight, I'll crush it, but I don't want to let it go, either. 'Thanks for coming to find me last night,' I say.

'Thanks for having me. More fun than Josh's dopefest. Can I ring my mum in case she rings Rosemary's?'

'Yeah, of course.' I show her to our hopelessly old-fashioned landline.

'Thanks. I've hardly got any credit.'

'Sorry – is that from calling Theo last night?'

'Sort of. But it's worth it. Otherwise I'd've been stuck at that party.'

We shudder.

Katie picks up the receiver and pokes at the phone.

'You have to dial.'

But she doesn't get it and I have to show her.

'God, it takes forever.' She pats one of mum's weird sculptures on the head. 'What are you doing today?'

My palms have gone sweaty; I hope my face isn't as red as it feels. 'Nothing special.' I busy myself patting the dog. 'I have to clean up. You could hang out – but you don't have to do any cleaning or anything …'

'Cool.'

Cool. Just like that. Cool.

Katie's mum doesn't mind if she's at mine or Rosemary's as long as she's 'somewhere safe'.

I ring to tell Mum I'm home and Aunty Jean deigns to put my mother on the phone.

'How was church?' Mum says, laughing at me.

'Oh, it was great,' I joke back. 'I'm getting baptised this afternoon.'

'Oh, yes?'

'Yes!' I say, as earnestly as I can. 'I don't want to be left behind after the Rapture, Mum. And I don't want you to be left behind, either. Join me, repent your sins, wash away your evil ways, and—'

Mum's voice is flat. 'You're not serious, right?'

'Relax, mother, I remain a sinner.'

———

So, everything is peachy, but the fracture inside is bubbling and charging – how dare Keek tell my secret? He crossed his heart. How dare he?

———

I can't believe how many dishes I've managed to use in one weekend. Katie entertains me with Herb impressions while I wash them. I laugh until my stomach aches.

'I thought you liked them,' I say between sighs.

'I do like them. Most of the time. But not nearly as much as they like themselves. Ha!'

The laugh-pain in my stomach churns into rottenness. 'I hate Cho,' I say.

Katie tosses a teaspoon in the sink. 'She's probably jealous.'

'Jealous? What does she have to be jealous of? I'm not the one who stole her best friend.'

'You and Keek were pretty tight.'

'Yeah, but friends. Or so I thought.'

'Yeah, but ...' Katie looks away.

'But what?'

'Well, he had a massive crush on you.'

'Keek?' Even the water circling down the plughole looks sceptical to me. 'No, he didn't.'

'Yes, he did.'

'No way.'

'Yes way.'

'No—'

'Clover, the only one who doesn't reckon, is you.'

'Well, I hate him.'

Katie's mum rings. 'She'll be here in an hour, but I'll see ya tomorrow,' Katie says, hugging me.

I hug her back and a big sigh escapes me. It's so good to feel safe with someone. I think of Robbo and the other Herbs. They'll be having a field day with what happened at the party. My missing one-night-stand father is probably common knowledge by now. I wonder if Keek and Cho have heard. 'If I ever go to school again,' I say.

'You have to go to school.'

'I don't think I can.'

'You have to. You have to find out who lied, Keek or Cho, and then you have to tell them what you think, right to their face. You can't let people say things like that about your mum, Clover. You have to stand up for her. And who knows what Robbo is saying? People saw you run out of that bedroom. He's going to have to say something, especially as everybody thinks you already – you know.'

'We didn't.'

'I know. But Ellen told everybody that you did.'

'What's her problem? Why does she do that?'

'To make herself feel better about having humped half the football team, I guess.'

'And why does she do *that*?' We head out the back on our way down to the kiddies' park. The flywire slams behind me. Why hadn't her experience with Robbo cured her forever?

At the boundary of our garden, Katie rubs the stone belly of the buddha. 'Slut?' she speculates.

I'm not convinced. Why does somebody suddenly become a 'slut'? They dump her, one after the other. It can't be fun. 'Why does she keep hooking up with them?' I wonder out loud.

Katie leans in towards me. 'She said she's done things that made her want to vomit.'

'What things?'

'You know.'

We shudder, but there's a kind of delight in it. 'Anything can happen when you're drunk,' I say.

Katie lifts her shoulder and purses her lips knowingly. 'But it isn't about getting drunk. Ellen is a *stalker*.'

And now there are people at school saying I'm a slut, and I'm still a virgin. And why should I care? But I do care.

Katie climbs up the short ladder to sit at the top of the slide. 'I think Ellen wants to make Robbo jealous.'

'I hate Robbo, too,' I say.

'Rob Marcello,' Katie slides down, 'is a slut.' She skids off the end faster than expected and lands on her arse. 'Shit,' she says, then laughs such a big loud laugh, I have to laugh too.

'Yeah, but no one cares that Rob sleeps around. No one talks about it as if it's a bad thing. None of those guys get put in a bad light because they've done it. It shits me. I mean: why *is* it a bad thing? If Ellen was having a good time, why should anyone care?'

'Forget about them. At least until tomorrow.'

But I can't. In a rush of revenge, I tell her about 'Hercules'. We stroll back and play cards until her mum beeps in the driveway.

⁓

It's after ten when Mum gets home. Lucille goes nuts and celebrates by peeing on the rug.

'That's the third time she's done that this weekend,' I complain, glad Mum is back to clean it up.

'I wonder if I should take her to the vet for a check-up, poor darling.'

'You've cut your hair.'

She stops stomping on paper towel and does a turn. 'Do you like it?'

'Yeah.' But it's weird because she looks younger and sort of ... modern. 'You're wearing make-up.'

Mum laughs. 'Your aunty can't help herself.'

'Was it fun?'

'It was. It really was. Jeannie and I haven't laughed like that since uni days. And we danced our butts off. How about you?'

'I was fine,' I lie.

'And how about you and Alison, hey?' She's happy and relaxed, even though she's tired and dealing with dog pee. 'How were the Larders?'

'Yeah, Alison.' I hand her another roll of paper towel. 'They were all right.'

'Good,' she says. 'I suppose I'd better call them and say thank you.'

I'm sweating. 'You know what they're like. You'll be on the phone for hours, talking about Jesus. It was only a sleep over. Just write a thank-you card and I can give it to Alison at school.'

Mum kisses my cheek. 'Good thinking, 99.'

I dawdle to school and chuck the thank-you card in someone's wheelie bin on the way. When I get there, the knot of kids shocks me with its noise. It's like walking through treacle. The shouted word – *fight* – pushes its way through the fug. Punch-ups don't happen that often at Fernwood – I've never seen one before. My bag is heavy on my shoulder and my mouth goes dry. Maybe I should get Fitzy or even go home and leave them to their prehistoric bullshit. I hope it's boys. Then I see – as if the knot of bodies parts especially so I can see – Rob Marcello punching the crap out of Keek.

At a run, I hurl my bag at them. It bounces off Rob's shoulder. He turns towards me and Keek wriggles out of his grip, but he doesn't run off. He leaps on Robbo and punches him hard, twice.

A roar comes out of me – a prehistoric response of my own, I guess, and I wade in, grab at Rob and push Keek away. I'm screaming, not even words, and inside my fear and rage and the blur of faces, I glimpse Natalie looking pale, and Rosemary and Ellen smirking.

Keek's face is bright red and streaked with dirt. 'Stop it! Stop it!' I bawl in his face. My spit flies out to join up with his tears.

'Clover—'

Fight.

'Please go.' My voice is hoarse and high-pitched. It hurts my throat. 'Go!'

Keek grabs up his bike from the dirt and is gone. I round on Robbo, who shouts, 'That's right you little fucker, off you run.'

'I hate you,' I scream, and try to punch him.

He grabs my wrists and holds me off. 'Settle down. It's not my fault your faggot boyfriend had a go. He's lucky I didn't kill him.'

'Yeah,' shouts Pete Tsaparis. 'He's lucky Robbo didn't kill him.'

I struggle against arms that could toss me up a tree. 'Let me go.'

'I didn't even want to have a go at the little shit.'

'He'd better watch his back,' pipes in Pete.

'Why should I believe anything you say, you pig?' I spit the word. I wish it were a knife plunging into Robbo's heart. Wish I were a teacher to kick him out of school. Wish I were my dad – big enough to humiliate him with a look. Or better still, smash his stupid laughing face in.

But it's the crowd that's laughing, not Rob. He shoves me away and I land in a heap. 'Whatever,' he says. 'I'm over it. Come on boys.'

And off they go. The three Herbs follow and I wonder where Katie is. Only Natalie looks sorry. The crowd breaks up. Mark Creswell, Trung and Alison Larder sit near me on the asphalt.

After a long silence, broken only by the bell and my sniffling, Mark says, 'Want a carrot?'

'No thanks.'

'I'll have one,' says Alison. Then, like an afterthought, 'We're late.'

Mark says, 'Yes, we are,' and crunches, thoughtfully. I sit up and lean against his bulk, soft and warm, and sniff.

'What happened?' I ask, though a big part of me doesn't want to know.

Alison untangles herself from Trung's arms and sits in his lap. Why had I thought it strange that they were going out together? Why shouldn't they? I envy them. Mark takes a second peeled carrot and observes, nodding, as Alison tells the story.

'Robbo told Rosemary that Keek told Cho that you have crabs and Cho told her brother and her brother told him and Robbo said he turned you down because of the crabs and that you freaked out and ran off drunk from Eldrich's party calling Cho an effing slut and that you were going to cave her head in and then Katie Marshall told Rosemary she's full of shit and everyone thought Rosemary was going to cave *her* head in, but Sutcliff caught Katie swearing and sent her off to Berty and then Rosemary told Cho that you were going bash her and Cho told Keek and Keek and Cho had a big fight and then Keek told Robbo to eff off and Robbo told Keek to eff off, but he wouldn't and that's when you turned up.' She sighs a big breathy sigh and kisses Trung. 'Did I miss anything?'

Trung shakes his head. 'Nah, that's about it. But Keek was off his nut. He definitely threw the first punch. Keek, I mean.'

'Keek doesn't fight,' I say. 'And I've never bashed anyone in my life.' And, crabs? It's like hearing a story about somebody else.

Mark nods sympathetically. 'Sure you don't want something to eat?'

Trung stands up, pulling Al up with him. 'We'd better go. My parents will die if I get detention.'

'They won't die,' says Mark.

'No, seriously,' Trung replies, earnestly. 'They'll die.'

I can't help noticing that getting up makes Mark puff like he's climbed a hill. Trung offers him a hoist up, but he shoos him off.

223

'Tell Katie I'm sorry she got into trouble,' I say. 'Tell her to please not get in a fight with Rosemary. I – will you make sure?'

Alison shrugs. 'I'll try.'

Trung shakes his head. 'As if they're going to listen to you.'

'I'll make sure,' says Mark, and I hug one of his arms.

I'm a coward, but I can't stay at school. I go home, tell Mum I don't feel well and let her put me to bed.

I don't feel well.

———

Later, wrapped in my doona and cuddling a hot water bottle, I ring Katie. 'Rosemary didn't hurt you, did she?'

'Nah. Robbo told her not to.'

His name makes my guts ache. 'Rob?'

'Yeah. I told him Hercules told me to tell him to tell her to back off. And he reckons he's sorry. He even asked me to tell you that.'

'Did he?'

'Yeah. But now he's going out with Rosemary.'

Is that what it's all been about? Me, Katie – all of it? I think of Rosemary's smug face. They deserve each other. Lucille treads circles on my trailing doona and settles with a sigh. 'Shit, Katie. Are you okay?'

'I'm okay. Ellen's more upset, I reckon. What about you?'

'I don't care. I hate him. You smell, dog.' I push her off.

'Keek and Cho broke up.'

It's as if the phone zaps me. 'Why?'

'Dunno. They had that big fight and now they're broken up.'

'Did you talk to him?'

'No. But you should.'

'No.'

Unfazed by rejection, Lucille pushes her nose under my hand for a pat and fixes her worried eyes on me. How does she know when I feel like crying?

'When are you coming back to school?' Katie says.

'Tomorrow.'

But I don't feel well the next morning, either.

Mum is suspicious. 'Are you sure nothing happened while I was away?'

'Like what?'

'Oh, I don't know. Drugs?'

'Good one, Mum. I've got the flu or something.'

I'm happy to stay in bed, to prove it.

———

I can only keep up the staying-in-bed thing for so long. I get restless. Lucky for me, Mum has work and I spend most of the time watching TV at Mrs T's. But I can't resist an invitation to Katie's on Saturday, even though it jeopardises my chances of having next week off too.

Katie's house is strange. Lots of grass-mat flooring and a fake palm tree in the corner. Is no one normal?

'It's my dad,' she says, handing me a Milo in a pineapple-shaped glass. 'He collects Polynesian kitsch.'

'Why?'

Katie rolls her eyes. 'There is no sane explanation for parents.'

We sit in her room, which is as neat and girly and blonde as she seems at school. Her major interests seem to be make-up and Justin Bieber. 'I talked to Keek,' she says.

'Oh, yeah. What did he say?'

'He said he doesn't think you'll ever speak to him again.'

'He's right. Did he say why?'

'No.'

I'm sweaty and disembodied, sitting here staring at her dressing table with all its compartmentalised eyeliners and hairclips and lip glosses. If I tell her I lied to her about my parents, she won't want to have anything to do with me. I feel my pulse beating in the silence.

'Don't be a dick.' She shoves me with her pink-socked foot. 'What's going on?'

'What Keek told Cho about my mum getting pregnant on a one-night stand. It's true.'

'So, your dad doesn't live in England, then?'

'I don't know where he lives.'

'Gawd, it's like *Home and Away*. A bloody saga.' Katie flops back on her pillows. 'Your mum's all right, Clover. I wouldn't freak out too much. My parents got married because they were pregnant with my brother – Mum'll tell you. She's always reminding Dad. And Robbo hasn't said anything to anyone about that side of things. Not that I've heard, anyway. Just the crab story.'

I cover my face with my hands and tip sideways, groaning.

'At least Sanda's saying he doesn't know anything about it,' she offers. 'Says if anyone has a problem they should go see Robbo.' She pats me. 'I don't think he meant to hurt you.'

Doesn't want me to tell everyone his middle name is Hercules, more like it. 'Maybe,' I concede. 'But he knew all those dickheads were in the hallway listening to us. Probably watching, too. Yek.' I feel slimed by the thought.

Katie pokes me. 'What about Keek?'

I don't want to talk about Keek. 'How are Rosemary and Robbo going, anyway?'

'They're like an old married couple, bickering away. She's so jealous. She doesn't let him get away with anything. I think the only reason she hasn't tried harder to hurt me is because he told her not to. They'll probably grow old and fat together.'

'She already has a fat arse,' I say.

'And he's got a fat head.'

I love Katie when she's gleeful, but her face falls.

'What's wrong?'

'Rosemary is mad with me for yelling at her at that stupid fight. She's got this Facebook thing going about whether I should be allowed to hang out at the footy or not.'

'What thing?'

Katie drags over her laptop and brings up Facebook. 'Look at this.' It's a long inbox message from Rosemary, calling me and Katie total sluts and crapping on about loyalty and how miserable she's going to make Katie's life if she doesn't 'prove' that Rosemary's her best friend by apologising for 'being such a liar' at the fight.

Rosemary's status says *Bitches who lie about there mates should stay the fuck away from Fernwood FC*, and a whole lot of people have 'liked' it. There's a conversation about it on her wall and I can almost feel the knives stabbing out of the screen into Katie's heart.

For the first time in my life, I'm glad my mother is so uptight about Facebook. There's a *vibe* coming out of the computer, heavy and mean and ... *forever*.

'That's the wrong "there",' I say.

Katie shoves me gently with her shoulder. 'I don't think that's the point.'

'It's horrible. I'm sorry.'

'Will you be there on Monday?'

'Maybe.' But I know I'm going to stay away as long as humanly possible. 'Be sick too, and come around to mine.'

Katie closes the laptop. 'Maybe.'

⌘

It's Sunday afternoon and I'm working up a sore throat for tomorrow.

Mum knocks on my bedroom door and peers in. 'Keek's here.'

'No. I'm not talking to him.'

'Well, you'll have to tell him that yourself. Now sort it out, you two.' She shoves him in and shuts the door.

I open it again and tell him to get out.

But Mum's still there. 'No,' she says. 'Clover, I don't know what's going on, but it takes guts to come to someone's house and say you're sorry, so ...'

I glare at her, and she tapers off.

'So good luck,' she finishes, and leaves us to it.

I'm not saying anything. I can't even look at him. I sit at my desk with a black pencil and draw a heavy-lidded eye.

'I ...'

I draw a knife around it so the eye is in the blade, near the hilt.

'I'm sorry.'

I make the knife stab into a heart. But not a cheesy pretend heart – a real one with ventricles and atriums, aorta and veins.

'You don't understand.'

I throw the pencil, my beautiful black Lyra pencil, right across the room. 'You got that right.'

Keek's voice rises. 'We were drinking and, I don't know. She was upset and ...'

I pick up a crimson pencil and colour in the heart. That's what I love about Lyra pigment: the harder you press, the richer the colour. The blood from the heart fills up the eye.

'I was trying to ...'

I retrieve the black. I need it to outline the blood, dripping from the wound, dripping into the crack.

'Fuck, Clove, please don't ignore me.'

'You promised.' My voice breaks open and the tears show through and I hate myself for being so weak and stupid to trust anyone, ever. Especially Rob. I flush to think that Keek must've heard I'd been in that sleazy bedroom with him.

'I didn't mean – I was trying to *explain* you. She promised she wouldn't—'

'*Explain* me?'

'Fuck.' He sits on my bed and puts his head in his hands.

'Explain me? Explain what?'

'Why you're so …' He trails off, grappling with fresh air.

'So what? So *what*?'

Then he shouts. 'So angry!'

'I am not angry.' I yell, of course, and feel my face burning and my eyes bugging out of my head.

Mum bangs on my door. 'Clover!'

What the hell? It sounds like she's kicking it. I fling it open, furious, but her arms are full of Lucille wrapped in a towel.

'What's happened? What's wrong?'

Mum's face is hard, as if she's frozen. 'I don't know.' She points with her chin to the kitchen. 'Get my keys and open the car.'

I follow instructions. 'Mum, I'm scared. What happened?'

I get in the back. Mum leans in and passes in Lucille, who shivers and moans on my lap.

Keek stands on the nature strip with his face full of tears. He looks about ten.

'Get in, Keek,' Mum says.

He gets in beside me. The dog shudders and he puts his hands on her. 'Lucille,' he says.

Mum looks at us in the rear-vision mirror. 'I don't know what – she got up and peed everywhere – but it was like water. Then she started walking in circles – staggering.' Mum starts the car twice and it makes a bad sound. 'Shit,' she says. 'Calm down.'

We arrive at Animal Emergency the same way everyone after us arrives – tearful and desperate. And we wait the way everyone waits; quietly. Mum, Keek and I have our hands on Lucille. She shudders from time to time, then stillness. We freeze, waiting for breath.

A man whose dog has already disappeared down the corridor can't stop himself from crying, comforted by the awkward patting of another man. They are older, like grandfathers. I want to draw them. The vet nurse emerges, looking grim. The crying man's face is too scared and hopeful to bear. I lay my cheek on Lucille so I won't have to see, but I can't block out the sound of his heart breaking.

Keek's phone rings. It's his dad. When he goes outside to talk, I watch him through the window, my cheek still on Lucille. Keek's hair is a fireball in the sun. A corona. Rob and school seem small and cold and far away. Not warm and close and real like Keek, coming back in to sit next to me, his leg pressing mine. I want to say something, but my throat is a desert, my voice cattle bones in the sand.

A different vet nurse introduces himself. Lucille is gone from under me, carried by a man wearing a pale-blue cotton suit with white rubber shoes. The shoes whimper on the linoleum as they disappear down the corridor.

Nothing to do but watch hell and salvation unravel, or read *The Australian Women's Weekly*.

Mr McKenzie is in the doorway. Mum glances up at him, then away. I think for a minute he's going to beckon Keek from there, without a word, but he comes in and sits on the other side of Mum, leaning forward to speak to us.

'Hey son. Clover.' He touches my mother's arm. 'Anything I can do?'

She dissolves like sherbet in the shower and Keek's dad puts his arm around her and holds on and her face falls like cloth against his collarbone. Like the toll of a melancholy bell, I'm struck by the thought that my mother has no mother.

Mum sits up and sniffs, pulling herself together, but Mr McKenzie keeps his arm around her, the back of his hand near my shoulder, close enough to see its ginger hairs. Keek and I exchange a glance of mortification; he's as stiff and uncomfortable as I am. We're rescued by the vet, inviting us down the corridor to where Lucille lays on a metal table.

There is nothing she can do; Lucille is going to die. She'll 'put Lucille down' here and now, if Mum agrees.

'Is she in pain?' Mum asks, her hand on the dog's head, her thumb stroking one ear.

'I can give you something for the pain,' the vet says. 'But her kidneys are barely functioning. It can only get worse. Eventually, nothing you could administer at home will be strong enough to stop her suffering.'

'But she might die naturally? Before that happens?'

The vet concedes with a noncommittal nod. 'She might.'

Mr McKenzie carries Lucille to the car and we take her home, to the lounge, to a bed fit for a queen; fit for dying naturally.

Mum sits by the bed on a footstool, stroking Lucille's head. I sit on the floor, one hand on the dog, the other on my mother. 'She looks terrible, Mum.'

Mum offers a grim smile and squeezes my hand but seems inward, locked up, gone to some place I don't know. 'I've seen worse,' she says.

⸎

Aunty Jean is in England and will be for the next month. I never thought I'd miss her, but I do. She sends a bunch of flowers and a get-well card addressed to Lucille Stinkbottom. Mum smiles. Mrs T, back from Sydney with a fistful of baby photos, is in and out all day, bearing food, tutting at the dog. She is in favour of euthanasia.

'Selfish,' she says, wagging her finger.

'It's my decision.'

I've never seen Mum arc up to Yiayia before. I want to run in and wave my arms, make them stop, but I'm fascinated, too.

'How much longer? Another day? A week? It's wrong.'

Mum massages her temples. 'I can't do this today.'

But Mrs T isn't one to take a hint. 'Your mother—' she begins.

Mum's face blooms red. 'Don't tell me about my mother. You don't ... You're not my mother. Go home.' She catches herself. 'Please.'

But it's too late. Even I feel the stab in the guts, watching. My grandfather died in a drink-driving accident not long after my grandmother passed away from cancer and if Mrs Theopopolous and her family hadn't helped her, Mum would never have been able to take over the mortgage and keep the house.

Mum is already sorry. 'Yiayia ...' she says, but Mrs T holds up her hand.

'I see when I'm not wanted.' She points to Lucille. 'But that poor animal ...' She tuts again, shakes her head and stomps away. It's a dignified stomp and I know she's holding back tears.

Mum says, 'Shit,' and goes to her room.

Lucille sighs.

⁓

Tuesday morning, day two. Mum gets washed and dressed for the first time since Sunday and looks like she means business.

'Are we going to the vet?' I ask, my voice choppy with tears.

Mum puts her hand on Lucille's shoulder and runs it down her bony back. 'No,' she tells me. 'School.'

I can't push her to let me stay home again – it would be like pushing her off a cliff.

***

We pass Keek riding to school and I wait for him on the street near the gate. A cigarette is essential, so we're late when we walk into maths together. There's a ripple of assumption from Rosemary's corner.

It's a test. Mr Arkwright nods tensely for us to sit. Even though he's only about thirty, Arkwright wears 'slacks' up to his chin and his shirt tucked in. He hurries to point out the few seats available. Keek peels off to sit next to big Mark.

Katie, sitting with Nat, waves. Rosemary nods to the seat behind them with a look that's almost a smile. I've seen that smile before, offered to others – it says reconciliation is possible, for a price. I lock eyes with Katie and give a little wave back, willing her to forgive me. I know rejecting Rosemary will make life hard for her, but I can't pretend the rest of the Herbs are my friends. One way or another, they're going to make my life hell, but I can't suck up to them. I just can't. And besides, they'll never accept Keek.

I turn away and take a seat next to Alison Larder. It's the turn of a kaleidoscope: everything has changed.

Alison is feverishly lost in some mathematical conundrum, but after a moment, she turns her head and takes me in slowly, as if I've grown a third eye; nods the slightest of nods and goes back to her test.

While I'm getting out my pens, two messages arrive at my desk; one slipped sideways from Alison, who doesn't waver from her impossibly neat and undoubtedly correct workings-out. It's an invitation: *Dear Clover, please come to my 17th Birthday Bad-taste Costume Party,* with various uninspiring sleepover details and a no-alcohol message from her parents. The other is a screwed-up note thrown hard at the back of my head that says: *Ur ranga boyfriend is DEAD.*

When we file out of class, Pete Tsaparis pushes past, lifting Keek by the elbow, shoving him forward. Keek doesn't say a word, but a wash of red creeps up his neck.

'Don't be a dick,' says Katie, shoving Pete in turn, but she follows the Herbs.

'Katie—'

Katie stares over my shoulder, as if I'm not there. 'You should've come to school yesterday.'

'I—'

'If you had Facebook like a normal person, you'd know what's going on.'

'What happened?'

She twitches, meets my eyes and says, 'Two days is a long time in cyberspace.' Her eyes drop, down to her jumper, and she picks off a few pill-balls of fluff. 'Anyway, it doesn't matter. It's just how it is.'

'I—'

Katie pushes my hand off her arm. Not mean, but firm, her eyes to the ground. 'Rosemary's right. I nearly lost all my friends because of you.'

'Lucille's dying.'

Katie's hand flies to her heart, her eyes flicking back to mine. Rosemary, spying from their little knot further off down the corridor, sends Ellen, who says, 'You all right, Katie?', as though Katie might be in danger of catching something.

'Come on,' calls Natalie – I'd like to think, sadly – and they're gone.

───✦───

When I get home, Mum's got her face in the dictionary and the proofs for a bridal magazine spread over the dining-room table. She's sighing and moaning over them, despising 'the commercialism of it all', circling and annotating the mistakes.

'Hi love, how was your day?'

'I hate school, I'm never going back.'

'Mm, okay. That's good.'

'What?'

She shakes her head and looks at me properly. 'What?'

'I said, I'm leaving school.'

'Oh, God, Clover. Not now. I can't cope with this right now.'

'*You* can't cope.' A wave of red anger, like lava, pushes up from somewhere dark. '*You* don't want television. *You* don't want Facebook. *You* don't want me to have a mobile phone. You don't even know my dad so you don't care where he is. Well, fuck you.'

'Don't.'

'You want to control every tiny little thing about my life!'

'Please don't do this.'

'I'm not a little kid anymore. I live in the real world, Mum. Do you know what a freak I am? Even Year Sevens are on Facebook now.'

'That doesn't make it right.'

'I don't care about right! Do you understand? I'm not ten – I'm sixteen and I can make my own decisions. You can't make me go back.'

Mum's face has already crumpled and now the tears fall. 'I want to protect you—'

'*Control* me.'

Mum wipes her eyes. 'Okay. You're right. You're not a little girl anymore because I can assure you; the little girl you were would never speak to me the way you just have. And don't ask me to apologise for the way I've brought you up. Don't you think it would've been easier to plonk you in front of the tellie, to give in, feed you crap, go with the flow? You think I haven't missed out on things, trying to …' She pushes herself up from the table. 'It doesn't matter. I don't even know what I was trying to do anymore.'

Lucille barks, once.

'I'm going to see to the dog. I'll think about Facebook and the phone, but you are not leaving school and that is that.'

She hardly says anything all night, and we have eggs on toast for dinner.

I hear her up late, worrying about me on the phone to Aunty Jean, who's no doubt suggesting she sell me and use the money to fly to England. 'I'm working from home,' Mum says. 'Yes, bridal, really.' She laughs – or is it a groan? 'I suppose, it's cruel, for an old maid like me. Thanks for that.' Her voice tightens. 'No, no I … She'll know when it's time to go.'

I don't want to go to school, but I don't want to stay home, either – I can't breathe. I hang around, procrastinating. Mr McKenzie and Keek turn up to visit the patient and give me a lift. I think my mother arranged it, worried I won't go. Lucille is quiet, uncomplaining, with eyes of infinite question.

'She's dying softly,' says Mum, shut up in her tower. When Mr McKenzie puts his hand on her shoulder, she covers it with her own and they crouch there, easily, as if all things in the tragic universe are in order.

'Let's go,' I say to Keek.

'Yeah,' he murmurs. 'And I've got something to show you.' He kisses the dog one last time and heads out to the car.

I linger, suddenly unwilling to leave. Lucille wags her tail. Two thumps. Her eyes are on me. I kiss her head, afraid I'll never see her again. She sighs and closes her eyes. It's permission to go. Or an instruction. Mr McKenzie ruffles my mother's head, as though she's a kid, and follows me out.

In the car, I say, 'So show me.'

Keek nods at the back of his dad's head. 'Later.'

It doesn't take much to convince Keek to piss off from school. 'Let's piss off,' I say.

'Okay.'

Keek reckons he's an expert at forging his mum's signature. I'm nervous as hell about handing in my note five minutes after he's submitted his about 'the dentist', but Mrs Stubbs in the office is dealing with flooding toilets – clogged by an outbreak of Year Eight toilet-paper madness – and waves me off with barely a look. I'm almost disappointed. After leaving Katie on her own, at the mercy of Rosemary and Thyme, I should be punished.

Outside the gate, we assess each other. 'Where should we go?' I ask. 'The bowl?'

'Check this out.' Keek pulls a little red book out of his bag.

I turn it over in my hands. *The Skate Park Grind Guide*. 'What's this?'

'The Skate Park Grind Guide.'

'Yes, Einstein, but so what?'

'It's got every bowl in Victoria – with photos. And look.' He opens it up and there's Fernwood. 'You're famous.'

There's my art in the little black-and-white photo – and it looks amazing.

'Sadly verminous with bikers,' I quote, amused, reading Fernwood's entry and its fascinating facts about spines, rollovers, grindable lips and hip-to-hip transfers. It's like they're describing a living body. My eyes light on words that wing that little brown bird back into my tree: *Graffiti gives this bowl definite character*.

Keek taps on the page. 'Apparently our bowl is a lot like Fitzroy bowl.' He seems to think this is significant.

'Character,' I murmur.

Keek says, 'And public transport directions for every bowl in Victoria.'

I return from my fantasy of being the world's next Banksy, even though I know I'm not even half as good, and if I'm honest with myself, I prefer a pencil. Or a brush. 'What are you suggesting?'

'Let's check them out.'

'What? All of them?'

Keek offers an exaggerated shrug.

'What about your bike?'

'I'll get it from home.'

'What about your mum?'

He shrugs again.

───⌐───

Keek steals his own bike with no problems at all, adds fifty-seven bucks from his piggy bank to the heist and by lunch we are on the train, eating falafels, headed for Fitzroy.

By the time we get there, it's almost time to turn around and get back before our parents wonder where we are. And I want to see Lucille. But it's exciting to be in the city, without Mum; with Keek. On the train, we gravitated into a new way of being together: my legs slung over his. His arm is around my shoulder as we walk into the Edinburgh Gardens.

'That tram ride down Brunswick Street proves that Melbourne is really a giant art gallery,' I say. 'Promise me we'll check out some art for every skate park.'

'That would take months,' he says. 'What about school?'

Beyond the gardens, I feel the swell of the city. 'I'm done with school.'

'Oh, yeah,' says Keek. 'Have fun telling your mother.'

As far as I know, nobody in the office has questioned my phone call informing the school that I'll be away sick for the rest of the week. I guess it's because of my excellent impersonation skills, and my long history of absences. And they're used to Keek staying home because of his mother.

'But I defs want to sit that English test on Monday,' he says.

I shrug, but it comes out as more of a shudder.

'They'll forget about us,' he says.

'What if they don't?'

It's Keek's turn to shrug.

I've never had trouble getting Mum to buy me art supplies, so I've used them to make myself refillable pocket-sized tins and a couple of deodorant-bottle felt markers from instructions Keek found for me on the internet.

So many suburbs. So many bowls. Police or no police; it's an opportunity too good to resist, but I can't use 'Kandas' anymore. I get out the sketchpad and throw around a few ideas. I choose Jonez because in a strange way, it feels like reclaiming myself from Rob ... and it's so good to write, it sets a tingle in my bones.

But even with the whole day, and saying we're going to the park after school, we're still only going to have time for one or two locations a day.

———— ʠ ————

Thursday is day four and Lucille lies on her bed and sleeps. Or stares at us. Her mouth is dry and her lips keep sticking to her teeth, giving her a hapless look. We give her water from a teaspoon and Mum changes the bedding every few hours. But it still smells, so she burns incense and scented candles. The house feels closed, warm; claustrophobic.

Lucille does wag her tail when I give her a pat, or coax her to eat a few crunchies from my fingers, her bony head as smooth and warm as ever. Leaving her is scary because every time could be the last time, but it feels good to get away from the house and on the train with Keek. I use his phone to ring Katie, but hang up when she answers. I don't know what to say.

EIGHT

When I get back late on Friday afternoon, Mum hands me the bad-taste birthday invitation. 'You should go to Alison's party,' she says. 'She rang.'

'Where did you find that?'

'In your room.'

'What were you doing in my room?'

'Picking up washing off your floor.'

I suspect she was snooping for evidence of graffiti crimes. She won't find any. Not in my room. I've done a couple of less-than-inspired paintings at home as camouflage, but she's suspicious of my paint-affected fingernails. Not even a nailbrush can get them clean.

'You've left art-mess all over the lounge and got pastels on the carpet again,' she complains, then nods at the invitation. 'Friendship goes both ways, you know.'

I wish I could tell her about Katie. About the lovely – and scary – people Keek and I have met on the train, at different parks. That today, Keek met a bunch of riders and nearly broke his neck learning a crazy new trick he'd never seen before, and I had time to create a cool little stencil dog character. 'Save the Creek' has morphed into 'Retrieve the Planet' and the dog has the globe of the earth in its mouth.

But I can't.

And Keek can't tell his dad about the cool concrete he's found, or about the bowls that are so rough they make Fernwood seem like luxury, or the truth about where the scrapes and bruises come from.

Keek rescues me from having to lie about my day at school by ringing and asking if I want to come over to watch TV. I practically run there.

❧

I'm totally jealous of the huge flat-screen TV attached to Keek's bedroom wall. The rest of the room is bare except for electronic stuff, his computer, the bikes – of course – that hang on a different wall, and horizontal stacks of books. 'Why don't you put them on shelves?' I ask, having knocked one over.

'It's a system,' he says, righting and sorting them, restacking with definite obsessive-compulsive tendencies.

'There's something wrong with you,' I observe.

But he stings me with, 'What? Because I'm not clumsy?'

It's been a big week and I'm happy to snuggle up on Keek's bed for Friday night television. I show him Alison's invitation. 'She rang to see if I'm coming and guess what my stupid mother said?'

'Happy birthday?'

I give him a withering stare. 'She said, of course I'm coming.' At the time, I'd been relieved Alison hadn't given me away by asking if I was sick or something. But now I'm annoyed. 'It's tomorrow night.'

'Let's go.'

'It'll be boring as!'

'How do you know?'

'It's God-bothering former lesbian Alison Larder, Keek. A-l-i-s-o-n.'

Keek is finding pleasure in my outrage. He studies the invitation. 'It's her dad who's a God-botherer. And don't be such a bigot – so what if she's a lesbian?'

'Bigot? What kind of a word is that?'

He tuts, mocking me. 'Did you not study *To Kill a Mockingbird*?'

'So now you're Atticus Finch? And as if Aunty Jean would let me be a bigot about lesbians.'

'Then maybe you should think a bit harder about what you say.'

Ouch.

But it's hard to stay annoyed with Keek when he has his little-kid face on. 'Look – we have to dress up,' he says cheerily. 'Bad taste. What will we go as?'

'I might go as Alison Larder.'

He laughs. 'The superbrain's all right. Why are you so mean about her?'

'I dunno.' I flop back on the pillows. 'Because she makes it so easy, I suppose.' A news update comes on. I hate the way they do that in the middle of other shows. 'Mute it,' I say over the sound of manicured voices and machine-gun fire.

'That's what we can go as.' Keek is excited. 'Dad's got a couple of ski masks and I think he's even got some camo stuff.'

'What are you talking about?'

'The party. Let's go as suicide bombers.'

'What?'

His eyes spark. 'You heard me. Can't get much more bad taste than that.'

'That's not bad taste! Bad taste is like ... a woolly brown jumper tucked into pink high-waisted nanna slacks, or something. Or going as, like, Tinkerbell.'

Keek directs me to the television screen where there are explosions and smoke and terrified people. 'That, CB, is bad taste. And I know just the thing for the bomb.'

'Or tan leather lace-up shoes,' I counter, weakly.

Keek grins. 'Suicide bombers.'

'You want to go to Alison Larder's supervised, no-alcohol, bad-taste fancy dress sleepover birthday party as a suicide bomber?'

'It's perfect.'

'But you hate parties.'

'No, I don't.'

'Yes, you do.'

'No, I don't.'

'But you never go.'

At these words, an octopus of regret swims from its secret cave in the sea of my guts. I wish its tentacles could grab the words back. I think of Rosemary's party; Thyme telling Keek I was off up the road with Robbo. Of that horrible room at Josh Eldrich's. I'm like Lysander in Mum's annual version of *A Midsummer Night's Dream* – I'd been totally obsessed with Rob Marcello, but now I 'repent the tedious minutes I with him have spent.' I'm about to try some Shakespeare, but Keek rescues me.

'I'm never invited.' He grabs the remote and the sound blares back on. He turns it down and stares at the screen.

'Do you ever wish you were still with Cho?'

Keek flops back and smacks his head on the wall. 'Ow,' he says. 'No. But I miss riding with her – them. It kinda weirded it all up.'

'You're still friends with the others, aren't you?'

'Sorta. It's awkward now.'

All the unsaid stuff is a fog, cutting us off from each other.

'It doesn't matter, Clove. Come here.'

I use Keek as a pillow and he puts his arm around me. The fog thins and disappears. I want to say, 'Are you my boyfriend?' But it's so perfect just as it is. Friends who start going out, break up.

'I reckon I could make a fair bomb out of egg cartons and an old phone charger,' he says.

───※───

The next afternoon, Keek rolls up to my place with plastic bags full of 'costumes'. He holds his own oversized pants on with a belt and rolls up the legs, but his dad's 'commando' pants are way too big for me. I stick with Mum's cargo pants, generally relegated to gardening. It's truly embarrassing. We both wear ski masks, but push them up like beanies.

'That's the most uncomfortable thing I've ever put on,' I say.

'We only need it for effect when we arrive,' Keek says, strapping my 'bomb' to me with black gaffer tape.

'Do I have to wear this?'

'Yes.'

A puffy sleeveless jacket, fingerless gloves, Mum's old walking boots and a double row of little cardboard tubes threaded on string and painted gold complete my ensemble. 'Ammo,' says Keek. He wears the same, but with his dad's old motorcycle boots.

'Clunking around in those great clod-hoppers,' says my mother. 'The whole idea is ridiculous.'

'Are you going to be all right?' I worry.

Mum taps on my fake bomb. 'Are *you* going to be all right? I'm deeply dubious about the ethics of these outfits.'

'It's a bad-taste party,' says Keek. 'It's *meant* to be dubious.'

'I still think you could've borrowed a pair of matching tracksuits from Mrs T.' Mum kisses my cheek. 'Sleeping bags? Pillows? Toothbrush?'

'All sorted.'

'Well, have fun, but not too much fun.'

'It's alcohol-free, Mum.'

'Yes, I saw the invitation. The Larders are so full-on. Apparently the only ones who are going to survive the apocalypse are the congregation of Fernwood Evangelist Church and those they save. But they're very nice.' Mum laughs aloud.

Mr McKenzie arrives to give us a lift to the party. 'Bloody hell,' he says when he sees us. 'There's something very disturbing about you two being dressed up like that.'

Keek presses buttons on the dead mobile phone he has attached to his bomb and says, 'Boom!'

His father shakes his head.

'I hope the Larders aren't offended,' says Mum. 'Not to mention the racist overtones.'

'How, racist? We could be from anywhere,' says Keek.

'How not racist?' Mum adjusts my ammo.

Keek frowns. 'It's meant to be ironic, not racist. I mean, isn't the racism in the assumptions?'

'Well, perhaps.' Mum seems swayed by this argument. 'But such acts are about desperation, not bad taste.'

Keek shakes his curls. 'The whole shebang is bad taste.'

'Then go as soldiers,' Mum says. 'It's not funny, is it, Dave?'

Mr McKenzie says, 'Leave me out of it. How's the patient?'

Lucille remains Lucille, long-suffering eyes, cold ears and warm bones. Keek and I have to negotiate our bombs to lay on the floor and pat her while Mum and Keek's dad disappear into the kitchen for a cup of tea.

'It will be a week, tomorrow,' I say.

'Mrs T talking to your mum yet?'

'Yeah, but she won't come around. Says she can't bear to see "what's going on". She thinks we're cruel.'

I run my finger over Lucille's bony skull. Is it cruel? The Dalai Lama says it's the right thing to do. And Mum's not pretending she's going to get better or anything.

'Mum says looking after Lucille while she dies, after all these years of Lucille looking after us, is the least we can do.'

'What do you reckon?' His hand brushes mine as we stroke the dog.

I kiss Lucille's nose. 'I reckon I love you,' I say.

Lucille licks dry lips that stick to her gums, revealing her teeth and letting out a stinky plume of serious dog-breath. We roll away with moans of disgust. When we recover from the smell, I give Lucille teaspoons of water and Keek rustles up his father.

***

'Behave yourself, kids,' says Mr McKenzie, lumping our sleeping gear out of the boot. 'See you tomorrow afternoon.'

'Thanks, Mr McKenzie.'

Keek says, 'See ya, Dad.'

I like seeing them give each other a hug.

It's a strange feeling, rocking up to the Larders' front door. It must've been hard for Alison, I realise, coming back and finding everything the same, but completely different. Especially me.

Keek shoves me. 'Cheer up, CB.'

I don't think Mr Larder has a clue, but Mrs Larder remembers me. 'Hello there, Clover,' she says. She peers out the front door. 'Has your mother gone without saying hello?'

'No, my friend Keek's dad dropped us off, Mrs Larder,' I say. 'Mum asked me to send her love.'

'Gosh, how formal,' she laughs. 'All the kids

call me Margaret. Well, tell your mother that we send our love and remember her in our prayers. And this must be Keek, then.' She holds out her hand and he shakes it.

There's plastic matting protecting the carpet and we follow it as she ushers us downstairs to the rumpus room. They don't seem to register our bombs. 'Uncle Sam needs You,' jokes Mr Larder. 'Boys sleep to the left, girls to the right.' In between is a large square of carpet, a trestle table of food, balloons, streamers and Alison dressed entirely in red – red shoes, red tights, red skirt, red jumper, red ribbon in her hair. Red earrings.

'What are you?' says Keek.

'A period.'

Keek is confused, but I laugh. Then his mouth falls open, shuts and he turns red too.

'I was gonna wear tampon earrings, but Mum wouldn't let me,' says Alison. She seems proud.

'Well, happy birthday,' says Keek, handing over the chocolates and our homemade birthday card.

'What are you?' Alison asks. 'German back-packers?'

'Suicide bombers,' says Keek.

'You don't look Japanese.'

'No, modern ones,' I explain, but she is confused. 'Anyway ...' I shake off the idea that Alison knows nothing about anything except abstract mathematics. 'Where is everyone?'

'Trung and Mark are coming at half-past from Trung's basketball final and Youth Group finishes then too.' Great. It said seven p.m. on the invitation. Me, Keek and Alison Larder – maybe I should've let Keek make a real bomb after all.

'Do you want to play darts?' says Alison.

Alison is a fiend at darts and so is Keek. I've been the early victim in two games of *Killer* by the time the kids from Youth Group arrive. There are about twelve of them and they all seem to have gone for emo or hip-hop as their version of bad taste – fascinating. But none of them have pulled it off. Their 'essence of dag' makes their outfits not so much amusingly bad, as just bad. But then again, I'm hardly in a position to judge.

Trung fairly bounces into the room wearing pale orange velour. 'We won!' He and Alison do a victory dance.

'Is that your mother's tracksuit?' I ask, laughing.

Trung takes a bow. 'Grandmother's.'

Mark hasn't dressed up. 'I'm wearing a fat suit,' he says.

Alison chews loudly on a celery stick that she waves at me and Keek. 'So are you two going out or what?'

Keek's face is as red as Alison's menstrual jumper. I look at my shoes and remember how stupid they are.

Mrs Larder calls, 'Come on!'

Rescued, we follow her outside to whizz sparklers around in the dark. Keek and I stay out there to have a smoke and Mark loiters and smokes with us. I have a glimmer of how my mother must feel about me smoking. 'Should you be doing that?' I say.

Mark looks at me in his steady way. 'Should you?'

Keek looks at me. I look at Mark. We all shrug.

When Mrs Larder calls us for cake, Keek practically skips in.

'Maybe we'll be seeing you in church?' she says to him, smiling.

He smiles back. 'Maybe, Margaret.'

'Does she even know what he's wearing?' says Mark under his breath.

At ten-thirty p.m., Mr and Mrs Larder set up beds and Mr Larder rattles off a prayer. The youth group kids bow their heads and close their eyes. It goes on and on. Keek, Mark, Trung and I enter into the frozen jiggling hysterics of suppressed laughter; it's like being in a bubble and absolutely, collectively *getting it*. I steal a look over at Alison and as soon as our eyes meet, it's as if we've reached over and held hands. She lowers her eyes, conquering herself, and I can only hope I don't snort. A warmth rolls over me and I hope she feels it too.

I let out a big shuddery sigh of relief when Mr Larder finishes, thanks us for coming and wishes us a good night. I'm not the only one who has to laugh out loud before I can recover.

'How are we going to get these things off?' I complain, tugging at my costume. Keek has wrapped so many tape layers, my 'bomb' is immovable.

'Yeah,' he says. 'I may have gone a little nuts. We'll have to get scissors.'

'You ask, seeing Margaret is your new best friend.'

'You.'

'It was your bright idea.'

Mark calls out, 'Alison, got any scissors?'

Alison calls, 'Mum, can you get scissors?'

'Yes, scissors, of course. Hang on.' Mrs Larder kisses Alison and a few kids on the top of the head. She hovers for a moment and I wonder if she's going to kiss me too, but she pats me instead. I don't know if I'm disappointed, or relieved.

'Lights out,' she calls from the top of the stairs. I guess there aren't going to be any scissors.

There's shuffling, laughing and calling of good night and then, nothing. I wait for something to happen. Something does. Alison wriggles herself, sleeping bag and all, to where Trung is.

'Pass the lollies,' someone says, amid private giggles and shuffling about.

'Don't make a fuss,' Alison tells the room. 'I promised Mum we wouldn't, and tomorrow we're going bowling, remember, and I don't want to mess that up. Besides, I'll die if she comes down here.'

'Me too,' says Trung and there's a general laugh.

The room settles into quiet. Keek and Mark and I are the only ones left sitting up. It's almost psychic, our collective decision, and we move as one to creep back outside.

'Is this it, do you reckon?' Keek says.

'Yeah.' Mark lights another cigarette. 'I think this is it.'

We sit there for a while. The upstairs lights flick off.

'I think I'm gonna go home,' Keek says.

I want to, but feel bad. 'What about Alison?'

'Says you who wasn't even going to come.'

'Shh. Yeah, I know. But it's been ... you know.'

'Say you're worried about your mum and Lucille and I'm going to walk you. Alison won't mind.'

'I *am* worried about my mum and Lucille.'

'Then it's sorted.'

Alison doesn't mind. 'I'll say a prayer for Lucille,' she whispers, and kisses my cheek.

I hug her, tight. 'We'll come back tomorrow and go bowling. What time are we going?'

'Leaving here at ten-thirty. You'll miss out on breakfast. Pancakes. You sure you don't want my dad to drive you?'

We're sure.

Alison sits up. 'Don't get into trouble,' she says.

It doesn't take long to walk home. Before we turn into my street, I pull up on a brick fence. 'Let's have a smoke.'

Keek sits next to me, his arm against my arm, his leg against mine. 'Sure.' But we don't get out our cigarettes, we just sit there. My heart is beating fast, as if I were about to step up to a patch of beautiful bare concrete.

Keek says, 'I'm sorry, you know, about Cho—'

'No, me. I'm sorry any of that—'

We lunge, we bump, we go on the wrong side of each other, we laugh and then we get serious and everything is still and dark and Philip McKenzie kisses me. Then we rest our foreheads together and breathe, and smile, and kiss some more.

After a while, he says, 'Let's go see Lucille.'

Turning the corner, we see Keek's car parked in my driveway. The butterflies in my stomach plunge into an abyss. The fracture stirs.

'Lucille,' I say, and we run past the cars, through the side gate and in the unlocked back door.

It's candlelit, the scene. Lucille wrapped in a soft blanket, sprinkled with flowers, surrounded by tea-light candles and incense, only her face showing, eyes unseeing; the futon mattress pulled up at her altar; Mum and Keek's dad rising, untangling; wine glasses and screwed-up tissues, a saucer with butts – smoking? And that smell? Mum and Mr McKenzie smoking weed? Lucille dead? Mum pulls her top up over her bare shoulder.

'She's gone,' Mum says.

The fracture roars. This isn't real. It isn't what I'm seeing, hearing; the slur in Mum's voice, her unfocused eyes. 'Are you drunk?'

'A little. I wasn't—'

Lucille gone. I don't want to look at her. Don't want it to be true. Don't want Mr McKenzie to be standing there like a big embarrassed lump, the T-shirt under his open shirt tucked up, showing his hairy stomach. I see his feet. Bare feet. The rumpled mattress.

'You didn't stay for the sleepover, then,' he says.

'What are you doing here?' says Keek.

'Being a friend.'

I run. I hear Keek shout, 'No! Stay away from us!' Then he's with me, past me, running down the footpath, away.

At his house we stop, panting. Everything between us feels wrong. Stained. If I could, I'd run home. It's like we're – related – and we've kissed. My mum has wrecked his family.

'I'm telling Mum,' Keek says. Even his voice sounds different now, hard.

'Do you hate me?'

Keek swings around saying, 'I fucken hate everybody,' and kicks at their letterbox until it shifts on its pole and leans over the drive. He rubs at his forehead. 'Not you, Clover. No.'

He runs up the front porch steps two at a time and I follow.

The TV is on in the lounge room; its glow, and what seeps through from the kitchen, the only light. Mrs McKenzie is asleep on the couch; a couple of boxes of pills and a half-empty vodka bottle sit on the coffee table. Candace glares from the shadows.

Keek sits and mutes the TV. He shakes his mum's shoulder. 'Mum?'

She groans and rolls over. 'Yes, sure,' she says. 'In the fridge.' The room darkens, then flares with blue brightness.

'Mum, I need you.'

'She hasn't taken an overdose, has she?' I ask, my voice a squeak.

Keek checks the packets. 'No. There's only a few missing.' His hand closes over the box.

Headlights flash into the room, and there's a nasty scraping of wood and metal. Mr McKenzie slams out of the car to swear at the letterbox. Keek grabs the vodka, says, 'Get those smokes,' and stuffs the box of pills into his pocket. At the last second, he grabs the other packet too.

'What are you doing?' I say.

'Hurry up.'

We make it out before the back porch light comes

on and stop dead in the shadows. Mr McKenzie shines a feeble torch. 'Keek?' The dog at his thigh barks and I jump. 'Settle old girl,' he says and goes inside.

'My paint's in your shed,' I whisper. 'I need it.'

'I gotta get my bike anyway.'

We fumble into the shed using Keek's phone as a light. My backpack is safe where we'd hidden it, but no bike.

'Fuck,' says Keek. 'My bike's on Dad's car.'

Mr McKenzie comes into the shed calling, 'Phil, is that you?'

But 'Phil' is already on the footpath. I have to scurry to keep up with him. 'Where are we going?' I say.

'Nowhere.'

'Where nowhere?'

'Train.'

'We haven't got any money.'

'We've got bowling money, remember?'

It's a graveyard at Fernwood station. A bored security guy flashes his torch at us before heading off to patrol the carpark. It isn't until we're safely on the last train to the city that I remember our outfits. Keek echoes my thoughts.

'Either these costumes are the shittiest job ever,' he says, 'or that guy just made a breach of national security.'

Night-black train windows reflect us back into ourselves. The whole world is this ugly, empty carriage; the grey, the fluorescent lights, the muted clank and rumble. I spray FUCK THIS on the wall and window, as big as I can.

We change carriages. An old drunk sleeps across three seats, still and silent as if he were dead. Keek unscrews the bottle and takes a slug. With a face like he's sucked on a sour lolly and stubbed his toe at the same time, he hands me the bottle.

Straight vodka is about as far from a vodka Cruiser as you can get. I manage a couple of swallows. 'That's foul,' I say when I get my voice back.

He takes another drink. 'It's not as bad the second time.'

We pull up at a station. Keek hides the bottle, but no one gets on. When the train lurches off, he pulls out the pills.

Where the vodka had burned, I suddenly feel cold, down to my stomach. 'What are they?'

He holds up one packet. 'For sleeping.' He holds up the other box. 'For waking up.'

Keek's phone rings, making me shiver with nerves. He says, 'Dad,' and turns it off. He punches out two 'sleepers' and six 'wakers' and hands me half. 'Happy mothers' day.'

I stare at the pills. 'I'm scared.'

He shakes the pills in his palm. 'Prescribed by

a doctor.' Keek spits out the words. 'Can't get safer than that.'

'My mum doesn't think so.'

Keek says, 'Yeah? Well I don't give a fuck what your mum thinks,' and slams them down with a slug of vodka.

I don't want Keek to go wherever the pills will take him, without me.

———

The train rattles along. It's nearly an hour's travel from Fernwood to the city. We suck down the vodka between stations, waiting to see what will happen to us.

The drunk sits up once and stares, bleary eyed. We stare back. No one speaks. He sinks back down and snores twice, then silence.

An old lady gets on, dragging a battered shopping trolley, intent on counting and recounting a pack of tiny cards; and a pair of metal-heads in full regalia, drinking beer. We stagger through the connecting doors until we find another empty carriage.

Keek says, 'Sometimes I hate him.'

'Your dad?'

'My brother.'

He crumples. I sit next to him, my arm around his shoulders.

'You don't know what it's like.' He rubs a sleeve across his face, but the tears keep coming. 'Everything

I do, everything I say – it's all about him. All my life I've been compared to him. One day, I'll be older than him. That's all my eighteenth is about, to her – I'll be older than Matt, he'll never be eighteen, and Dad—' He slaps his palm against a pole and it rings faintly, a lost chime of childhood. 'He's never fucken there. And when he is there he gets angry and then they fight and it's still about Matt. I hate them.' He puts his head in his hands. 'Hate them.'

I hold him as the sobs come harder. A group of party-people get in, see us and change carriages.

Keek's breathing slows. He sighs and rubs his face. 'Sorry.'

'No,' I say. 'Don't be sorry.' I take the bottle and drink. It's still foul, but comforting; a cleansing burn. I pass it back and watch Keek finish it off; then kiss him. I can't get my body close enough to his; the only safe place in the world. I want him to touch me and when he does, something in me explodes. This is what it means, I think, to want someone inside you. We hold each other and the train chugs on, clanking through the night.

⁓

It's energising to cross between carriages while the train is moving, and a relief to get away from the sound of the empty vodka bottle rolling around on the floor, but this is the last one. I tag it gently, lovingly. A great wave of calm and wellbeing washes over me.

'You know what I want to do?'

'What's that, CB?' Keek hooks my legs over his, leaning back; his tears, everything bad, seems far away.

'I want to paint Lucille and Retrieve the Planet somewhere it'll be seen. Where it'll matter.'

'Like, where?'

'Dunno. Somewhere big.'

Keek kisses me. 'Sounds like a plan,' he says.

The train pulls into Flinders Street station. Blood pounding, I have the jitters. I'm thirsty, thirsty. I need space, air, a drink of water. We lurch off the train. Lurch, stagger, crash into each other and laugh.

'Settle, settle,' I say.

The platform is quiet, but we stop to collect ourselves in the hopes of making an inconspicuous exit. I manage to buy some water from a vending machine, but have a hard time swiping my Myki. Keek dashes through with me.

A man's voice calls, 'Oy!' but we are gone, running up Flinders Street.

We stop to catch our breath, then weave through the thin crowd, past St Paul's Cathedral, through the deserted square, up past the theatres and over to Bourke Street. At Spring Street, we stand across from the billion steps of Parliament House with its three flags flying.

A busker plays *Stairway to Heaven* on an acoustic guitar and it all comes flooding in: Mum and Mr McKenzie, Lucille, school, Robbo and the Herbs, Keek's brother, the sound of old trees falling.

'Like there,' I say, pointing at Parliament House.

'Like there, what?'

The fracture rumbles. Power. That's what its imposing size, those many grey stairs are about; the flags flying over cold stone. I gaze around. Further down the street, a guy hunched over in a blue duffel coat spews as he walks; not even into the gutter, but along the footpath at the edge of the buildings. My stomach lurches. He wipes his mouth and keeps walking.

Keek shudders and says, 'Jesus.'

It's crazy; acres of concrete and asphalt and misery. In a swoop of pictures, I imagine how the space, the land, might once have been. Like it used to be down at the creek, maybe, but bigger, older, deeper, alive with night noises. We aren't far from the river, people would've lived here. Just lived. But now the whole place is polluted: tar and concrete, endless offices, trees like prisoners, and no one minds – but if Keek and I lit a campfire, the cops'd be all over us like a plague. I can't see one star. When did people get so afraid of outside; need to flatten everything into smooth hard lines, block out starlight, sunlight, the moon? My heart collapses in on itself with sadness.

Keek says, 'I think I'm having a heart attack.'

'Me too.'

We sit and smoke, clutching our chests.

A gust of wind blows takeaway food rubbish across the street to the lowest step of Parliament House. It was the Victorian government that wrecked my creek. They could've saved it, could've figured out another way, but they care about all the wrong things: not the environment, not art, not kids. They *say* they care about stuff, but then they take away money from everything good and give it to ... I don't even know who they give it to. Not schools. Not hospitals. What do they do in there? I've seen Federal Parliament in action on television at school – if we kids carried on like that, we'd be expelled.

'What's wrong with them?' I say. 'They're meant to be like – like *parents*, looking after things, but they just fuck about, obstructing, confusing, lying, cheating.' I nod, my head heavy with importance. 'The piece ...' I stop myself from crying. 'Retrieve the Planet. There.'

Keek looks over to Parliament House, all oblongs and pillars and square edges. 'Parents,' he shouts, his voice slurring, then screams, his body jerking with the effort. 'Fuck you!'

'Shit. You scared me.'

The busker packs up his guitar and leaves. I'd give him money, but can't negotiate my pockets.

'I could be dying.' Keek's voice is liquid calm, now, and rolling out of him. We sink together like

269

melted sadness. 'And it'd still be about stupid dead stupid Matt.' He yells again, a wordless roar of ragged anger, his body rigid in my arms, and slumps. 'I wish ...' And his longing hugs the air. 'I don't hate him, Clove. I don't hate him.'

He cries in my lap and I stroke his hair until a big sigh rumbles out of him. He sniffs mightily, rubs his face on his sleeve and rolls on his back with me as a pillow. A delicate wave of tears ripples from his lips to the curve of his chin and back, but then he smiles at me.

'I've always thought you were pretty, Clover Jones. Even at primary school.'

Keek takes my hand and kisses my palm. It's the most wonderful thing that has ever happened to me.

'Don't cry,' he says. 'Shit, I gotta sit up.' He sits up, burps and then laughs. 'Let's do your crazy art thing.'

We stuff around, struggling with the annoying tape on our ridiculous costumes, kissing, taking more pills and arguing over our grand plan. We finally agree that it has to be the huge slate wall left of the foot of the stairs. Keek will handle the stencils, I'll paint, then we'll run in opposite directions and meet at St Paul's. The security guy patrolling the steps seems to have disappeared, but we'll still have to be quick. I pull the gear out of the bag; only a few tins and mostly homemade, but they'll have to do.

It seems like such a smooth plan. An antidote.

Keek pulls out the stencils and drops them.

I'm annoyed. 'Don't unroll them here—'

An amplified voice drowns me out. 'Victoria police. What's going on?'

Keek says, 'That's not in the plan.'

The street is empty. Everything is strange and far away, as if I'm looking through binoculars backwards. 'Are they talking to us?'

'I fucken hope not,' says Keek. 'Let's go.'

We go, but the voice says, 'Stop.'

We stop. There's a divvy van on Spring Street. People gather behind it like extras in a film.

'Stay where you are,' instructs the voice. 'I'm Senior Sergeant John Ellis. How about you tell us what's going on.'

'As if we know what's going on,' Keek laughs. It's infectious. Keek cups his hands to his mouth and shouts, 'We're representatives from the Bad-taste Party and we have a list of demands,' and semi-collapses next to me.

'What list of demands?' I want to know.

'Retrieve the planet.'

'That's not a list.'

'What's your name, son?'

Keek shrugs off the voice with an irritated, arm-waving dismissal and insists to me, 'It is a list.'

'One thing can't be a list,' I insist back.

Keek gets to his knees and shouts, 'We have one demand.'

'Get on the ground.' The threat is palpable. It blasts through the fog.

Keek drops and we grab each other, crunching cardboard. His fake-bomb mobile digs into my collarbone.

'I'm scared,' I say.

Keek nods. It's like finding out your nightmare is real.

More voices.

The sky is a smear of grey with a brownish tinge. I see one star.

People say things, but I can't understand them. I don't want to. I say, 'Keek, please ...' But the words bubble out like toasted cheese.

The star disappears, swallowed by streetlights and pollution along with the rest of the Milky Way. I think of Mum, down the creek on summer nights with Lucille free off the leash, my little-girl hand in her firm mother-hand, pointing up at the stars, telling me stories. Where will it end, the tree-killing, the asphalt: when there's nothing left but ugliness? I sit up to throw the deodorant-bottle paintbrush, yelling, 'Retrieve the planet.' As it leaves my hand, a cop looms over me and sprays me in the face. Paint splatters on concrete. My eyes and face are burning. My hair, my neck, my chest.

Keek screams, 'Fuck,' and flails away from me.

I scream too. I'm blind. Hands on me, yanking my

arms behind my back. I struggle, but the chasm opens and I fall forever.

———

Keek and I ride to Canberra on his bike. We climb a tree and Alison Larder says, 'Philip McKenzie, a goose walked on your grave.' We break into Parliament House and hide in a potplant with Lucille. At night we sneak into the House of Representatives, but we lose the dog and Keek goes off down the creek, calling and swearing. When I finish writing, right across the box around the Speaker's chair, instead of *Retrieve the Planet*, I've written *How Dare You?* Then Alison says, 'Hey Jones, it's your dad.'

But Al has never called me 'Jones' and it's my mum, with a face fairly divided between worry and relief. Oversized shower-curtains. I'm in hospital. I've never been in hospital before, but I know this is hospital. My head is filled with dishwashing water, but my eyes are jagged with fire.

Mum takes my hand. 'Thank God.' Her jaw tenses. 'Don't ever do this to me again. Running off like that …'

Dread spreads with the ache of my body, my burning scalp. 'Keek?' My voice is a croak.

'He's okay.'

'Mum, my eyes are burning.'

'It's the capsicum spray. They're all red and swollen.'

'Capsicum spray? Why did they do that to me, Mum? I didn't do anything.' The tears make my eyes sting worse. 'I want to go home.'

'Oh darling.'

'I want to go home.'

'You're under arrest.'

'But we didn't do anything.'

She brushes hair from my face and dabs at my tears with a tissue. 'You're in the hospital and there's a police officer sitting out there. They say you'll have to go straight from here to a police interview. We might even have to wait for a lawyer and ask for bail.'

'Bail?'

'Bail means I can't take you home until ...' She takes in a deep breath and lets it out slowly, but tears still hammer at her voice. 'Until they sentence you. Otherwise ...' She crumples.

'Otherwise what?'

'You'll be locked up.'

The nausea I've woken with is growing. 'But we didn't do anything.'

Mum blows her nose. She pulls a piece of paper from her bag and reads from it. 'Public nuisance, affray, bomb hoax. Reckless behaviour. Causing public fear of explosion. Attempted criminal damage and using a drug of dependence. That's the list of things they told me you might be charged with.'

'But we didn't do anything.' Well, we got drunk. Yes, I know we got drunk. A bitter taste at the back of my throat prompts other memories – Keek's mother, her pills, his tears. I fish around for more, but all I can come up with is residue from the dream I woke up with. 'We didn't do anything,' I say again, as if saying it will make it true.

She holds me with a penetrating look. 'Sometimes things look worse than they are.'

I know she's talking about Mr McKenzie and that makes me think of Lucille. I dissolve into tears, the uncontrollable kind that come when you're six and have hurt yourself falling out of your tree. Tears that demand someone – your mother – make everything better. A wave of gratitude embraces me with her arms, accompanied by a wash of sadness because she can't fix things anymore.

'I'm sorry,' I manage.

'Oh,' says my mother and I hear a glimpse of how much she loves me in that encircling sound. When she can speak, she says, 'We're going to be all right, Clover. We'll get through this. We're still uncurled, we'll get through.'

'Uncurled?' Even now, my mother is as weird as ever.

'Your grandmother curled up. Before she died. She ...' Mum's eyebrows and shoulders briefly weigh up the alternatives. 'Curled up. I don't know how else to describe it. Shrivelled sounds so … Anyway, we're not dead. We'll get through this.'

'Where's Lucille?' Asking is like popping a blister, when the skin is left raw.

'Wrapped up. Waiting for you to get out of here. David's dug her grave. Under the lemon tree. It's kind of him.'

'So are you two …?'

She looks away. 'I don't …' Her shoulders rise and fall in a rolling stretch. She holds my hands and kisses them. 'Don't worry about it. We're friends.'

I almost feel sorry for her.

'So, is he mad?'

'Probably.'

A cheerful nurse shoves the curtain back and proceeds to prod and poke me. But she can't do anything about the burning except give me a damp face washer. Then a doctor. Then another cheerful nurse. I answer the same questions many times, guessing that somewhere else in the building, in another room of curtains, Keek is doing the same.

Then come the police.

———

It's humiliating, being arrested. The police are not sympathetic to my feelings.

'You made your bed,' says the officer who drives us, me hungover and crying, back to the police station. 'Don't blame us if it's uncomfortable.'

They've already been to our house and confiscated stuff – books, the computer, art supplies. Not even Yiayia could stop them. Imagine not believing Mrs T?

They think I'm lying about everything and won't let me see Keek or tell me anything about him. It is already too easy to doubt myself – I can barely remember getting off the train. The dream has faded and when I picture the events, we *did* paint Lucille fetching the world back from the brink of destruction, painted it big – but I'm not sure where. But we haven't made any mark at all, apparently. And anyway, our non-graffiti is the least of our problems.

'Bomb hoax is a serious matter,' says Senior Sergeant Ellis, pushing himself back on the cheap chair, crossing his ankles and folding his arms over his paunch. 'Affray,' he adds, as if that were supposed to explain everything.

I think my mother is going to scream, but she presses her palms into the table. 'I think it's clear,' she says, 'that the kids did not intend a bomb hoax when they wore the costumes to the party.'

'But they did google homemade bombs and they didn't stay at the party, did they?' Ellis taps his forefinger on the neat crease of his shirt sleeve and I feel a horrible urge to rip his tapping finger off his hairy hand. 'Instead, they took themselves off to threaten the seat of government in this state; shouting abuse, threatening damage. Thousands of dollars have been spent, Mrs Jones, in the interests of security, because of your daughter's idea of a joke.'

'I prefer Ms Jones, if you don't mind.'

Ellis sits up and points his pen at her. 'It's time you both faced up to the seriousness of what she's done.'

'I'm tired,' says my mother. 'What happens next?'

Ellis pulls his clipboard to him. He nods at me, sharply. 'What did you think you were going to achieve?'

In an avalanche, I see international headlines: Graffiti Girl sends Message to the World. I see my father's hands – smooth, not hairy and white like Sergeant Ellis's – pick up the paper and see my photo and know. I see him rush to the airport ready to find me, and Mum. The neediness of my own delusions creeps redly up my neck.

'Nothing,' I say.

'Right,' says Ellis. 'We've decided to give you a summons, so think yourself lucky. That means you will be released on the condition that you appear in court on the date specified in the summons to answer the charges. If you do not appear when required to do so, you will be arrested and brought to the court. Do you understand?'

No. I don't understand anything except that I'm scared. We haven't done anything. We're no threat to anyone or anything. If only Keek hadn't used all that bloody tape. The wires and the mobile phones made the cops crap themselves. It isn't fair. We haven't done anything. And even if we had, it would only have been free art. Art can't hurt anybody. Can it? My eyes and scalp are still burning. It's horrible. So horrible I can't help but cry. I hope Keek's all right.

'I'll repeat the question: do you understand?'

Mum puts her hand on my arm. 'Come on love,' she says softly.

'Yes,' I say.

'We'll give you a charge sheet with details of the charges against you.' He turns to my mother. 'You'll find pamphlets from Legal Aid near the front desk there,' he nods out to the police station proper, out into the rest of the world, 'or the court will appoint a lawyer on the day. They'll explain and give you advice about what to do next.'

He ticks something on the papers in his clipboard, then taps his blue pen on the table in front of me. 'The police prosecutor will describe the events from our point of view, then your lawyer can explain your side of the story. So you better start thinking about that, Clover, what your side of the story is, because nothing you've told me today is very convincing.'

———

At home in the shower, Mum helps me mash ripe tomatoes into my hair and on my face. 'This will neutralise the burning,' she says.

'Are you sure?'

'No.'

But to the relief of us both, especially me, it works.

The summons arrives in the mail less than two weeks later. Mrs T and I look on while Mum opens the envelope.

'Three weeks,' she says.

I ring Keek after school. 'They're doing our court thing on the same day,' I say. 'We're the "co-accused".'

'That's good, I guess.'

I want to see him so bad. 'Yeah, I guess.' I curl the phone cord around my fingers until they ache.

'I did that English test,' he says. 'You can still do it, if you want to. I asked.' I love Keek when he's being earnest, but the thought of school is like being filled with sand.

'I don't think I can go back. Mum's investigating other schools.'

'Yes, you can go back.'

'I can't talk long, coz of it being your mobile,' I say.

'Guess what.'

'What?'

'Ellen's pregnant.'

'No way. To who?' Poor Ellen.

'Well, there's the drama. Half the footy team are shitting themselves. But it's weird – it's like the go is that if you're not shitting yourself about Ellen, you're probably a virgin.'

'What does she reckon?'

'She won't say. But anyway, we're off the Herb radar – no one cares about us. Cho and that are all good. And Mark and Alison are amusing, now that I've totally accepted I'm a nerd.' He laughs. 'And they want to see you.' I hear him breathe into the phone. 'I want to see you.'

'I want to see you too. Is your mum—'

'Don't even ask.'

I take my questions out to Lucille and the big flat rock near her grave, but she doesn't think I should go back to Fernwood Secondary either. I feel a wash of pity and embarrassment for Ellen. She has a big mouth about who she's *going* to hook up with, but the only person that I know she's actually slept with is Robbo.

'God,' I tell the dog. 'That could have been me.'

Mum comes to share the rock. 'You okay?'

'Mr and Mrs McKenzie got married because of Keek's brother, didn't they?' I squint at my mother, willing her to tell me the truth. 'Because she was pregnant.'

'Where did that come from?'

'It's true, though. Isn't it.'

'Yes and no.'

'What does that mean?'

'It means they were young.'

'Would you please tell me?'

Mum breaks a stick into tiny pieces, drops them and peers at them like a fortune teller. They appear to indicate she should spill the beans. 'At school everyone thought Maria was away with glandular fever, being looked after by an aunty up north where it's warmer. Dave went all distant and weird, but I always thought … Anyway, then Maria came back and they were joined at the hip, but never seemed very happy together. He was quite an arse, to tell you the truth.'

'What about the baby?'

'I didn't even know there was a baby, for ages. Later, it came out that her family had pretended that her aunty had adopted him; nothing to do with Maria. As soon as Dave turned eighteen, even though Maria was still only seventeen, they applied to court to be allowed to get married without their parents' consent. They wanted their son.' Mum arranges leaves in a pattern around the soothsayer sticks. 'It was a big thing. Everything coming out. Then they moved away.'

'But they came back.'

'Yes, when Keek was – what was he, in Grade Three? Something like that. Dave told me recently that he made a few dumb investments, after Matthew's accident. He'd worked hard, you know. Earning money and studying at night. Then he had a breakdown and couldn't work and they went broke. And then his uncle left them that house.'

'And now Mrs McKenzie's stuck there.'

'Dave's never gone to school meetings or anything either. But you're right, she is stuck. I think she's ill. And lonely. He told me her family hasn't spoken to her since, not for all these years. Not even when she lost her son.' Mum shakes her head as if she can't believe her own words. 'Don't want anything to do with Keek. Nothing.'

I light the candle in its jar on Lucille's grave. The flowers have withered and Mum spreads them out like heartbroken mulch. Yiayia has left a beautiful little stone dog. The little dog cool in one palm, I cup a hanging lemon with the other and put it to my cheek.

That the lemon is alive on the tree strikes me as an amazing thing. I pull back, to stare; the lemon is growing before my very eyes, but I can't tell. The lemon will keep changing, but even if I sit here for a month,

I'll never see it grow with my naked eye. From where I sat, it would seem as still as a photograph.

Everything is moving and everything is still, both at once. Being alive is the same as dying. I sit back on the rock and poke with a stick at the few browning lemons, fallen and rotting. Once you're dead – that's a whole other thing altogether.

I think of Lucille, under the ground. It's impossible to imagine her there. Lucille disappeared with her last breath, Mum said, and I believe her.

But where?

Maybe Mrs McKenzie is comforted by the idea that her son is in heaven with Jesus, but it doesn't seem like it.

'Why is death so horrible, Mum?'

'I think it's only horrible for the ones left behind.' Mum taps at a lemon and sends it gently swinging. 'It's how we evolve: birth, death, new birth. The spirit can see the big picture, but the soul is attached – so no matter how right it might be for the one who has died, it still hurts.'

'What happens?' I say. 'You know, when we die.'

Mum whistles. 'You don't want to know what I think.'

'Yeah, I do.'

Maybe hearing that I mean it, Mum settles herself. 'Well, I think when we die, we excarnate – you know, the opposite of incarnate?'

I nod, shrug and shake my head. 'I guess.'

'Well, we leave the body behind and excarnate through the moon-sphere, Mercury, Jupiter, right out to the Saturn sphere, letting go or transforming everything connected to our earthly life.' She maps an arc in the air, like an invisible rainbow. 'You with me?'

'Yeah, sorta. Is that it?'

'No. When we've gone out through the planetary spheres and we're free,' she tracks the arc to its highest point, 'we see a vision of the great spiritual human being we're meant to become and according to that vision,' her hand traces the completion of the arc, 'we design our next life on the way back through the planetary spheres to earth.'

She folds her hands in her lap. 'Then, when we're born, we promptly forget everything that happened to us in our existence between death and a new birth – Dr Steiner calls it drinking "the draft of forgetfulness". And that's what I think happens when we die.'

'Right,' I say. 'Sounds like a lot of work.'

Mum laughs.

I sit back and cross my ankles. 'So you think if people have a bad life, they designed it that way?'

Mum picks a lemon leaf and rubs it with her thumb. 'No, I don't believe that. We're all here to learn love, Clove. And sadly, people and *peoples* don't always act in accordance with their higher selves – and they suffer; and cause suffering for others, preventing *them* also from acting in accordance with *their* higher selves.'

'But why are people allowed not to act however you said – to wreck everything and make others suffer? I mean, there's something seriously wrong with the world.'

'Yes.' She drops the leaf. 'I wish I could reassure you, but I don't know.' She frowns at the flame in the jar, as if it has hidden her thoughts, or is revealing them. 'I'd like to believe it's because we're developing a new substance for the world. A *spiritual* substance. Love. Truly human love … that embraces but is greater than romance, and family, and identity.' She brushes a yellow daisy with a fingertip. 'Love that's as real and miraculous as the wisdom in nature.' Mum straightens up and the daisy nods, a tiny sun against the dark turned earth of Lucille's grave. 'But it has to be made in freedom – a free deed of the heart – and if we don't have the choice *not* to follow our higher selves, then there's no possibility of developing that freedom.' She glances at me with a vague shrug. 'I don't know. We're not free yet, that's for sure. "No woman's free while her sister's in chains" as the old saying goes. More-or-less. Give or take a gender.'

'I don't even know what you're talking about,' I say, feeling irritated. 'How are we supposed to know what to do, then, if nobody's ever free anyway?'

'I don't know. I think it's got to do with the transformation of fear into love.' She sighs. 'If I'd known you were going to give me brain-strain, I'd've prepared a few notes.'

Fear. That's what is wrong with me. 'I'm cracked with fear,' I say.

Mum puts her arms around me and I slide down her body to rest on her lap.

'Remember grandma's Leonard Cohen record you used to love so much?' she says, stroking my hair. 'Everything that's not invisible is cracked, my love. How else will the light shine in ... and out?'

I cry, with the safety of Mum's hands on my head.

Eventually, I sit up. 'Will Mrs McKenzie come to court, do you think?'

'I hope so, for Keek's sake.'

'Me, too.' I pick up my own twig to crumple. 'So are you—?'

Mum takes a big breath. 'Dave and I are ... I mean, I think it's more than unfinished business from high school, but ...' She brushes her hair back with her fingers and twirls it into a knot at the base of her neck. 'We made a mistake.'

There's a softness to her, as her hair unfurls and falls around her face. She's ... beautiful. Her eyes seem so sad.

'He's married.' She sits up and tucks her hair behind her ears, my mother once again. 'He's married. And Maria would be utterly devastated by a divorce. And neither of us wants to drag us all into some horrible affair.' She flicks away tears with her fingertips. 'So that's that, then.'

'So—'

She cuts me off, standing to kiss me on the top of my head. 'Mrs T is coming over tonight. She told me to tell you she's coming for a sitting.'

'A sitting?'

'Yes. She says you promised to paint her hands.'

The next day, over baked mushrooms and salad, Mum says, 'Dave and I have been conspiring and we think we might have come up with something.'

'Oh, yeah, conspiring?'

'By email and over the phone.' She tuts at me. 'But don't think I'm going to start justifying myself every minute.' She moves the salt and pepper to lay out a school information pack unlike any of the others; it's like entering another world, other colours, the gentle, vibrant rainbow colours of Mum's watercolour paintings and the Steiner-school fair. 'Dave's been looking at the mortgage for me – or as he says, "bringing my finances into the twenty-first century" – and, well,' her face flushes red, 'because houses in this area are now worth a ridiculous amount of money, even old-fashioned ones like Mum and Dad's, and we have plenty of equity ... how would you feel about doing your VCE at a Steiner school? The one in the country – where we go for the fair. What do you think?'

My memories of Steiner-kinder are vague, warm and full of the smell of freshly baked bread; sitting with lots of children at a long wooden table and Mum bringing carrot cake for my birthday. I don't remember any adults talking. Just singing. Like a bunch of real-life Julie Andrewses. There was always a candle burning. The annual fair is also their Open Day, so I've seen samples of the stuff the kids produce in the high school – it's pretty impressive. And surely they wouldn't still be singing all the time …?

'We'd have to move.'

'Yes.'

'What about Yiayia?'

'She'll cope.'

'But you—'

'I'm ready for this, Clover.'

'But, Lucille is here.'

'No.' Mum puts one hand to her heart and the other over my heart. 'She's here.'

⁓

My lawyer, Janet, says in her clever, tired voice, 'A show of family and community support is important. It will make an enormous difference to the judge.'

She's older than Mum and doesn't dye her short peppery hair. She's kind, but I can't help feeling she thinks I'm a spoilt brat and there are more important things she could be doing with her time.

'The worst-case scenario is that they treat it as preparation for an actual act of terrorism,' she tells us. 'Then they might consider detention.'

My mother squawks and goes pale.

Janet says, 'But don't worry, please. There was information on your computer they might consider radical, but nothing connected with any particular organisations, so I can't imagine it coming to that. The main thing in our favour is that the kids were born here and are white.'

My mother looks like she's been stung by a bee. 'That shouldn't have anything to do with it, surely?'

Janet's voice is sad, and withering. 'In this scenario, it has everything to do with it. But no priors counts for a lot. Like I say, don't worry too much.'

❧

But we are worrying, all of us, when we arrive at the Children's Court and Janet is nowhere to be seen. I feel sticky with guilt as my mother, Aunty Jean, Mrs T and Theo offer up their belongings for the scanner and walk through the metal detector like people associated with a criminal.

To the right is the Family Court. We have to go to the left, for criminals. At a desk upstairs we're told my case will be heard in Courtroom Eight and we are instructed to wait.

There's a scattering of people already sitting in the waiting area. A guy with tattoos on his neck and broad shoulders fills out his suit. He smiles at Aunty Jean and winks. She smiles back, but nobody's smiles last long. Even Theo and his mother are subdued. A thin woman in a pink dress meant for someone younger hovers over two teenage boys, as mean as cat's piss. One of them has 'no remorse' tattooed over his eyebrow. When he catches me reading it, I look away.

Ten minutes later, Keek arrives dressed in a suit, curls gone, short back and sides. The boys shift in their seats and one whispers something to the other.

Mr McKenzie bodily hands his son to Mum, says, 'Can you keep an eye on him?' and rushes off, back down the wide stairs.

Keek pulls at his collar. The top button is already undone. 'Mum's in the car,' he says. It's almost an apology.

'You look nice, Keek,' says Mrs T, giving him a hug. 'So handsome!' Theo shakes his hand. Aunty Jean rubs the back of his head as if he's a dog. 'About time,' she says.

Keek without hair is surreal. I want to kiss his ear, his neck, but feel shy. It's like meeting him for the first time. Do I even know him? Maybe I don't, but I want to. I haven't seen him for weeks. But he doesn't hesitate. He hugs me, right there, in front of everyone. With one arm still around me, he turns to my mother. 'I never meant to hurt Clover.'

'I know,' she says, and I worry she's going to cry. 'Sometimes we accidentally hurt the people we care about the most. But we're on the same side now. Aren't we?'

Keek nods, but I wonder if he's convinced.

Two men in brown suits appear at the top of the stairs. One greets Keek with a handshake and introduces himself to the rest of us as Dan. He pulls Keek aside and sits down with him to talk. I want to listen in on what they're saying, but the other man approaches me.

'Clover?'

'Yes.'

'My name is Ray Fahid.' He shakes my hand, then Mum's. 'I'm here to represent you today.'

Mum says, 'Where's Janet?'

'Janet can't make it, I'm sorry. Unavoidable. But she's briefed me on your case and I've had a good chat with Dan on the way in. Without the complication of the hoax and affray, I would be confident of a Good Behaviour Bond without conviction.'

'And with the complications?' Mum asks.

Ray gives a quick headshake. 'It depends on the position of the police prosecutor. But I will do the best I can.' He takes me to another row of seats in the waiting area, nearer to the tattooed man. 'Now, Clover, can you tell me again – why did you leave the party?'

I tell him everything I can remember, staring at his bony knees pressed up against his suit pants while he scribbles furiously in his notebook.

A woman in a black suit pops out of a corridor and says, 'You may go into Courtroom Eight now, thank you.'

Ray tells us to bow to the judge when we go in, which we do, but the judge's chair is empty. A pair of glasses sit on the high bench, behind which is a computer and a microphone. In front of the bench there are desks with swivel chairs where somebody else's lawyers are sitting. The police prosecutor is there, pouring glasses of water, and they chat like old friends.

A teenage girl sits alone in the front row, her headband very yellow against her straightened black hair. A nervous couple sit behind her in the third row and the yearning from them is almost palpable. But she's in a bubble, a blank, switched off.

The rest of us take our places on black leather seats bolted to the green carpet in the pine-panelled courtroom. I count the chairs; seven rows of ten. Ray gestures that we're to sit in the fourth row, and wait. The tattooed man sits in the back row writing in a notebook. The woman in pink and her sons are in the fifth row back. Their turn after us, I suppose.

Ray nods at our group. 'There's a matter before the court, and then it's us. Dan and I will be back in plenty of time.'

There's a woman sitting in a booth below and beside the judge's bench. 'Who is that?' I whisper.

'The court registrar,' answers Theo.

The registrar picks up a telephone and says, 'We're all ready to go in Courtroom Eight. Vogel.'

A door behind the registrar opens and in comes the magistrate, a middle-aged woman with a gold brooch detailed with diamantes that say 'K' on the lapel of her tweed jacket. Or diamonds, for all I know. She enters through a loftier door than ours and ignores us from behind her high wooden bench.

'All rise,' says the court registrar.

We rise.

'The Eighth Division Melbourne Children's Court is now in session. Judge Karen Robinson presiding.'

Robinson's no-nonsense hair is the colour of steel. She takes her seat and picks up her glasses.

'Please be seated,' says the court registrar.

We sit.

The case before ours blossoms like a tumour. I bet the magistrate is wearing brown leather lace-up shoes. A longing washes over me not to be judged by a hair-sprayed stranger wearing brown leather lace-up shoes. I think about the judge's shoes because I don't want to think about the list of sad and hideous things the accused has done. According to the cops, her only explanation for the unprovoked violence was, 'Because I can'.

'She ran away from home at thirteen,' her lawyer pleads in his stuttery way. 'And became addicted to amphetamines and alcohol.'

Even now 'the accused' won't have anything to do with her parents, sitting two rows behind her like scarecrows. They flinch when they hear what she called the fifty-one-year-old Sri Lankan woman she pulled off a train and bashed, but I can't help wondering what they did to make her run away in the first place. It must have been something unbearable.

Mum wipes tears from her eyes. I look at the parents again. Maybe they just tried too hard.

The man shifts in his seat and glances over his shoulder at me and there's a shadow behind his eyes that's so creepy, I'm glad Vogel ran away.

The magistrate asks the accused to stand and she does, looking frail and innocent.

Judge Robinson takes off her glasses and grips the girl with her eyes. 'You have heard the summaries before the court.' Her amplified voice still seems quiet, her distaste palpable. 'Seeing you standing there, it's hard to believe you're the same person described by the prosecution. But hearing this repetitive anti-social behaviour and knowing that you have walked out of this court not once, but twice before, promising to attend group conferencing, but instead embarked upon such appalling and criminal behaviour, does not give me confidence in your rehabilitation outside the guidelines of juvenile detention.

'I take into account that you have pleaded guilty and show remorse. Up until now, the court has been fairly forbearing, but I seriously believe the best thing is to remand you. The community does not have to put up with this behaviour.' The judge puts on her glasses and peers at the computer screen. 'You can resume your seat.'

Vogel doesn't cry, not even during the sentencing, but her mother does; and so does mine. Courts and police can take you away and lock you up against your will and the will of the people who love you and there's nothing you, or they, can do about it.

The magistrate stands.

'All rise,' says the court registrar.

We rise. The judge ignores us, escaping through her private door. Keek helps me up. I'm crying. I want my life. I don't want the fracture to be a ravine that I fall into and disappear – I want it to open up and let the light shine through. Yamouni was right; even if no one understands you, you've got to make beauty from pain. Maybe it's impossible, but I want to try.

The registrar says other things after the magistrate leaves and people start moving around, but I can't hear them. I feel as if I've fallen under water.

Mum says, 'Ray and Dan are back.'

Keek's voice is a rumble, my ear against his chest. 'Is my dad with them?'

'No, not yet,' says Mum. 'But they'll be here, we have ten minutes. Do you want a drink of water? Clover?'

'Yes,' I say. 'I've got to go to the toilet.'

But I don't go to the toilet. I rush down the stairs and out to the street, searching wildly until I spot the McKenzies sitting in their car. I run to Mrs McKenzie's side, but it's Dave who winds down the window. I yank Mrs McKenzie's door open, shocking us both.

'Matt's dead,' I blurt. 'But Keek's still alive – and he needs you.'

Dave says, 'Now, come on—' but I cut him off.

'It's not Phil's fault, but it's like you're punishing him for it.'

Mrs McKenzie hasn't moved a muscle, but I see a tear slide down her cheek. I bob down and put my hand on her arm.

'Please, Mrs McKenzie.'

'Clover?' I stand. It's Aunty Jean calling from the courthouse steps. She claps her hands when she sees me. 'It's your turn,' she calls. 'Quick!'

'Go on, Clover.' Dave opens his car door. 'We'll be there in a minute.'

Aunty Jean pulls me close in a one-armed hug. 'I thought you'd run off,' she says. 'Your mother told me you'd never leave Keek to face all this alone.'

We have to go through the security rigmarole again and Mum's waiting to hurry me up the stairs. I give her a squeeze. 'I love you,' I say.

It's our turn.

At Ray and Dan's gesture, Keek and I sit next to each other almost in the middle of the front row, my family flanking off to our right; his seats empty on the left, waiting.

Our lawyers hand papers to the registrar who picks up the telephone and says, 'We're all ready to go in Courtroom Eight. Jones and McKenzie.'

Too soon, the door behind her opens. 'All rise,' says the court registrar.

We rise.

'The Eighth Division Melbourne Children's Court is now in session. Judge Karen Robinson presiding.' The magistrate takes her seat and picks up her glasses. 'Please be seated,' says the court registrar.

We sit.

The magistrate is reading something on her bench, glancing up now and then at the computer screen. No one says anything.

I can't help glancing back to the door, willing Keek's parents to arrive. The same door that swallowed Vogel in the company of two police officers, followed mutely by her broken parents. It opens, and in a shift of reality, there's Mr Radshaw, ushering in Mark, Alison, Trung and – my blood turns to fizz – Katie. They smile and nod and sit in the row behind us. There are whispered hellos and thanks for coming. Mark pats Keek's shoulder.

Katie says, 'Have you heard about Ellen?'

The court registrar says, 'Quiet, please.'

Mr Radshaw hands Ray a manila folder. He glances in it and hands it to the court registrar, who takes it and hands it on to the magistrate, who smiles briefly at Mr Radshaw over her glasses, but doesn't acknowledge us. Her eyes flicker over the contents of the folder, then back to the computer screen.

There's a plastic bag caught in the tree outside. I see it through the tall glass panels that face the atrium. Well, that's what Aunty Jean called it when we were downstairs. I can't listen to the whisperings of my friends. I can only stare at it. Flapping, trapped.

The door opens again and we all turn our heads. Mr McKenzie bobs at the judge, his arm around his wife, who is wearing sunglasses and leaning on a stick. Keek's leg keeps jiggling and his face is stony, and a blush creeps up Mum's neck, but I feel like cheering.

Keek's parents make their slow way to the front

row and sit themselves beside their son. The judge watches them, then leans down to the court registrar and has a whispered conversation before sitting up and addressing us.

'Yes, thank you,' she says. She addresses my lawyer. 'Yes?'

Ray shrinks slightly. 'Plea of not guilty on the bomb hoax, Your Honour. Plea of guilty for all other charges.'

Robinson turns to Keek's lawyer who says in a louder, bored voice, 'Plea of not guilty on the bomb hoax, Your Honour. Guilty for all other charges.'

She nods and takes off her glasses. 'Now, I'll have the charges.'

The police prosecutor begins with, 'My submissions are that there is one charge of theft, withdrawn.'

The judge swings her glasses on to refer to the computer screen and says, 'And that leaves – eight charges.'

'Yes,' says the police prosecutor.

'Seven, for Jones, Your Honour,' pipes up Mr Rahid.

'That's right,' says the police prosecutor. 'Only McKenzie is being charged with possession of a drug of dependence.'

The judge nods, folds her specs and gestures to him to proceed. He launches into the horrible list of our crimes: public nuisance, affray, bomb hoax. Reckless behaviour. Causing public fear of explosion. Attempted criminal damage and using a drug of dependence.

I feel myself shrivelling. In a flat, storytelling voice, the police prosecutor recounts our supposed rampage. Refers to us as 'the accused and the co-accused'. I can't believe he's even talking about us. I hear my friends and family drawing in their breath; they've probably all changed their minds and are sure we should be locked away. Especially me.

'The accused and the co-accused were subsequently interviewed and offered no reason for their behaviour.'

Unlike my mother, who has clutched my hand and is breathing heavily, the magistrate seems unfazed. 'They are the matters?' she says.

'Yes, they are the police matters.'

Robinson peers over her glasses at Keek's lawyer.

'The accused and the co-accused come before the court as first offenders,' he says and Ray nods. Dan tells them our ridiculous story, emphasising that we had no intention of being a public nuisance, causing affray or sparking a bomb hoax and that the whole evening was a series of unfortunate choices, entirely out of character for the pair of us. 'They are accompanied today by their respective parents and close family.'

The judge interrupts him to glare. 'Parents who should be aghast.' Mum shrinks. Mrs T takes her hand. The judge takes off her glasses. 'What sort of children use a symbol of global pain for their entertainment?'

Dan says, 'Yes. But thoughtless, Your Honour. Not malicious.'

'They are remorseful, Your Honour, and show a clear understanding of the issues,' pipes in Ray.

Robinson wipes her lenses with a tissue. 'Am I right in thinking the substances of addiction cited belonged to the co-accused's mother?'

'Prescription, Your Honour,' says Dan.

The judge ignores him. 'You want to say something, Mr Rahid?'

'Thank you.' He indicates Mr Radshaw. 'Your Honour can see the upper-school coordinator of Fernwood Secondary College, here to support the accused and co-accused.'

Who could have known I'd ever genuinely want to hug hairy old Radshaw?

Robinson indicates the row behind us with her pen. 'Schoolmates, I presume?'

'Yes, Your Honour.'

'There are letters of support,' Ray reminds the judge.

Robinson says, 'Yes, thank you, Mr Rahid,' but she may as well have said, 'shut up'.

A silence.

The air is heavy. Judge Robinson is deciding. She looks up from her files, glances at me, at Keek, adjusts her glasses and peers into her computer. My whole life is suspended in the faint glow of that screen.

The magistrate asks us to stand. We stand and Keek takes my hand. Then the sky cracks open and the light shines through.

Parting the hanging fronds of the weeping willow, free in the sunlight, I feel a … reverence. But melancholy, too. There's a sign up; the block's been sold. They'll probably chop down this old tree. I feel guilty for hoping I'm gone before it happens. I don't think I could let it be killed without a fight and I'm afraid of getting capsicum-sprayed again; of falling into the clutches of the police. I give the tree a hug. 'But I will, if I have to,' I whisper.

I press my cheek against the trunk and feel relieved to be able to, and sad, imagining what Vogel is doing today.

Katie says, 'You always were a weird one,' and feeds a piece of cracker to Alison's new rat, who's made a nest on Al's shoulder. 'We should do something to celebrate.'

Keek reaches up to grip the branch above his head. 'Let's go to the movies.'

'Yes.' Alison grins. 'And I can sneak Hilbert in.'

'I can't believe your mum let you get a rat,' I say.

She laughs. 'She didn't. But it was love at first sight.' Al pats the rat. 'Wasn't it, Hilly? There wasn't much she could do about it, especially after I convinced Dad he helps me study – and now, as an added bonus, having the cage in my room keeps her out of there. She can't stand it.'

I'd forgotten what a wicked laugh she has.

'She carries it everywhere,' Trung complains.

'Him,' Alison corrects, righteously.

Mark strokes Hilbert's nose with an enormous thumb, but his eyes slide to Trung. 'Jealous are we?'

Trung remains unimpressed. 'You could at least have called him after a mathematician people have heard of.'

Alison screws up her nose. 'Not Einstein.'

'Yes, Einstein.' Trung offers the rat a crumb. 'Isn't that right, Steiny?'

The name is a trigger. 'I'm going to Steiner,' I rattle out. 'The one up the mountain.'

Everyone looks, except Keek.

Katie says, 'How will Sutcliff ever live without you?' and laughs, but our chins wobble with lurking tears. She hugs and then shoves me. 'God, don't make me cry, you'll wreck my make-up.'

Mark adjusts his back against the willow's trunk. 'Do they take criminals on good behaviour bonds?'

'Without conviction,' Alison adds, kindly.

'Apparently, they do.'

Alison looks at Keek who hasn't moved, hasn't said a word. 'How far away is it?' she asks me.

'About half an hour, by bus. Maybe longer.'

Trung says, 'Longer.'

'I'm scared shitless, but it's got small Year Eleven and Twelve classes. Lots of art.' I slip my arm under Keek's and around his waist, knowing I've been a coward to not wait until we're alone. 'It's not that far. Bring your bike on the bus. It's not, like, England, which was my mother's other bright idea. And look.' With my spare hand, I reach into my pocket and brandish my new smartphone. 'Not that I have a clue how to work it.'

'Give me that,' says Trung, and Alison, Hilbert, Mark and Katie hang over his shoulder while he attacks the screen with his thumbs.

Keek looks at the phone. Finally, he looks at me. 'Well, that's definitely it, then.' He pulls away from me and reaches for his bike.

'What's definitely it then?' I want to know, a sudden ice-cream headache in my chest.

'Time to learn to ride, CB.'

'What?'

'Well, I'm not dinking you up and down freakin' mountain country.'

'I will. I promise.'

'Done.'

We shake on it.

He wheels the bike out from under the willow fronds with one hand and leads me with the other.

'Now?' I say.

Keek nods. He kisses me once, on the lips. 'Calmly, easily.' He kisses me again, more than once. 'Now.'

ACKNOWLEDGEMENTS

Love and thanks to my beautiful daughter, Georgia, and Leigh Wilson (aka Seao) for keeping me on the straight and narrow, and to Tasha, the quintessential old black staffy.

Thank you, thank you, Allen & Unwin publishers and design team – particularly my editor, Jodie Webster: your kindness and experience has made publication a joy as well as a privilege, and your deft, sensitive touch has brought out the best in the book.

Many thanks to Cath Crowley, Ali Arnold, Sophie Cunningham, Clare Renner, Sally Rippin, Dr Olga Lorenzo, Ania Walwicz and Penny Johnson for your wisdom and encouragement; and to the lovely folk at Varuna, the writers' house, especially Catherine Therese and Maria Katsonis; to the RMIT PWE cohort 2008–2010, chiefly my dear Jacinda Woodhead, Benjamin Laird, Elizabeth Reichhardt (& Stu), Scott Marriott and Rose Hudson; the writers' conversation: Kaye Holder, Jennifer Hansen, Ann Bolch, Lu Sexton & Rowan McKinnon; and those gorgeous writerly women: Trish Bolton, Lucy Treloar, Kate Richards, Jenny Green and Dana Miltins.

Heart's gratitude for the love and support of friends and family, especially Sally, Jacci, Jenni, Leah,

Joey, Dawn and Carolyn, my sisters Julie, Paula and Denise, and my darling Mum & Dad xxx.

And thanks Clover and Keek for carving your lives into my imagination and revealing your story to me.

ABOUT THE AUTHOR

Clare Strahan is a Melbourne writer who once rattled out a novel on a manual typewriter by candlelight. She is also a drama tutor with a passion for Shakespeare, a graduate of RMIT's Professional Writing & Editing, a writer of fiction and poetry for humans of all ages, and has published in *Overland*, where she curated their first fiction anthology and assists as a contributing editor. She is a freelance editor, creator of the *Literary Rats* cartoon, and flutters about the twittersphere as @9fragments.

Clare is a signatory to writersforrefugees.com